A Nashville Spicy Christmas

Casey Morales

WWW.AUTHORCASEYMORALES.COM

Cast of Characters

ANDRÉ MARTIN: PSYCHIATRIST, FRENCH, married to Nick Dunlap

Annie: Former Broadway star, avid baseball fan

Carson Beasley: Taekwondo student in Cooper's dojang

Cooper Hawk: Grandson of the late Marjorie Polk, number cruncher turned taekwondo dojang owner, partner of Nate Stringer

Dario: Cooper's butler aboard ship

David Reese: Member of Congress (TN-D), married to Joe Gibson

Ethan: Former resident of Buckeye Ranch in Cleveland, Ohio, adopted by Nick and André

Gabe Rossi: Owner of Pawesome Dog Training Academy, married to Tyler Hyatt

Jack: Flight attendant on Delta flight

Joe Gibson: Political campaign operative, married to Congressman David Reese (TN-D)

Kervin: Former minor league baseball player for Columbus Clippers and teammate of Nick Dunlap, married to Zack

Miguel Nuñez: Police officer, former minor league baseball player and mentor of Nate Stringer, married to Sam Prescott

Mila: A baby

Nate Stringer: Minor league baseball player turned Memphis Mango, mentored by Miguel Nuñez while in college, partner of Cooper Hawk

Nick Dunlap: Major league baseball player for Cleveland Guardians, adopted father of Ethan, married to André Martin

Sam Prescott: Owner of mechanic shop, married to Miguel Nuñez

Stephan Breeden: Memphis Mango catcher, friend of Nate Stringer

Tyler Hyatt: Mechanic in Sam Prescott's shop, married to Gabe Rossi

Zack: Former minor league baseball player for Columbus Clippers and teammate of Nick Dunlap, married to Kervin.

A Quick Word Before You Begin . .

.

Hi. I'm Cooper.

(Yes, I just waved at you, even though I know you're reading a book and can't see my Forrest Gumpish gesture. You'll just have to get over it because I'm generally a very kind and friendly person, and I like you because you're reading my story; well, it's really all of our story ... or is that all of our *stories* ... I'm not sure. Anyway, I waved. So there. Consider yourself well greeted and accept it for the loving, caring gesture it was ... is ... should be.)

You probably already know my friends. That Casey Morales guy wrote about them in other books. Isn't it kind of forward for an author to just write your story? I mean, they were good stories, and I'm worth getting to know, but really, he could've asked first. Never mind that I'm a figment of his imagination and there wasn't anyone to ask until he wrote me into existence. That's a pesky detail.

He still could've asked.

For the few of you who are rebellious by nature and haven't read all the books prior to picking this one up, let me introduce you to my adopted family.

First, there's Nate.

He's the love of my life and light of my world. He's the best human being I know; though he's merely an above-average baseball player. That's why he didn't make it from the minor leagues into the biggies, or whatever they're called. Between you and me, I'm glad he didn't make it. He now plays for the Memphis Mangoes, a sort of Harlem Globetrotters for baseball, and he's having a blast. His days are spent practicing insanely funny routines, shooting TikTok videos with his teammates, and working out like any other baseball player. In the three years I've known him, I've never seen him so happy, and that makes *me* happy—like, really happy.

Sam and Miguel introduced us.

Sam is a mechanic. Well, he's more than that. He owns a mechanic shop in Nashville. Does that make him more of a business owner, or is he still considered a mechanic? Miguel is his husband. He's a cop. He also played minor league baseball and was Nate's mentor when my man played for Vanderbilt University.

And oh ... my ... gawd ... is Miguel hot.

He also happens to be the smiliest cop on the planet. I mean, seriously, this guy's cheeks must hurt at the end of the day. I wonder if Sam gives him little cheek massages to make them feel better. That would be nice. Awkward, but nice.

Tyler (we call him Ty) works for Sam. How can I describe him? If Miguel is toothy, everyman handsome, Ty is cover-of-the-sexiest-magazine-ever, dripping-sensuality-on-a-stick, every-man-and-woman-on-the-planet-wants-to-jump-his-bones hot.

It's seriously not fair. Seriously.

On top of that, he's nice. He could at least be a jerk so I could hate him properly—but no, he had to be a nice guy on top of being Henry Cavill-but-thinner-and-slightly-less-built sexy.

(Yeah, Ty makes me talk in hyphens. When you see him, you'll understand.)

Ty married his beau, Gabe, about a year before I met them. Gabe is deaf, but his lipreading skills are off the chain. (That means incredible.) Come to think of it, Gabe might smile as much as Miguel, which is creepy and unsettling, considering Miguel makes my face hurt just watching him.

Gabe is cute.

Then there's Nick.

He used to play baseball on the same minor league team as Nate, but Nick is much better (at baseball … I have no idea how good Nick is at, um, other things involving balls and bats, and Nate is fabulous with his bat … and my balls … and his balls … and my bat … darn it, now you got me all … never mind).

Nick got transferred from Nashville to Columbus, Ohio. We all thought that was a bogus move by the team to get rid of the openly gay guy in a town that doesn't exactly fly the rainbow flag above city hall during Pride. Nick was pretty torn up at the time, but it ended up being the best thing.

While playing for the Columbus Clippers, he met André, a French psychiatrist who works with at-risk kids at this place called the Ranch. No, it's not an actual ranch. I was disappointed when I learned that too. I expected children riding cows or steers or whatever children ride on ranches, but no, it's just called that.

Very disappointing.

Anyway, as Nick and André were dating, they both fell in love with the cutest little boy who didn't have a family of his own. His name is Ethan. They ended up adopting him right before Nick got called up to play for the major league baseball team in Cleveland. They're an amazing, beautiful family. Seriously, they make me cry, and I'm not generally a crier, unless you bring up my grammy, who passed away, but that doesn't happen very often, but crying over how sweet Nick, André, and Ethan are does, and I turn into a blubbering mess … in a good way … in the best way. I love them.

You know what? The whole gang is an amazing, beautiful family.

I don't think I've ever talked about them like this before. It feels good to say it out loud.

We really are a family. And we're amazing.

Oh, wait, I almost forgot the pair who started this whole thing.

I'm not sure any of us would've met without Joe having wild, meaningless monkey sex with Sam. (Don't judge, they're adults, and it was hot. Like, slam-me-harder-while-you-do-that-thing-with-your-tongue hot.)

Sam started developing feelings, but Joe is this bigwig political consultant who helps candidates get elected and he had fallen for his boss but hadn't admitted it to himself yet (you can judge that part. It's suspicious).

David was his boss. He was running for governor of Tennessee, but got outed on the debate stage near the end of the race. I guess he had a thing with a guy in his military unit years ago, before he married a woman and it all came out (that sounds so messy when you say it out loud). He lost that campaign pretty badly, but his district sent him back to Congress. I guess congressmen can sleep with anybody and keep their job—not that I'm complaining. David's great, and he loves Joe to the moon and back.

Joe refusing to date Sam freed him up to fall for Miguel, which gave Ty hope when he met Gabe, which started this giant snowball of love rolling downhill where it slammed into us one after the other.

Isn't that how love works? It's just a giant snowball. A big, mean, cold, icy hunk of frozen water aimed right for your face.

Okay, it's better than that, but winter is coming and I'm in the mood for a snowball fight.

Buckle up, kids. This story's going to be fun!

Cooper Hawk

PS (from your author, not Cooper): This book involves a reunion of a large found family that is now scattered across six couples, three cities, two children, and several single folks. To help avoid confusion for those who haven't read the previous Nashville Spicy books, along with a traditional chapter tag indicating whose head we're in, I've included the husband/partner's name in parentheses.

Chapter One

Cooper (and Nate)

Carson's fist was a blur as I bent backward to avoid the blow. His hair, more orange than red, blazed as he spun and pushed off, sending a kick toward my chest. He was fast, especially for a skinny fourteen-year-old, but I was his master.

I reached out, grabbed the trim of his dobok, and threw my weight backward. The tall toothpick of a boy was caught off guard. His arms flew wide as he tried to right himself, but my weight and momentum were too much for him.

"Shiiiiiit!" he screamed, his voice cracking, as I crouched and rolled onto my back in a backward barrel roll, tossing him easily over my head and out of the circle. By the time he'd risen, I had already popped into a ready position facing him with both fists raised. He shook himself off and assumed his own ready posture.

I straightened, lowered my fists, and cocked a brow. "You are out of bounds, *jey-jah*," I said, looking pointedly at his feet a good two strides outside the white perimeter.

Carson glanced down, then immediately snapped to attention, slammed his fists together, and bowed deeply. "Thank you, *sabeom*."

The honorific of a master still rang strangely in my ears, despite running the dojang for more than a year. The clear adoration in the eyes of my students felt even more odd, though I understood. I'd competed at the highest levels—well, almost the highest level. I'd been knocked out in the final Olympic trial before making the US team. Moreover, as a master of a dojang with as many stripes on my belt as the boy had knuckles on his fist, his respect was appropriate, if a bit awkward.

"You did well today, Carson. Your mom is waiting." I pointed toward a row of comfortable couches where parents watched practice. A woman whose hair was somehow more sun-kissed than his waved when she noticed us looking her way. "Tomorrow, we'll work more on balance. When you are at a severe disadvantage in weight, balance becomes even more important. You made my job easy by falling over."

Carson grinned, and his face nearly split in two. "I did kind of tip over."

I laughed. "Tip over? I'd say you threw yourself at that wall over there, head first. Not a good look, my friend."

He beamed. Carson's dad left when Carson was five. His mom spent time in and out of hospitals and court-mandated treatment centers for addiction issues. I marveled at how the boy smiled and carried himself with a confidence I knew he didn't always feel. It made me want to spend more time with him, to push him to be better, to put my arm around him and let him know there were people in the world who cared, who wouldn't leave.

Instead, I donned my own dobok, cinched my belt tight, and welcomed him into my fold. Carson spent virtually every day the doors were open on my practice mats, at least ten hours each week, most weeks more. I tried to give him a "scholarship," to let him train for free, but his mom paid me for one hour each week. It's what she could afford, and she was too proud to let me waive that.

I understood that pride.

"*Sabeom*, see you tomorrow," Carson said as he turned to retrieve his backpack from a chair where students sat to watch their peers. He'd hit a growth spurt this year, and his legs were too long for his body. It was like watching baby Bambi wobbling from one end of the gym to the other. I couldn't suppress a grin.

All the other kids had left an hour earlier, and the only sounds in the gym were the whirring of the big-ass fans and the grunts and groans of our sparring.

I'd been turned to face Carson and hadn't heard his mom cross the floor. Bony fingers snaked down my shoulder to grip my bicep, squeezing as if testing a grapefruit at the supermarket. She knew I was gay, but that didn't matter. Her hands always found my biceps, or sought some excuse to pat my chest—and to leave her fingers on it a little too long.

"Oh, hi, Mrs. Beasley," I said, trying desperately not to jump off the mat.

"Hi, Cooper," her voice purred. "You look so good out there ... with Carson."

Heat flooded my cheeks as her hand left my arm and pressed against my chest.

"Thanks. I mean, he's great. Your son is great. Carson. He's your son. Of course, you know that, and you know he's great, but really, he did great. Sorry about the whole throwing him around thing, but that's kind of what we do here, you know, in taekwondo. We throw people and things, and break them. Things, we break things, not people. Unless by accident. Sometimes they break things like arms or legs or things ... you know?"

Her eyes weren't quite as glazed as they'd been the last time I'd seen her, but her nails were a bit longer. She curled her fingers so they dug through the fabric of my dobok, teasing my chest in a way that would've been pleasant if she'd been, well, *a man*, and not the mother of one of my students. I took a couple steps back, freeing my chest from her claws—I mean, nails, ... fingers ... from her fingers.

"See you tomorrow, Coach Cooper," she singsonged, as she looped her hand into Carson's arm and pulled him toward the door.

"It's *sabeom*, not coach, Mom," Carson said with a heavy note of adolescent annoyance.

"Of course it is, dear," she said, glancing back and winking.

I nearly peed myself right there. And my dobok was white. That would've been terrible.

Mrs. Beasley couldn't have been more than a few years older than me. Why she flustered me so badly was a mystery. Nate thought it was funny. He thought the blush that flooded my face and neck and arms and toes—and *everything*—each time she grabbed me was even more hilarious. I loved him, but my man was useless in defending my honor with cougars, and, while I might've been capable of beating most men into submission, I was no lion tamer.

Cougars scared me. They had claws ... and teeth ... and boobs.

The bell on the front door tinkled, letting me know Carson and his mother had left. I padded over to the wall and began shutting off the lights. One row after the next winked out with each switch. I paused at the last bank that illuminated the center ring.

This was *my* dojang. I was the master here.

It hadn't been that long ago that I worked in a cubicle, crunching numbers for a boss who cared more about whipping his subjects than making them better employees. Except for him—and a coworker or two—I liked my job. Numbers were fun. But having my own dojang and getting to help kids every day—that was like living a dream.

I glanced back as I clicked off the last of the lights and locked the doors. My phone buzzed before I could press the button on my key remote to unlock my truck. A tiny caterpillar tap-danced in my chest when I saw a text from Nate.

God, I loved that man.

NateStringerOfficial: You done beating up children?

HawkeyeBB: Never. There's always more to punish, although I'm not sure training counts as punishment. It's actually more of a reward, especially coming from a master. Have I mentioned how weird it is to be called that? I know, it's been over a year, but still, it feels weird. Good, but weird. Speaking of feeling good, I need you naked.

NateStringerOfficial: I'm ignoring everything before the word naked. Yes. I will be stripped bare and oiled up when you get home.

HawkeyeBB: Please don't. You know how much I love squirting all over you.

HawkeyeBB: Oil. I love squirting oil all over you. Your body. All over your chest and arms and ... everywhere.

HawkeyeBB: I didn't want you to think I meant actually squirting all over you with my private part thingy.

HawkeyeBB: Although, now that I say that, I kind of want to do that too. It looks so hot against your dark skin, all creamy and gooey.

NateStringerOfficial: I can't decide if we're going to have sex or ice a cupcake.

HawkeyeBB: CUPCAKES! Yes! I'll stop by the Donut Den on my way home. That's a great idea.

NateStringerOfficial: You're killing me, Coop. Get home. I missed you today.

And just like that, I forgot about cupcakes.

I punched in the code and opened the door. Our house was strangely quiet and dark. Even the kitchen, which served as the center of our universe on most days, stared back all shadowy and silent.

"Babe? You here?" I called out, setting my gym bag down by the door.

No answer.

I took the stairs two at a time.

The guest bath was open and empty. At the end of the hall, our bedroom door stood open. A dim glow flickered from somewhere within, but I heard nothing.

"Babe?"

Still no reply.

I was suddenly nervous. That wasn't unusual for me. I got nervous when I held my pee too long. But this was different, more fear than nerves. I wasn't sure what there was to be scared of, but some sixth sense told me to clench, so I did.

When I peeked through the doorway, those nerves morphed into a completely different racing of my heart.

Nate had spread giant beach towels across its surface and lay in their center, completely naked. The light of a dozen candles scattered throughout the room flickered in the oiled surface of his rich brown skin. The only part of him that wasn't glassy slick was his head and face, which rested with closed eyes on two fluffy pillows. A gallon jug of massage oil sat on the nightstand.

I stood in the doorway and stared.

He was stunning.

And he was *mine*.

His eyes fluttered open. "Hey, you. Sorry, I know you wanted to squirt all over me, but I decided that meant the icing, not the oil. Hope you like it."

"Sweet baby Jesus and the llama and alpaca."

He spat a laugh. "Jesus didn't have a llama ... or an alpaca."

"He should have," I said, stepping into the room. "Nate Stringer, you might be the most beautiful man to ever don the slickyness."

He chuckled. "Don the slickyness?"

"Yeah, it's a thing. At least, it is now."

He sat up on his elbows, flexing his abs as he did. My cock pulsed at the sight.

"Coop, I love you. Now, shut up and get naked."

"Oh, yeah, naked. I forgot I had clothes on," I said, ripping my T-shirt over my head faster than anyone ever had in the history of T-shirts and head-ripping. In seconds, my dick flopped free and slapped against my stomach. I was so fucking hard already.

"Happy to see me?" His grin was predatory.

"You have no idea."

"Oh"—he reached out and stroked me, the oil sending shivers across my skin—"I have an idea."

I was still struggling to kick off my tennis shoes when I felt the warmth of his mouth surround me.

"Oh, fuck, Nate."

He swallowed me down to my balls, and I nearly tumbled over. His hands gripping my cheeks and pulling me into him were the only things keeping me upright.

"Babe, wow. That feels—"

He pulled back and ran his tongue around my head. I was so sensitive. My whole body trembled.

He smiled up at me, and the sight of his crinkled eyes just above my cock sent my heart sprinting. I ran my fingers over his head, scratching his scalp the way I knew he loved. His eyes grinned further, then he dove again, resuming his swallowing and teasing.

Oil coated my fingers as I trailed them across his shoulders and neck.

A moment later, he scooted to the edge of the bed and stood, wrapping his arms around me and pressing himself as tightly against me as possible. A squishing sound made me giggle.

"Think this is funny?" he reproved playfully.

A second later, he'd spun me around and shoved me onto the bed on my back. I watched as he grabbed the KFC-bucket-sized jug of oil, popped the cap, and poured it like he was filling a Fry Daddy onto my chest.

"That's so cold!" I squirmed.

"Shut up and take your medicine."

I smeared oil that had pooled across my chest. It gleamed in the candlelight.

"Gotta admit, my nipples look hot all oiled up," I said, grinning.

He capped the oil and set it on the table, then climbed over me and sank his teeth into my right nipple. I nearly leapt out of the bed.

"Ahh!"

He reached up and pinned my arms. Our bodies slid against each other, and his cock slapped mine as he wiggled his hips back and forth.

I started to say something, but his teeth left my nipple and smothered my mouth in a ravenous, tongue-forward attack of passion and lust.

I could barely breathe. I didn't care.

Consuming Nate, letting him consume me, was all I could think or feel. His body blazed with heat and sweat, making the oil ooze between us with frictionless pleasure. He let his full weight settle onto me, and I felt his cock throbbing and pulsing. A warmer wetness coated where it pressed, and I knew he'd leaked himself all over me.

"Cooper Hawk, I fucking love you more than anything," he growled, his breath filling my nostrils with the heady scent of our peppermint toothpaste. "I want to make you feel so good."

He scooted down, gripped my legs with his hands, and hauled them over his shoulders. He'd poured so much oil on me that it dripped from his chest where we'd pressed together, dribbling trails through the curly patches of black hair on his pecs and stomach. I poked one bead with a finger, then gripped his chest and squeezed as much as his hardened muscle allowed.

"God, I love your body. It feels so—"

My breath caught as he slid inside me. There'd been no warning, no prepping, no easing in. The oil granted him entry and he took it, shoving the length of himself until my balls squished against his stomach.

"Oh shit!" I called.

I ran both hands across his chest, then gripped his arms. Corded muscles resisted my touch, sending yet another thrill through my chest. He looked so fucking hot in the candlelight. I wanted to lick him and eat him and fill my soul with his presence. I couldn't get enough of this man until . . .

He drew back and slammed into me harder. Then again, and again.

Nate's eyes flared with need. His whole body pulsed with desire.

He braced himself with his hands on my shoulders, then shoved into me even harder.

"Fuck me, deeper, please," I begged.

And he did.

Nate was normally more passion than heat, but that day he slammed me so hard I saw stars.

"Your cock is so hard," I said, my head rolling against the pillow.

"You're going to take all of it. Every. Last. Inch." He punctuated each word by slamming into me like some maddened lumberjack mutilating a hunk of wood with his axe.

Fuck, I wanted to be mutilated.

His pace quickened.

His breath shortened.

His abs tightened and he gritted his teeth.

"Wait!" I cried.

He froze. "Are you okay? Was I hurting you?" he said through labored breaths.

"I'm good. You weren't hurting me nearly enough." I grinned at his stunned face. "I just don't want this to end so ... quickly."

He smirked for the first time since I'd come home. "You saying I'm a minute man?"

"If you keep going, you'll be more like a seven-minute man. I need a lot more than that tonight. I want the cake and the cream and the cherry on top—which reminds me, I've been meaning to try this new cherry-flavored lube. I saw it on ... never mind. It looks tasty, and it's supposed to heat up as you ... you know. It sounds like fun, and I really want to slather your asshole and lick it out. Would you like that?"

Nate stared down, still throbbing inside me, his smirk now more an amused grin. "You can pop my cherry anytime."

I cocked my head. "I love you, babe, but you haven't had a cherry in years. There's nothing to pop, unless you count the sound your ass makes when I pull out. That's definitely—"

"Coop! Are you calling my ass a noisemaker?"

I shrugged. "It does *pop*. I think it's cute."

"Cute. Great. That's what every man wants to hear about the sounds his asshole makes after sex."

I giggled. "Do men really think that much about the sounds their assholes make?"

"Absolutely. I think," he said, then shoved his now semi-hard dick inside me. "All this talk about pooping sounds made Little Nate take a break. See what you've done?"

"Can't see it, but I can feel it. It's cute too," I said, then switched into little kid voice. "Wittle Nate taking a nap. Aww."

He shoved my chest and pulled out—soundlessly. "Jerk."

I reached up, grabbed his shoulders, and flipped him so our positions were reversed.

"Little Cooper isn't tired," I said, glancing meaningfully at my fully erect dick.

He followed my gaze, and his eyes widened. "He's so pretty."

"He's hungry for some popping," I said, lifting his leg over my head as he'd done mine moments before.

"Oh, babe, I'm not sure—"

Whatever he was going to say died as I shoved in just as hard as he'd done to me.

"FUCK!"

I pulled back and slammed into him again, using all my taekwondo-enhanced leg and hip strength.

"Easy, damn," he called out, one hand reaching up to grip my arm and beg for mercy.

There would be no mercy.

I slammed into him again and again, and his protests died. His fingers pinched my nipples, and bolts of lightning seared my skin.

I grabbed his other leg and tossed it over my shoulder, then hefted his body and shoved a pillow under his lower back to give me a better angle.

When I slid forward the next time, Nate's eyes rolled back, and I knew I'd found his prostate. I could feel it against the head of my penis, a tiny punching bag screaming to be jabbed.

I squeezed his legs tight with my arms and pounded his ass, savoring every moan and the way his chest heaved with each thrust. His nails dug into my skin as he grabbed my hips and urged me deeper.

But rather than speed up, I slowed until my movements were slow and steady, then I spread his legs and leaned forward to graze my lips against his. His eyes shut, and his fingers found my hair, kneading and pulling as I slid in and out. I swallowed his breath, fed on his tongue, gave myself wholly and completely to the yearning of the moment. Every thrust of my hips pressed our oily bodies together and slid my cock past the last of his inner walls.

His cock was wedged between our oily stomachs, so each time I pressed forward, it got its own thrust.

"Damn! Babe ... God. You're gonna make me—" His arms flew around me and he held me close. "Shit! I'm coming ... babe!"

I shoved harder and faster. My own abs tightened, and I welled deep inside. I was so close.

His body convulsed and he clung to me, as if afraid he might fly away in his ecstasy. Warmth and moisture shot between us, and I felt each pulse as his balls emptied against our oil-slickened bodies.

Still, I pressed inside him, deeper, harder.

"Nate!" I called out.

"Fucking fill me up, babe." I shoved deeper, and the first waves of pleasure forced me upright. I slammed my hands to his shoulders and pushed up, then pressed myself in again, flowing freely into the man I love until nothing was left to give.

Spent, I fell atop him, and he wrapped his arms around me and kissed my neck.

"I love you so much, Coop," he whispered in my ear.

"I love you too, babe."

Chapter Two

SAM (AND MIGUEL)

THERE'S SOMETHING ABOUT POPPING a hood and taking an engine apart that fills my soul. I'm not sure if it's fixing something broken or the feeling of grease under my nails. I've always loved working on cars.

I did not open a garage to work on paperwork. Paperwork sucks.

Accounting sucks worse.

Around five thirty, Ty appeared in my office doorway. "You look like shit, boss."

I peered up with just my eyes, a glower that didn't deserve a raise of my head.

"Easy. Don't shoot." Ty put up his hands. "I mean, you usually look pretty shitty, but today must be something special. You look extra shitty. Or should that be shitty deluxe, like a pizza?"

"There are moments when I truly hate you," I grumbled.

Ty flashed a brilliant smile and flicked his shoulder-length hair dramatically. "No, you don't. You love me with every fiber of your being, and that grates at your nerves. I get it. I'm hard not to love."

"No. Really, you're not. In fact, I'm finding not loving you pretty easy right now."

He chuckled and stepped in, flopping into the beat-up leather chair I'd had since college. "Working the books today?"

I nodded, tossing my pen on the ledger.

"It's good to be the king," he said.

"Until it isn't," I said, my ancient office chair screaming as I leaned back. "Something I can do for you? Shouldn't you be heading home to lover boy?"

His face brightened further at the mention of his husband.

"Lover boy won't be home until late, something about an owner running late for their pickup. That happens about once a week. Drives him crazy."

"I bet." He scanned the photos covering the far wall, most of happy customers with their repaired cars or trucks, a few of our mutual friends, our shared family. "What are you guys up to this weekend?"

Ty shrugged. "No idea."

I snorted.

"What?"

"It wasn't that long ago that Ty the Terrible would be planning his next conquest around this time on a Friday. Now look at you, surrendering to marital bliss and the will of your better half."

His brow rose along with one finger. "First, he *is* my better half. There's no question about that." A second finger popped up. "And second, I would be planning multiple conquests, thank you very much. Friday and Saturday night each deserved their own victory."

"Victory or victim," I teased.

"Victory," he scowled. "There were never victims, only the next willing hottie in line to sample the fabulousness that is Tyler Hyatt and his magic cock."

I groaned. "I could've gone years without hearing you say that."

He laughed. "Magic? Celestial? Euphoric? Pick your adjective."

"Annoying. Infinitesimal. Un—""I don't even want to know that last word," he groused. "It's the eighth wonder of the world, even if you are too wrapped up in Smiley to understand that."

I grunted.

"How is our favorite cop? We haven't seen you guys in a few weeks. Feels like forever."

"He's great. Been working like a dog and comes home beat, but he loves it." I watched Ty look back to the wall of pictures, his gaze lingering on an older woman we both knew years before. "How are you boys? Still enjoying your honeymoon?"

He smiled without turning toward me. "I hope that phase never ends. It's been almost three years and it still feels new."

"Like your conquests?" I meant it as a jibe, but his face was sober when he turned back toward me.

"That's my past, Sam. Thank God it's in the rearview mirror. Gabe is the best thing that's ever happened to me, and I'd die before screwing this up."

I crossed my arms and cocked my head. "You don't miss the scene at all? Even a little? I hear Palm Springs is coming up soon."

The circuit party in Palm Springs had always been Ty's favorite. He'd talk about it for months, then spend hundreds on new shirts he'd likely never wear, save to hang off a belt loop while he wiggled to music and lasers.

"Is it?" he asked, and to my utter astonishment, I believed he hadn't realized it was. "That's so not my world anymore, and no, I don't miss it at all. It was fun for a while, but, I don't know … it was so … hollow, like nothing meant anything. I didn't get that at the time. Hell, you tried to tell me as much, but I wouldn't listen."

"Damn straight—on both the me telling and you not listening."

He rolled his eyes. "Yes, Mom, you were right."

I grinned. "Mothers always are."

He shook his head. "I don't regret any of it. Well, most of it. There might've been a few things I regretted—but it's just a chapter in the book of my life, and I've moved on."

"Oh, God," I said, gripping my stomach. "Now he's waxing poetic. I'm gonna hurl."

He snorted and looked away again. Something on the wall kept drawing his eye. Then he spoke in a reverent whisper. "Do you ever think about her?"

"Who?

"Marjorie Polk."

"All the time." My eyes drifted to the framed photo of the white-topped woman with the effervescent smile and stern gaze. "She bought my freedom when she paid off the shop. Miguel does okay as a cop, but we'd still be clipping coupons and juggling bills if it wasn't for her."

"You remember her smile?"

I startled. That was a very un-Ty-like question.

"Yeah."

He closed his eyes. "I can still see her walking up to the shop, that ruby red car behind her. Can't believe she left that to you too."

Marjorie had willed her husband's 1955 Bel Air, a car he cherished for decades before he passed. That car, with its ailing engine, brought us all together.

"Still runs great. Miguel and I take it out for a spin on nice days, drop the top. Feels like she's in the back seat with us sometimes, giggling like a little girl."

"She left us Coop too," Ty said wistfully. "I didn't know what to make of that kid when he threw up all over your office."

I laughed despite the heavy topic. "He is known for his word vomit."

Ty chuckled. "I love that guy. He might be the best of us."

"Us?"

"Our family," Ty said without hesitation. "That's what we are, Sam. You know that."

I thought a moment, then nodded. "Yeah, I guess we are."

Chapter Three

Miguel (and Sam)

Fridays weren't usually painful; at least, not until the sun went down and the kids went crazy. Any cop would tell you those were long nights. Thankfully, my day shift ended as the sun winked below the horizon, but just after the worst of the weekend, rush hour subsided.

I climbed into my cruiser and let my head fall against the rest. *Maybe I'm more tired than I thought.*

My phone buzzed, and I realized I'd almost fallen asleep. I glanced down and smiled at the notification.

Sam the mechanic: Put the handcuffs away and get your ass home.

Me: I thought you liked my handcuffs.

SAM THE MECHANIC: OKAY, CHANGE OF PLANS. BRING YOUR HANDCUFFS HOME ... AND YOUR ASS.

ME: HA. I'M IN THE CAR. SEE YOU IN TWENTY.

SAM THE MECHANIC: LOVE YOU. LOVE YOUR ASS MORE.

ME: IT LOVES YOU TOO.

I stared at the screen a few seconds after he sent his last text, grinning like a goofy boy passing notes in class. Sam the Mechanic was how I'd entered his name in my phone when we'd met, and I'd never changed it. It still made me grin.

The first time I saw Sam, almost five years ago, he'd put on this air of the gruff mechanic, painfully straight, uninterested in anything but cars and his shop. It's the role he plays with his customers, so I guess it made sense. Technically, the police department was the customer that day. We'd screwed up by taking a murder victim's car to his garage by mistake, and he'd been as caught off guard as I had been at our chance meeting.

Still, I remember his eyes the first time they locked onto mine. He'd stepped out of the shop, and the setting sun shot straight through a tree to warm his face. I'd never seen pools of blue so deep and rich, almost electric. I remember wondering if he wore colored contacts, but details jump out when you're a cop, and I couldn't find any evidence of lenses. My searching for them made him blush and turn away. My heart still flutters seeing the tough mechanic melt before me.

My phone buzzed again. This time, it wasn't Sam.

NateStringerOfficial: Yo, dude.

Nate was one of our closest friends. I spent a couple years mentoring him when he was in college at Vandy. I was in the minors and he thought I was a god. Now, he calls me Dad. I'm not sure which fits better.

The Nashville Sounds released Nate, ending his hopes of a major league career, but the Memphis Mangoes, a sort of Harlem Globetrotters of baseball, picked him up. Their antics now littered TikTok and Facebook feeds almost as much as piano-playing cats.

Me: Did you just "dude" me? You give up baseball for surfing?

NateStringerOfficial: Sorry, in Mango mode.

NateStringerOfficial: The guys are a trip. You'd love hanging out with them.

ME: I'M ABOUT TO BE IN BANANA MODE … OR IS THAT CUCUMBER? ZUCCHINI? HEADED HOME TO SEE SAM.

NateStringerOfficial: EW. I DO NOT NEED TO KNOW ABOUT MOM AND DAD PLAYING WITH EACH OTHER'S … FRUITS AND VEGETABLES. I'LL NEVER GET THAT NASTY IMAGE OUT OF MY MIND.

ME: HA HA. YOU'D LOVE IT IF YOU TRIED IT. TRUST ME. YOU COULD BOUNCE A QUARTER OFF SAM'S ASS. AND HIS EGGPLANT IS PERFECTION!

ME: BESIDES, HOW DO YOU THINK LITTLE NATES ARE MADE? YOU DIDN'T JUST MAGICALLY APPEAR.

NateStringerOfficial: I NEED ONE OF THOSE AIRPLANE BARF BAGS, STAT!

NateStringerOfficial: Besides, if you two have figured out how to make little Nates, we're going on Oprah. You get a Nate … and you get a Nate … EVERYBODY GETS A NATE!

I was laughing so hard, I nearly dropped the phone.

Me: God, no. The world can barely handle the one Nate we have.

NateStringerOfficial: That's for damn sure.

NateStringerOfficial: How is Mom, anyway? Feels like forever since we saw you guys.

Me: It's been almost a year—not that we keep track or anything. You just don't love your parents anymore. Ungrateful heathen children.

NateStringerOfficial: That's us. Rotten bastards running naked in the streets and fornicating.

Me: At least I taught you well.

NateStringerOfficial: LOL right.

NateStringerOfficial: Anyway, I actually had a reason for texting.

Me: Talking to your parents isn't reason enough? Got it. I see how you are.

NateStringerOfficial: You really are Dad, you know that?

NateStringerOfficial: Coop and I were talking. We really miss you guys. Memphis is great, and he's killing it at

THE TAEKWONDO THING, BUT WE'RE PRETTY ISOLATED HERE.

Something in his text plucked at my heart. Nate wasn't rough around the edges like Sam, but he rarely opened up and talked about his feelings. Even after the Sounds released him, when he hit his version of rock bottom, it was like pulling a deeply embedded splinter to get him to talk.

ME: YOU OKAY, NATE? TALK TO ME.

NateStringerOfficial: OH, YEAH. DIDN'T MEAN TO WORRY YOU. SORRY. WE'RE GREAT. COOP IS AMAZING, AND I LOVE BEING A MANGO EVEN MORE THAN I DID PLAYING IN THE MiBL.

ME: BUT?

The dots danced, then stilled, then danced again.

NateStringerOfficial: IT'S JUST KIND OF LONELY. WE'RE IN THE OFF-SEASON, SO A LOT OF THE GUYS ARE BACK HOME WITH FAMILY.

ME: I get that. The off-season was always kind of weird for me too. Like I didn't know what to do with myself.

NateStringerOfficial: Exactly!

ME: You could come home, stay here. Stay as long as you like. Sam would love to see you.

NateStringerOfficial: I could never do that to Coop, and his gym doesn't shut down for the holidays until the week before Christmas.

ME: So, come home for Christmas. How long will Coop's dojang be closed?

NateStringerOfficial: Until after New Year. Two weeks, give or take.

ME: That's perfect. Drag Coop's ass home to see your parents. You're long overdue.

NateStringerOfficial: You know, it's not a bad idea. You're not nearly as dumb as you look, Dad.

ME: Hey! Watch it, kid. I look plenty dumb.

NateStringerOfficial: Prosecution rests. Read that bit again and you'll see why.

NateStringerOfficial: Let me talk to Coop. Love the idea of hanging out for a couple weeks, especially around the holidays.

NateStringerOfficial: Please tell me Mom isn't decorating the house already. It's not even Thanksgiving.

ME: We got the tree last week. Lights go up tomorrow. Let there be holiday cheer!

NateStringerOfficial: Is it too late to reconsider the visit?

ME: Very funny. By the time we're done, it'll look like Santa threw up everywhere. It'll be amazing.

NateStringerOfficial: Ew. I'm definitely reconsidering. Chunks of elves isn't pleasing to the eye.

ME: Santa would only spew elf chunks if he'd eaten his helpers. I don't know about your St. Nick stories, but cannibalism was never part of my holiday cheer.

NateStringerOfficial: Unless the elf was hot and had a gigantic cock. You'd eat him then.

Me: Swallow, never chew.

NateStringerOfficial: Oh, god. I'm going to hurl. Tell Mom hi.

Me: Yes, dear. Love you boys.

I chuckled, waiting for another reply, but the dots remained firmly in their tight little row, so I tossed my phone on the passenger seat and fired up the cruiser. It hadn't been a bad day, but back-to-back text chains from my two favorite men made it a lot better.

I smiled all the way home.

Chapter Four

Sam (and Miguel)

Sam usually turned the porch light on at night, especially when he knew I was coming home late. He argued I shouldn't walk into a dark home, that I should always see that he loved me and was there waiting.

For a gruff mechanic, he was about as sweet and gushy as they came. And I loved every minute of it.

When I pulled into the driveway and clicked the garage door open, the porch light was dark. I paused a second before pulling forward, eyeing each of the street-facing windows, unable to find any lights on in the house. Sam's car was parked in its usual spot on the left side of the garage.

My gut, trained by years of police work to suspect anything out of the ordinary, began to churn.

As I stepped through the door that led from the garage directly into the kitchen, I was again surprised by how tidy things were. At this hour, Sam normally had ten pots or pans scattered across the stove and countertops. He was a decent cook, but created more mess than any one human should when prepping a meal.

There wasn't a single pan anywhere in sight. The house was utterly dark and eerily quiet.

I resisted the urge to call out, instinctively resting my hand on the grip of the sidearm on my hip, then stepped slowly through the kitchen, past the living room, to the bottom of the stairs. Every room was the same: dark and empty.

Panic began to well in my gut as I climbed the stairs, careful to step slowly on the edge of each to avoid creaks and groans. Something danced above, a flicker of light, some tiny glow that felt … off.

I reached the top of the stairs. Our bedroom was dark, and I could just make out the still-made empty bed.

We kept the hall bathroom and guest room doors closed, and only blackness crept through the crack beneath them.

There was only one place left to check.

I could feel the weight of a massive stone pressing down on my chest as I stepped into the bedroom. The flicker I'd seen before reappeared from the partially opened door to our master bath. It looked like a beam, maybe a flashlight, but then it danced.

I gripped my gun and flicked it free of the holster.

The house remained deathly silent, though my heart's pounding filled my ears.

When I reached the bathroom door, I paused, listening. Still nothing.

I drew my weapon, steeled myself, and shoved the door open.

"Whoa! Don't shoot!" Sam yelled. He was partially submerged beneath a sea of bubbles in our oversized soaking tub. One lone candle, about the size of my thumb, flickered from the window sill above. "That's not the gun I hoped you'd draw on me when you got home."

I blew out the breath I hadn't realized I'd been holding and holstered my gun. "Dear, God, Sam. You scared me half to death."

"Surprise," he said, pulling his sudsy hands free of the water and doing jazz hands to match his goofy grin. "I ordered Chinese, told them to hold the delivery until nine. I thought you might be all hot and sweaty after a day's work and need help to clean up. I'm a good back scrubber."

I leaned against the vanity and looked down at the beautiful, bubble-covered man before me. Sam's thick black stubble was a couple days past its usual expiration, forming the beginning of an impressive beard and offsetting his ocean blue eyes. His body was covered by the soapy water, but the upper half of his impressively hard chest, glistening wet, sat above the waterline.

The rumbling fear that churned my gut a moment before shifted, and a very different gun below my belt began to stir.

"I am kind of dirty," I said, pretending to sniff my arm. "You might need to scrub inside too."

His grin turned lecherous, and he hefted his hips out of the water and stroked his already hardened cock. "Good thing my body has a tool for that."

I wanted to be turned on. I really did—but the bubbles covering his dick made me laugh.

"What? I was trying to be all sexy."

I snorted. "You are all sexy, babe, but those bubbles ... "

He glanced down, and his expression became pained, only adding fuel to my laughter.

"Shut up and get naked," he growled as his crotch sank back beneath the surface.

"Yes, sir. I've been looking forward to seeing you and ... Mr. Bubbles all day."

"Oh, fuck, no. You are not nicknaming my cock Mr. Bubbles."

"Too late. Already did. It's cute." I gave him my widest grin.

He glowered, then one lone finger rose from the bubble ocean.

"Wow. You have birds down there too? This is quite the bath."

His other hand rose with another bird.

I let my heavy-duty belt drop and stripped out of my uniform as quickly as possible. When the last sock flew into the bedroom and I turned, fully naked, to face Sam, his eyes widened appreciatively.

"You're so fucking hot," he said.

I tried not to blush. After nearly five years together, Sam still stole my breath. His compliments were even more overwhelming.

"You're not so bad yourself," I said.

"Step over here and stand in front of the tub for a second."

I did as instructed. The moment I was within reach, he leaned forward and took my waking cock into his mouth. There was no gentleness, no caress or kiss. He opened and consumed everything he could shove down his throat. I arched my back and tried not to fall over, pleasure radiating throughout my body like lines of eager ants racing back to their hills. His hands rose from the tub to grip my hips. Warmth pressed into my skin with his touch, and water dribbled down my legs.

Still, Sam shoved me inside his mouth, again and again, until my semi-hard dick was pulsing with need.

"Step in," he said, offering a hand as I lifted a foot over the tub's rim.

We usually lay back-to-chest in a bath so one of us could hold the other, but this time he guided me to sit facing him with our legs overlapping.

"Wow. That water feels nice," I said.

He leaned forward, gripped the sides of my head with both hands, and pulled me into a deep kiss. One hand remained firm, while the other released my head and fingers began gently rubbing my scalp. I let out a low moan.

"That's my boy," he said. "I'm going to take care of you tonight. Now, turn around so I can wash your back."

I had just gotten comfortable, but did as instructed, awkwardly twisting until my butt settled between his legs. Sudsy water trickled down my back as he scrubbed with a swollen sponge, first on my shoulders, then my neck, then down my back. Sam's touch was gentle, deliberate, as he washed the day from my skin. When he finished my back, he leaned forward and reached around to bathe my chest, planting kisses on my neck as he did.

The sponge floated to the far end of the tub as Sam's hand teased the muscles of my stomach, then drifted lower to play with my tip. I leaned my head back, resting it against his shoulder, and he bit into my neck and gripped my shaft.

"That feels so good."

His teeth moved from my neck to my earlobe, and he bit—hard.

"Ow!"

"Let's get dry so I can make you dirty again," he growled in my ear.

"Yes, sir," I said.

"What do you want me to do to you?"

My skin tingled at the question. "Anything you want."

I stood and stepped out of the tub, then helped him do the same. When I reached for a towel, he batted my hand away and unfurled one he'd grabbed, then began gently dabbing the water off my chest.

"Oh no. You need to tell me. I want to hear it."

My mind whirled. "I want you to kiss me."

His dabbing paused, as his lips found mine, his tongue slipping through to press inside.

It amazed me, after all these years, how such a simple kiss could turn my insides to mush. If his arms weren't holding me up, I might've melted all over the bathroom floor.

He stepped forward, our lips never parting, and pressed me against the vanity. Every part of our bodies pressed against each other; I felt how much he wanted me. The contagion of his throbbing and pulsing infected my body and addled my thoughts. All I could feel were his lips pressing into mine, and his cock—

"You're leaking," he panted, his hand drifting down so a finger could lap up my pre-cum. I shivered at his touch, then watched as he lifted his finger to his lips and licked it clean. "I love appetizers," he said, as much with his eyes as his words.

"I want you inside me," came out before I realized what I'd said.

His eyes flared, and firm hands gripped my shoulders and wheeled me around to face the mirror. I'd barely looked back before he'd opened the middle drawer and lubed up his hand with the spare bottle I'd forgotten was in there. Slick fingers split my cheeks, as he rubbed others up and down, teasing my hole.

"Fuck!" No longer gentle, he shoved a finger inside me. "Ah! Damn, babe."Ignoring my body's resistance, he drew the finger out and shoved two in.

I lurched forward and arched my back.

He twisted his hand around so his fingers faced down, then crooked them so the tip of one teased my prostate.

"Oh shit. That's—"

He jerked his fingers out, yanked my hips back, and thrust his hardened dick deep inside me. I hadn't even heard him wet it, and now he was deeper than a proctological exam by a sadist.

"Holy fucking shit," I yelled.

He pulled back and slammed me again, and again, and again.

By the fourth or fifth thrust, my ass had finally relaxed, and pleasure joined pain. Sam's hands reached around and grabbed my chest, squeezing, nails digging into my skin as he pushed himself harder and faster.

One hand released, then gripped, my hair, yanking my head back so he could kiss my neck then smother my mouth.

Our tongues speared and thrust in time with his cock, and my whole body began to tremble.

"Do it, Sam. Fucking fill me up. Shove it in me," I shouted.

His grip on my hair tightened as his thrusting grew stronger and faster. I hadn't thought his cock could grow larger, but it felt like all of Sam was crawling inside me. And still, I wanted more.

"Harder!"He shoved my head down, bending me over the vanity so he could get a better angle, then thrust with all the strength of his meaty legs. It felt like he'd struck a lung.

"Holy shit, Sam!"

His hand clawed at my hips, pulling me into him with each push. "I'm getting close," he growled. "You're fucking mine, Miguel."

"Prove it. Make me yours."

His breathing grew louder, almost a groan. His body tensed behind me, his cock throbbing inside me, then the flickering candle burst into a brilliant sun as he released himself into my body.

"I'm coming!" he hollered.

I straightened and bowed back so my head was against his forehead, then grabbed my cock and began stroking. With him inside me, a gentle wind could make me come, and I shot all over the sink in a second.

Still, he thrust into me, slower, emptying the last of himself, enjoying the hyper-sensitive twitching of a fresh release. When his body shivered, he pressed inside and held himself there. Strong arms wrapped around and held me tight, as his lips found his favorite spot between my shoulders once more.

"God, I love you," he said through ragged gulps.

"What did I do to deserve you, Sam Prescott?" I whispered through my own raspy breaths.

When he answered, I heard the snarky voice I'd first fallen in love with in the parking lot of his mechanic shop. "You don't, but you're the best I could find at the moment."

I glanced in the mirror to see a shit-eating grin teasing his mouth, then a few teeth poked through as he found his jibe more amusing.

I clenched with all my strength on his softening cock. "Asshole."

"Is that an expletive or an offer?" His smirk widened. "Don't threaten me with another good time."

As I shook my head, he pulled out, and while I knew he stood behind me, I suddenly felt incomplete. There was nothing in the world that made me feel whole like one of us being inside the other.

I spun and kissed him again. "Let's get cleaned up. That Chinese food should be here any minute, and I'd rather not let the delivery guy see your Cream of Some Young Guy."

He groaned. "How long have you been waiting to use that? It's terrible. No points."

"Aw, come on. That's worth a few. At least a point or two for effort."

He grinned and flicked my dick. "One point because I love your cock. No points for the joke."

Right on cue, the doorbell rang.

Chapter Five

Tyler (and Gabe)

By the time I walked through the door, it was dark outside. Fall was clinging on by her nails, resisting winter's call, but I sucked in a grateful breath as the warmth of our home flooded into me.

"Hey, buddy," I said, kneeling down to wrap my arms around Dom in our ritual greeting. His black and white fur blurred to gray as his tail nearly wagged his whole butt off. A smile bloomed in my chest as his slobbery tongue found my ear.

"Eww, Dom. No tonguing my lobe."

His wagging intensified, and his tongue struck home again.

Audie bounded into the room a second later. If anyone but Gabe or I had entered, she would've been all teeth and hackles. Like most German shepherds, she had a protective streak stronger than a pro football team's offensive line guarding a quarterback.

"Hey, baby girl," I said, grabbing a handful of wiry black and brown fur.

Dom slammed his head into my chest.

"Don't be jelly. There's enough of daddy for both of you," I said as the beast rammed me again, this time hard enough to topple me onto the floor.

"Alright! Who's hungry?" I asked, knowing it was the only question that might free me from our pernicious pups. Affectionate, playful wags exploded into excited hopping and pleading whines. Dom spun in circles like he was chasing his tail.

I struggled to my feet, then strode into the kitchen. "Who wants good dinner tonight?"

The whining turned into howls. Gabe had found a powdered gravy online that came in three-gallon jugs, enough to feed the entire neighborhood some meaty goodness. Add a little hot water, and dry food became a meal of doggie royalty—or so Dom and Audie thought. They lost their little brains the moment either of us said "good dinner," our code for "we're adding the gravy tonight."

When the monsters were happily gobbling up their supper, I headed upstairs to our bedroom to shower and change. I'd cleaned most of the grease from my nails back at the shop, but the stink of car guts always lingered. A photo on the nightstand caught my eye and I paused before entering the bathroom.

Gabe stared back at me, his dark floppy hair blowing in the Mediterranean breeze. His smile still sent my heart fluttering, like some schoolgirl about to get her first kiss. The picture was from our first visit to his home, where I'd met his parents and brother. It was also when I'd surrendered myself completely to him and asked his father for permission to marry Gabe.

I traced a finger across his cheek, feeling only glass, but my chest warmed all the same.

It's funny how frozen moments in time hold such power over our hearts.

I returned the photo to its rightful place and stepped into the bathroom, cranking the shower as hot as it would go. When I stepped in, the rush of heat across my skin sank into muscles I hadn't realized were sore. I pressed my palms to the wall opposite the showerhead and enjoyed a few moments of blissful peace beneath the steamy stream.

A light attached to the wall above the toilet flickered, as did a dozen other strategically positioned lights throughout the house. Before I met Gabe, I never even thought about little things, like how a deaf person would know if a phone was ringing, or if someone was standing outside the front door. The flashing light likely meant Gabe had just walked in, so I shut off the water and began toweling down.

"Hey, babe," his voice drifted from downstairs. It had taken me over a year not to yell back at his call. Little things were funny.

I reached over and pressed a button, sending the lights throughout the house dancing in reply. A moment later, the clomp of his boots sounded against our hardwood stairs.

"God, I love your outfit," he said, his eyes roaming up and down my body and the towel loosely wrapped around my waist.

I tossed the towel into the bathroom and stepped close enough to pull him to me. "And I love everything about you, Mr. Rossi."

Our kisses had always been warm, sweet even, but three years into our relationship, they'd taken on layers of meaning I'd never known before. I brushed hair back from his forehead and reveled in his smile.

"Welcome home."

"Thanks." His beam brightened further. "I stink."

I chuckled and made a dramatic show of sniffing his neck.

"Yeah, dog poop isn't exactly the fashion scent this year." Gabe owned a dog training academy, and came home smelling far worse than any mechanic might after a long day's work. "My turn for a shower." He shoved my chest, and I stumbled to fall onto the bed. "Whatcha want for dinner?"

I arranged a pillow behind my head and scooched upright. "We haven't been to the store this week. Might be a pizza night."

He leaned down and kissed me again. "I love how you open a pizza box."

I was a classically trained chef, but Gabe took every opportunity to poke fun when I leapt at a shortcut in the kitchen.

"Careful, or I'll unbox you right now and you won't get that shower."

His brows shot up, then he shoved me back down onto my back. "I'm filthy. No hanky-panky until after pizza and *Survivor*."

"Yes, dear," I said with a smirk.

He leaned down and took my cock in his mouth, swirling the tip with his tongue, then let it flop free and darted into the bathroom.

"Asshole!" I called out, a little breathless from the unexpected rush of whatever flooded a man's groin when it got sucked.

"I'm deaf. Can't hear you. Please leave a message at the beep," he yelled back, and I was certain he'd been facing me to read my lips when I'd shouted.

An hour later, we sat cuddled with our feet touching on the ottoman and a pizza box spread across both our laps. Fuck plates.

On TV, Jeff Probst stopped a challenge due to an injured competitor, and the screen faded to black for a commercial break.

Audie sat faithfully by Gabe's side, while Dom was glued to mine. Four eyes rose and fell as we took each bite. Gabe reached down and scratched Audie's ear, then gave her a small piece of crust.

"She's about to turn ten. Can you believe it? Feels like yesterday she was a pup in a shoebox. God, she was cute."

"I bet she was," I said, leaning over and kissing Gabe's temple. He pressed into me, and we lingered with our heads touching. "Someone else has a birthday too."

He turned to face me with a questioning gaze.

"Sorry. Someone else has a birthday soon too," I repeated.

He smiled and nodded. "The big three-oh. Guess I'll have to start acting like a grown-up."

I nearly spat a piece of pepperoni. "You've owned your own business since you were twenty-one. I think you have the adulting thing down already."

He grinned. "Maybe. Still, moving up a checkbox feels … weird. Kind of daunting."

"Moving up a checkbox?"

"Yeah. You know, on forms. They put age ranges by little boxes. I'm moving up to the thirty-something box."

"Damn, I didn't realize you were getting so old. Do I need to get you a walker? Would you like wheels or tennis balls on the bottom of its legs?"

His elbow dug into my ribs as he giggled. The sound of his awkward laughter nearly brought tears to my eyes every time I heard it, like hearing a baby giggle. It just warmed my soul.

"Well," I continued, once he was done spearing me with sharp parts of his arm. "What do you want for your birthday? Should we go somewhere? Do something?"

"A trip sounds great, but I can't really leave right now. I'm down a worker at the academy." He thought a moment. "I'm not sure I really need anything."

I rolled my eyes. "It's your birthday. It's not about *needing*."

His eyes widened, and he lifted the pizza box to shift to face me. "I know what I want."

"Name it. Anything at all," I said.

"I want you to cook an enormous meal and for us to have Sam and Miguel over. Annie too." He paused, then added excitedly, "And Ben. God, how could I forget him? He would love it."

Ben was a deaf kid I'd been mentoring through the Big Brother program for years; although, once he'd met Gabe, I took more of a backseat role in the relationship. They bonded as only deaf people could. Still, he felt like a son to me, and the thought of him joining us made me smile.

"Definitely add Ben," I said. "We might need to ask the guys to host. Their place might be more comfortable for all those people."

He nodded absently, as his eyes drifted far away. "I wish the others could come. It's been forever since we've seen Coop and Nate."

I cupped his cheek, drawing his eyes back to me. "Me too." I started to move my hand, to reach for another slice of pizza, then spoke without thinking. "It's funny ..."

"What?" he asked, when I didn't go on.

"Oh, sorry. Earlier today, Sam and I were talking, just hanging out at the end of a long day. He brought up the whole gang, like he missed them too. He said something that really hit me."

"What's that?"

"He called us a family. All of us. Like, no matter how far away we are, we're still, I don't know, bound together. Sam and I have been family for years, but I guess I never really thought about everybody else like that …"

"But?"

I smiled as he read my thoughts. "But, when he said it out loud, it made sense. And not just the common sense of something that clicks. I felt it in here." I tapped my chest.

Gabe stared without speaking. His smile never faltered, and I thought moisture might threaten his eyes.

"I don't know. Maybe I'm being silly or mushy or—"

"You're being the man I love." He pressed his palm to my chest. "We *are* family, all of us. And I really miss them too."

Chapter Six

Nick (and André and Ethan)

Snow had battered Cleveland in an unusually early winter blast the day before Thanksgiving, dumping more than eight inches. Normally, the hearty midwestern city would shrug off such a paltry amount, but the early-season storm had caught everyone by surprise. The city hadn't yet activated their usual fleet of landscape trucks and snow plows, so arteries and minor roads alike were all but impassable. Schools closed (even though they were only supposed to be open a half-day), and most businesses hung a "Be back after Thanksgiving" sign hours before their originally planned break.

The Guardians' season had ended with a whimper in September, so my days were beginning to blur together. If it wasn't for the daily routine of getting Ethan out of bed, fed, and off to school, weekdays and weekends might've been lost too.

André's work never ended.

We'd barely moved into our new home in Cleveland before two different organizations offered him positions on their staffs. Psychiatrists were in high demand and surprisingly difficult to find. He missed the Ranch, speaking of the kids and staff often, but kept too busy to obsess on what we left behind.

My eyes fluttered open, and the comforting sound of André's deep, rhythmic breathing filled the air. He never quite snored, but his breath would catch at times, jarring me awake from even the deepest sleep. Despite those unwelcomed interruptions, his slow, almost melodic breathing that followed usually lulled me back into the world of dreams.

I propped myself on an elbow and gently traced my fingers through the thick mane of silver and black fur that covered his taut chest. André did have bulky muscles, like those who spent years pushing metal plates, but his passion for running kept his lean frame tight and his muscles corded. At forty-five, he had a better body than many thirty-somethings.

The morning's chill had his slightly oversized nipples standing at attention, and I couldn't resist the temptation to tease them. He mumbled something in his sleep, but didn't stir. The man could sleep through anything.

I leaned over and kissed his shoulder, intending to force myself from the warmth of our covers and get started with the day, but a wiry bundle of energy had other plans. Ethan bounded onto the bed like an Olympic pole vaulter—sans pole—into the tiny crack of space between our bodies, then bounced on his knees as if riding a miniature pogo stick.

"No school. No school. No school," he chanted, as if a half-day off was the sweetest treat he'd ever tasted.

I grinned and mussed his brackish hair that swirled and stood in only the way a nine-year-old's could after a night of fitful sleep.

André's eyes finally opened. "What is all this racket? Do you not know I am trying to sleep?" His thick French accent was cold syrup on our wintry day.

Ethan fell over, flopping onto his chest where I'd stroked only a moment before. "Aw, come on, Dad, get up. It snowed last night!" Childish glee threaded his every word.

"Snow? *Vraiment*?" André made a mock O with his mouth and widened his eyes.

"*Oui*!" Ethan said, using one of the few French words he'd learned in the past year. "It's amazing-ment."

André howled. "Amazing-ment is not a French word, Ethan. You offend all the French people with your loose tongue."

Ethan stuck his tongue out and tried to look down at it. "It-th not looth," he said, nearly biting his tongue as he spoke.

André reached up and tried to pinch it before the boy sucked it back into his mouth.

"Too slow," Ethan declared before pushing himself off André.

"Ow!" André bellowed. "You have bony knees, son."

"I want pancakes. And bacon," Ethan said, ignoring André's complaint.

"Don't look at me," I said, holding my hands up as though the boy held a gun. "He's the chef around here."

André gave me a sly grin, then shoved me under the proverbial bus with both hands. "I will make the pancakes, but only if your other papa bundles you both up and takes you outside to play while I cook."

Ethan exploded in a frenzy of bounces and ear-piercing squeals. "Can we, Dad? Really? Snow fight! Snow fight! Snow fight!"

As I laughed at his enthusiasm, I shot André a scowl, receiving a very French smirk in reply.

"I don't know the right French word to call you right now, but I'm thinking it in English. You hear me, Frenchie?"

André chuckled. "You called me Frenchie. That is bad enough. Now go take our son and make snow angels."

Ethan bolted out of our room before I could even stand. By the time I'd used the bathroom and wiped the sleep from my eyes, he was fully clothed and had his heavy coat snugly zipped to his chin.

"I'm ready. Hurry up!" he barked as I stared blankly into the bathroom mirror.

"Go get your gloves and your rubber shoes. I think I saw them in the bin by the door the other day."

"Okay," he chirped as he streaked away.

"You created a monster," André said through chuckles, as he entered the bathroom and wrapped his arms around my waist. He kissed between my shoulder blades, and I laid my head back to rest on his.

"You were supposed to be his doctor. If anything's broken, it's your fault." He tried to bite into my back, but the skin wouldn't give.

"He is not broken. He is beautiful. Perfect, even."

My smile was immediate and wide. "Yeah, he is."

"You healed him more than anyone, Nick. You know that, do you not?"

I spun around, careful not to shake his arms free. "I just talked to him, played with him."

"And that is what he needed. It was something we did not see, something we could not give him. You became his friend long before you were his father. Could there be anything more healing to a lost boy than that?"

I was suddenly overwhelmed by the love in this house—between André and me; between Ethan and both of us. The family of my youth hadn't felt this way. Staring into André's eternal gaze, I questioned the reality of that simple moment.

I choked back the lump wedged in my throat and squeezed his hands clasped around my belly, then felt the softness of his lips as they blessed my skin again. His hands unwound, and he made for the toilet.

"No offense, but I've been in here when you do your morning business. It's not pretty. I'm going to go tame our beast."

"*Bonne chance* with that. He will always be a wild one." He grunted. "Give me a half-hour. I will have his magical pancakes and bacon ready by then."

ALMOST AN HOUR LATER, Ethan and I stripped off the rubber liner over our shoes and shed our heavy coats. We were both breathing heavily from tumbling in the thick November snow. Ethan's cheeks glowed a brilliant red, and his breath puffed out in plumes before him. Still, his boyish smile never wavered. His was the exhaustion that only came with the raucous play of youth.

"Alright, you two. Pancakes are on the table and getting cold," André called from the kitchen.

"I don't remember him being so … mom-ish at the Ranch," Ethan said conspiratorially.

I only gaped a second before doubling over with laughter. Ethan's delighted giggles added to my chorus.

"I do not know what is so funny about cold pancakes. Come eat, young men."

Ethan's laughter bounded louder off the wooden walls of the mudroom, causing my own humor to grow in volume.

"Come on, before he uses your middle name," I whispered.

"Ethan *Jacob* Martin-Dunlap, get your skinny little butt into this kitchen!"

Ethan's eyes shot to mine, and his laughter paused as he processed what André had just yelled.

I cocked a brow, as if reproving, but couldn't hold back. As we entered the kitchen, my arm draped around my boy, tears rolled down both our cheeks.

"I let you two out of my sight for two minutes …" André waved a spatula at us, fanning our flames.

We took our seats and André began squeezing syrup onto his pancakes.

"My pancakes are cold," Ethan said in a simpering voice.

André shot him a death glare.

The boy looked to me, and I lost it, nearly spitting coffee all over the table.

"You two are as bad as Kervin and Zack," André mused.

"I miss Uncle Zack," Ethan said, shoveling his first bite of pancake into his mouth.

"Me too," I said. "It's funny. I lived with those guys, spent most of our days together then played games together at night. Now we go months without seeing them."

"Why can't they come up for Thanksgiving?" Ethan asked.

I glanced to André, then back to him. "That's a great idea. I wish I'd thought of it, but Thanksgiving is tomorrow, buddy. They probably already have plans."

"Have you asked them?" he persisted.

I looked back to André for backup, but he had focused all his attention on his bacon, like some food-crazed Frenchman on one of those cooking competition shows.

"No," I answered. "Guess I haven't."

"What if they don't have plans and they have to spend Thanksgiving alone, just the two of them? That would be really sad."

"Just the two of them. Not so sad when you say it out loud," André muttered only loud enough for me to hear, a curl forming at the corner of his mouth.

"How about this? Finish your breakfast and we can call them together. I'll put them on speakerphone so we can all talk to them."

Ethan brightened. "Play the kid card. I like it."

My eyes widened. When I turned to André, his were saucers.

"I didn't teach him that," I said.

"Do not look at me," André said.

"Guys, I'm right here." Ethan waved his tiny fingers. "I can hear you. Maybe I learn things from people *other* than you two. Ever think of that?"

"You are grounded until you are eighteen. There will be no learning from anyone else, especially about the birds and bees," André said, and I knew immediately he'd stepped in it. Ethan's nose scrunched, somehow rising to meet his furrowed brow. "What do birds and bees have to do with Uncle Zack and Uncle Kervin?"

I snatched my coffee off the table and raised it to my lips, desperately avoiding eye contact with André.

"Do you call it that because they're gay?" Ethan went on. "Wouldn't that make them both bees or both birds? Because they have sex, right?"

"Man, I'm full. That was great, babe," I said, shooting to my feet and grabbing every plate within reach to haul them to the sink.

"What do you know of sex?" André asked in his most clinically appropriate tone.

"Papa, I'm *nine*. I know lots of things."

"Alright, maybe I need to learn from you. Teach me what you know," André said, his tone soothing.

"Well ..." Ethan shrank under André's gaze. "They kiss."

"Yes?"

Ethan stared up, as if he'd explained sex perfectly—and completely. "They kiss each other like a mommy and daddy would, but they're boys."

"Alright. What else?"

Ethan's face went blank. He scrunched his nose again, then cocked his head. "That's it. Isn't it?"

I nearly dropped the dishes but managed to stifle my laughter until I was well out of the kitchen. I knew by fleeing the field I might never know the rest of the conversation, but given the preamble, that was a risk I was willing to take.

Bless André and his training.

A few moments later, I'd barely settled into my spot on the couch and raised the remote when Ethan rounded the corner and plopped down beside me.

"Are you ready?" he asked, as if continuing a conversation we were just having.

"Ready for what?"

He crossed his bony arms. "To call Uncle Zack. You promised."

"You did promise, especially after forcing me to have the sex talk," André said from the door, an amused grin playing across his face. "It is not every day a father talks to his son about *kissing*."

Thank you, baby Jesus. The boy thinks sex is kissing.

"Alright, scoot over here," I said, setting the remote on the end table and grabbing my phone. Ethan slid across the couch to nuzzle into me.

The phone rang four times before Kervin's voice spoke with a mechanical lilt. "Hello, this house does not participate in conversations with uppity major league players who abandoned their minor league brothers to poverty and poor pitching. Please leave a message at the beep."

André snorted.

"Hi, Uncle Kervin," Ethan shouted into the receiver that was only inches away.

"Hey, little man. I didn't need that ear anyway."

A muffled voice called through the speaker, "Hey, buddy."

"Uncle Zack!" Zack was Ethan's favorite person in the world ... behind André and me, of course.

Kervin mumbled, "Here, you take this. He'll want to talk to you anyway."

A second later, Zack's playful tones rang more clearly. "How's my best friend in the whole world? Are you ready for Turkey Day?"

"You know it. How's the hair?"

"Big as ever, and even more fabulous."

My mind's eye could see Zack waving his head back and forth to make his massive do wiggle. Zack's hair was so blown out most of the time he could barely squeeze it into his ball cap—and Ethan loved it. He really was a trip.

"Awesome, dude," Ethan beamed, then his voice fell. "I miss you, Uncle Zack."

A heartbeat later, "I miss you more than anything, little man. Seriously."

"You could come for Thanksgiving. Papa's cooking French queezy."

Zack snorted. "Queezy? You mean cuisine?"

"Yeah, that's it. French shit."

"Ethan!" André, Zack, and I barked in astonished unison.

"What? That's what Dad calls it."

André shot me a glare. I shrugged and mouthed, "Sorry."

"I bet he does. You should probably use a different word, okay?" Zack chuckled. "I wish we could be there, buddy, but Kervin's folks are making a big deal out of us visiting them this year. Maybe we can do something for Christmas."

An explosion of preteen enthusiasm exploded across Ethan's features as he looked from André to me. "Could we? Really? Please, Dad, Papa. Please."

André grinned at me, then stroked Ethan's hair. "We'll talk about it."

"That's French for yes, Uncle Zack!" Ethan practically screamed into the phone.

"No, I did not—" André began.

"I heard it. Totally does," Zack said, and I could hear him grinning. "We'll work on it, okay?"

"Yessir! It'll be awesome. You'll see," Ethan said.

"Alright, give Papa the phone. It's his turn to talk with Uncle Zack," I said, reaching down to pry the cell from his fingers, switch it from speaker mode, then hand it to André.

Ethan, satisfied his master plan was in play, darted out of the room to do Lord knows what. I slumped back into the couch cushions and grinned up at André.

He listened into the phone, then held it in front of him and switched back to speaker.

"... could even try to get the guys in on it." Kervin's voice sounded distant, like he was shouting toward the phone from across the room.

"It does sound like fun. Let me talk with the boss and see," André said.

"Holy shit, did I just get promoted," slipped out of my mouth.

André scowled. "Nicholas Dunlap, that is where our boy learned that word!"

Kervin and Zack's laughter sang through the phone as I stared pointedly at the speaker to avoid André's rebuking gaze.

"Alright, we need to get going. Kervin has a lot of cooking to do before tomorrow, and I'm supposed to watch and cheer from the sidelines. I think I'll make a margarita."

"Have a good Thanksgiving," André said. "It is good to talk to you."

"See ya, Zacky," I called.

"Later, dude," Zack chirped back.

"Stop saying shit," Kervin hollered in the background as the line went dead.

I tried not to laugh. I really tried.

Then André glowered again, and I lost all control.

Chapter Seven

COOPER (AND NATE)

"Boys, dinner's ready," I yelled from the kitchen.

Nate was no doubt showing Stephan the wooden decking that spanned one side of our house and spread across what would've been a yard to a privacy fence. Beneath the decking was a flowing pond filled with koi that never seemed to get enough to eat. No matter how many times we walked out and tossed them pellets, the ravenous little buggers still swarmed.

Like a team of gay wrestlers all oiled up and ready to go ... although, gay wrestlers wouldn't swim or jump over each other in the water, but their lips would be open, or, at least, their mouths would be, and the oil would make them kind of slimy if it was lathered all over their muscly bodies. But wouldn't that make those little tutu things they wore hard to stay on? Or was that the idea? To make it easier to slip off?

Yeah, they were like fishy gay wrestlers who'd been dipped in Wesson and were ready for the Fry Daddy ... or just their daddy ... or daddies. A team would need more than one daddy.

I giggled at my own inner silliness.

"Hey, babe. What's so funny?" Nate gave me a peck on the cheek, then snatched a roll from the basket in my hands and shoved it into his mouth. "I was just showing Steph the fish."

"Hey, no cheating," I scolded, swatting his hand too late to save the roll.

He gave me a bready grin and leaned forward like he was going to tongue me with his doughy mouth.

"Don't you dare!" I shoved him back.

He winked and scooted away.

"Cool koi, Coop," Stephan said. "Hear that, Nate? Cool koi, Coop? That's so rad."

Stephan Breeden was the catcher on Nate's team, the Memphis Mangoes. He was six foot three, lean and ripped, with wavy blond hair and oceanic blue eyes. If he didn't talk like a cross between a drunk Valley girl and a surfer high on pot, he would've been utterly hot. Instead, he was *oddly* hot—which was still pretty damn hot.

Nate chuckled through chews and Steph laughed at his own ... whatever that had been. I smiled politely and scurried back to the kitchen, where the turkey waited to be sliced. Everything else was on the table: green beans, sweet potato soufflé, rosemary and garlic roasted potatoes, gouda mac and cheese, fried okra, black-eyed peas, cranberry sauce, a ham from that honey-baking place that made my mouth water just driving by it, and three different kinds of pie.

"Holy shit, Coop, you cook for the entire team? This looks totally awesome." Steph's praise made something in my chest smile.

Then Nate added, "Babe, this really does look great. You didn't have to do all this work."

His hands snaking around to pull me into him, and the kisses he planted on my neck, made a completely different body part smile.

"Thanks, but I wanted to. This is our first real Thanksgiving together. Last year doesn't really count because we were at Sam and Miguel's."

His hands roamed up to grip my chest.

"As much as I don't want you to stop, this turkey won't slice itself, and you have a guest to take care of." I craned back and kissed him, then waved the knife toward the dining room, where Steph stood.

"Don't mind me, Coop," Steph said, nearly startling the knife out of my hand. "I'm enjoying the show. Could do with a few less clothes though."

Then I *did* drop the knife.

Nate laughed, kissed me one last time, then turned and shoved Steph back toward the dining room. "Get the hell out of the kitchen before he carves something other than that turkey."

Steph laughed. "Can't pay guys a compliment anymore? Damn. I miss the days when you could lick someone with your eyes and they appreciated the effort."

"No eye licking until after dinner," I shouted.

"Oh, hear that," Steph said. "We're one dessert away from some serious licking!"

Nate groaned. "God, why did I invite you?"

"Because I'm hilarious and I've got the hottest ass on the team."

"Not true," I said, carrying the turkey platter into the dining room. "Nate's ass tops them all."

"If Nate's ass knows how to top, I definitely want to see *that*. The idea kind of goes against the physics of—"

"Steph!" Nate bellowed.

Steph howled and shoved Nate's shoulder. "You're so easy. You know that, right?"

Nate raised his middle finger and glanced toward me.

I was redder than the damn cranberry sauce, and I swear Nate, who was genetically incapable of blushing, turned purple or crimson or some other non-tan-esque color.

Steph was harmless. He was that guy who could make you laugh, blush, and thank him for the embarrassment. No one ever knew what might fly out of his mouth, least of all him, but none of us could wait to hear whatever it might be. His personality was like some magnetic force, drawing everyone around him closer—like that gruesome crash on the other side of the road you simply couldn't resist slowing to gawk at.

He was like a good-natured golden retriever that didn't understand how running headlong toward a fence while chasing a ball would eventually hurt if he didn't slow down. All he saw was the ball, then *bam*. Fence.

Steph was one of four gay Mangoes; the *real* fruits on the team, they declared. He wasn't flaming or flamboyant, he was just unafraid to throw himself in front of any oncoming car or train or … comment.

When Nate first joined the Mangoes, after his hopes of making it into the majors had evaporated, Steph had been the first to wrap his arm around his shoulder and make him feel welcome. Nate needed that more than I'd realized. He'd been so lost.

Through his goofy, irreverent, utterly lovable kindness, Steph had become family. He didn't have any family of his own, so it only made sense for him to spend his holidays with us.

"Alright, then. Let's eat." I set the turkey down and stepped back to survey the spread. I'd done rather well, if I did say so myself. "We have wine, beer, tea, Coke, and I think there's a few of those natural energy drinks Nate likes. What are we having?"

"Red wine for me," Nate said.

"Sweet. Same," Steph echoed.

I nodded. "Red wine all around. I'll grab a few bottles. Something tells me we're going to need them."

ONE HOUR AND THREE bottles of wine later, we were beached on the sectional in front of our wall-sized TV.

"God, I'm fat and happy," Steph said, patting his non-existent belly.

"Fuck off. Your abs probably got better defined by eating all that," Nate groused.

"Aw, babe. Don't be jealous. Just because your six-pack has turned into a keg doesn't mean ours have to," I quipped.

"Damn. Score one for the Coopster. That was sick." Steph held up his palm for a high-five.

Nate had taken his off-season break seriously, avoiding the gym and enjoying the kitchen to the point that he had to suck it in just to squeeze into his pants in the morning. We both knew he'd have a six-pack the minute his routine resumed, but it was fun to tease him in the meantime.

"Ha ha. Very funny," Nate said, then glared at me. "I thought you were supposed to defend my honor."

I winked. "We're talking about your waist, not your honor, dear."

"Ouch. Where's Miguel when I need him? You might be a super-ninja, but he's bigger than both of you. He'd stick up for me."

I grinned. "Ninjas practice an entirely different art form. And they use swords—katanas—and they wear all black and masks and sneak around and assassinate people. Or they did way back in the day when ninjas roamed all over Japan, which, by the way, we are very far from in both time and space, so the whole ninja reference doesn't make any sense."

Nate and Steph stared. And blinked. And stared.

"I wonder how Miguel is. What are they doing today? Do you know?"

Nate shook himself free of my ninja-induced prattle. "He said they were doing dinner at their place. I think Ty and Gabe, and probably Annie, were going over there."

"Wonder if the guys took Ben too. He seems like a good kid. Kind of quiet though," I said.

"Coop! He's deaf." Nate's brows furrowed. "Of course he's quiet."

I laughed and smacked him with a pillow. "That's not what I meant, turkey. He's just kind of inside his own head a lot. But it's been almost a year since we've seen him, so maybe he's opened up. Gabe and Ty seem to be really good with him."

"Yeah, who would've thought Ty would make a great Big Brother?" Nate asked.

"He really is, isn't he?" I said.

We sat in silence for a long moment, watching whatever football game consumed the screen, then Nate muttered, as if to himself, "I miss the guys." I reached over and gripped his hand. "Me too."

"Who are you guys talking about?" Steph asked.

"Friends back in Nashville. Miguel was Nate's college mentor. Sam's his husband. Ty and Gabe are together. Gabe's deaf, and Ben's a kid they kind of adopted."

"We used to hang out with those guys all the time. Sam and Miguel are a trip," Nate said, his eyes lost in memories. "I wonder how Nick's doing."

Nate's sudden shift surprised me. He hadn't talked about his old teammate in months.

"Sorry," Nate said to Steph. "Nick was a teammate in Nashville. He got shipped off to Columbus 'cause the skipper didn't like him being gay. Nicky got back at him though. Smacked his way out of the minors and into a sweet contract with the Guardians."

"Livin' the dream," Steph said wistfully.

"Yeah," Nate agreed. "Moving out here was great for both Coop and me, but I really miss those guys."

"Why don't you call them? Or go see them?" Steph asked.

Nate cocked his head.

"Dude, you really are thick sometimes." Steph rolled his eyes. "It's the *off-season*. You've got a rich daddy over there. You can go anywhere you want, anytime you want."

Nate sat upright. "Okay, first, Coop's not my daddy."

"That's not what you said last night," I chirped, spanking his leg.

"DAMN! Kitty's got claws," Steph cackled.

"Please, don't encourage him," Nate begged. "Anyway, Coop has his gym."

"Dojang," I corrected.

"Sorry, dojang." I'd lost count of the number of times I'd had to correct him on that. I knew he thought of it as a gym with a fancy name.

"Don't you *own* said dojang, Master Ninja?" Steph asked. "Ninjas are—"

"Yes, they wear black and use steak knives. We got that." Steph held up a palm. "But, if you're the owner, can't you throw up a 'closed' sign and take time off? What's the point in owning a business if it doesn't buy you a little freedom along the way?"

A few heartbeats of silence were punctuated by the TV announcer losing his mind over a fumble.

"Why don't we call them? A phone call doesn't require vacation days," Nate said, snatching his phone from the coffee table, scrolling through his contacts, and punching Miguel's face faster than I could nod.

He hit speaker and laid the phone on the table.

Ring. Ring.

"You calling your mother on Thanksgiving? You missed me, didn't you? Aw, that's so sweet," Sam's gravelly voice grated against his sweet words.

"I thought you hated being called that," Nate said, a grin curling his lips. "And no, I missed Dad, not you and your dried-up pussy."

"I'll have you know, there's a cream for that, and it works wonders. Makes my cooter whistle sometimes when I walk though," Sam replied without missing a beat. "And you couldn't have missed your father because you texted just yesterday. Isn't that right, dear?"

Nate howled.

Steph glanced toward me, perplexed.

I was trying not to spill wine all over the couch.

"Whatever. Is there an adult there I could talk with?" Nate wheezed, struggling to contain his own amusement.

"You think Miguel is more of an adult than me? Lord, I thought we raised you to know better. Hang on, I'll put you on speaker. We just cleared the last of the table, and the gang is pulling out board games."

"Aw, look at you playing nice with your friends," Nate teased.

Sam's voice grew serious. "I'll have you know, there is no playing nice in Catan. I will crush my enemies like tiny, annoying, ready-to-burst little bugs.""Maybe it's a good thing we did our own Thanksgiving after all," I said, loud enough to get caught by the microphone.

"I heard that, little sensei. Don't make me drive down to Memphis. I will bend you over and—"

"What's all this? I heard the phone ring three minutes ago and you're already spanking each other?" Miguel's bubbly voice, accented by some degree of post-meal drunkenness, floated through the phone. I could hear his annoyingly cheerful grin through the speaker.

"Hi, Dad. Mom was being abusive," I called from across the couch. "He was talking about bending me over, and I swear that can mean more than just spanking. In fact, just the other night, Nate was bent over the—"

"Coop!" Nate shouted.

Steph doubled over, as Sam and Miguel's laughter made the speaker crackle.

"What? Nate's flexible. Isn't that a good thing?" I protested.

"Please, Coop, they don't need to hear—" Nate pleaded.

"Oh yes we do. We want him to describe it so vividly we can skip Pornhub later," Sam growled, low and sexy.

Tears were streaming down Steph's cheeks. "Is it always like this?"

I gave him a level stare. "It's way worse in person."

"You say that like we're a bad influence," Miguel said. "I'll have you know, I'm proud of the disrespectful, slutty men we raised you to be."

"Slutty?" Nate asked. "We're practically an old couple."

"Old couples don't bend one another over the—"

"Coop!" Nate shouted, flopping back on the couch with his hands over his face.

A female voice shouted something I couldn't understand.

"Annie is going to start singing if we don't get off this phone and start the game," Miguel said.

"I miss Annie," I said. "How is she?"

"Feisty as ever," Sam replied. "You'd never know she's seventy-two."

"The facelift and Botox help with that," Miguel whispered at nearly full voice.

"I heard that, Miguel Nuñez. Now get that pretty little ass over here so I can whoop it," Annie barked from somewhere in the distance.

"Prosecution rests," Miguel said. "At least she thinks my ass is pretty."

"And ... he went there," Sam said. Then his voice took on a serious tone. "You guys need to come visit. Really. We miss you two."

Nate sat forward and lifted the phone, as if to help the speaker convey how sincerely he agreed. "We miss you too." "Yeah, we do," I added. "We were just talking about finding time to come visit."

"You're always welcome. You know that," Sam said. "But I've got a crazy idea."

"What's that?" I asked.

"We want to do a cruise. Miguel's never been on one, and we're both long overdue a vacation. We've looked online and the prices are still incredible, especially the weeks before and after Christmas. Guess they haven't totally recovered from COVID yet." Sam's voice drifted into the background as he said something to one of their guests. "Sorry, Ty just said he and Gabe would be up for a cruise too. Looks like this could be a thing."

Nate looked to me. His eyes glittered with enthusiasm, and I knew if I didn't answer quickly, word vomit would coat my phone ... and likely the couch and coffee table and everything else within spewing distance.

"We're in. Absolutely," I said.

Nate reached over and gripped my leg. He was vibrating, and his smile ... it was my world.

"Alright, we'll do a little digging. Let's talk over the weekend. Good to talk to you guys," Sam said.

"You too. Tell Annie and the others we can't wait to see them too."

"Will do. Now, go bend Cooper over and stuff that turkey."

The line clicked dead.

Nate sat openmouthed, torn between responding to Sam's baiting and his excitement over the cruise.

Steph chuckled quietly as he watched Nate try to contain himself.

Chapter Eight

Nick (and André and Ethan)

André stepped around Ethan's chair and filled the crystal glass on its eternal stem with rich ruby liquid. I was pretty sure Thanksgiving wasn't a French thing, but sometime during his twenty-plus years in the States, he'd developed a passion for all things pilgrims and turkeys. He even wore a sweater of orange, yellow, and brown, looking more like an Old Navy model showing off their autumn line than a psychiatrist caring for children. Then again, we were at home. If he wanted to strut around looking like a silver-plumed stud, who was I to argue?

"Everything smells amazing, babe. You really didn't have to do all this."

He smiled, scooped the bottle before a drop could spill, then bent and kissed my cheek.

"This is our first Thanksgiving as a family. I wanted it to be special," he said, ruffling Ethan's hair as he strode back to his chair. "Let's see, starting from this end, we have escargot sautéed in butter, mushrooms in a brandy, butter, and rosemary sauce, green beans, asparagus—"

"What's that?" Ethan pointed to a circular dish with sliced vegetables layered in swirling, stacked circles and smothered in a bright red sauce.

"That is tian. It is a dish my mama used to make when I was little. I added tomato sauce for you, but most make it without."

Ethan glared at the dish like it was a wolf about to leap off the table and devour him.

"Trust me. You will love it," André said reassuringly.

Ethan's gaze didn't waver.

"These," André continued his table tour, pointing to an oval dish with something hidden beneath a savory layer of baked cheesy goodness, "are aubergines au gratin. And in the center is my favorite, turkey divan. One cannot celebrate Thanksgiving without turkey, no?"

"Oh no. Of course not," I chuckled. "Although, I'm not sure the original American settlers broke bread with the natives over anything this ... elaborate."

André tsked. "Then they should have invited a Frenchman. The tradition would be much more delicious today if they had."

I let my head drop onto the chair back as my eyes tried to roll out of their sockets. "I'm sure you're right, my little baguette.""What's a bag-it?" Ethan asked, scowling as he sounded out the word that clearly tasted funny on his tongue.

André scowled. "Baguette. *Ehht*, not *iht*. We do not use such disgusting sounds."

I snorted.

Ethan cocked his head.

A moment passed before he asked, "Like ick? That's gross. Is that why French don't use it?"

"*Exactement*!" André nodded dramatically, winking at me. "Now, let's eat before this gets cold."

Thirty minutes later, Ethan's belly was full and his attention span spent. "I'm done. Can I go play outside?"

"*May* I go play," André corrected. "Only if you take one bite of the tian."

Horror crossed Ethan's face as his gaze fell from André to his plate. One lonely scoop of the tomato-sauce-laden vegetables stared back. I watched, fascinated, wondering if Ethan might actually out-stare an inanimate object.

"Only one small bite, then you may go outside," André said, his voice soft but firm.

Ethan's hand reached up and gripped his fork. He stabbed toward it, as if testing to see if the animal was still alive. It wasn't. It was a vegetable dish, after all.

"It looks gross. I mean, icky." He drawled the *ih* sound, and André winced visibly.

I stifled a laugh.

Reluctantly, Ethan speared the smallest possible amount, barely coating the tines of his fork, and raised it to his nose. One sniff, then a second. His brows furrowed, and I swore he liked what he smelled but refused to admit it. Then the fork darted into and out of his mouth so fast I nearly missed it. There hadn't been enough on his fork to require a chew, so he simply swallowed and scowled.

"Well, what did you think?" André asked.

"It's okay. *May* I go play now?"

André shook his head. "Yes, wear your heavy coat, hat, and gloves. And don't forget your rubbers. You will eat that whole dish if you track mud into this house."

"Yes, *Mama*," Ethan grumbled.

I lost my battle with laughter.

André harrumphed and reached for his wine as Ethan flew from the table.

He raised his glass toward me in salute. "That is *your* son."

I smiled, raising my own glass and biting back a snort. "*Oui*, Mama."

As ANDRÉ PRESSED THE start button on the dishwasher, I wrapped my arms around his waist and kissed his neck, breathing in a saucy residue from his morning in the kitchen mixed with latent notes of our Irish Spring soap. It was oddly satisfying.

"That was amazing, babe. I don't deserve you."

"No, you are correct. You do not. Alas, we do not always get what we deserve." He spun in my arms to face me, planting his lips on my grin before I could reply.

My phone chirped from across the counter.

"Look at you, Mr. Popular. On a holiday, no less."

"I have a date later. He's probably just confirming the time," I said with a wink.

André did the most mature thing he could: he stuck his tongue out.

"There's the world-class doctor I know and love," I said, smacking his ass before stepping across the kitchen.

"Save the spanking for later. I feel like I will be a very bad boy tonight."

I froze and glanced back. His eyes were ablaze.

"Oh really?" My pulse skittered at the sight. "Guess you will be eating the whole casserole then."

He grunted. "I prefer eating something else whole."

I tried to say something, anything, just to keep the banter going, but words failed as my pants grew tight beneath my zipper and André fled into the den.

That man will be the death of me, I thought. *At least I'll die happy. And well fed.*

I woke my phone to find a text from one of my old teammates.

NateStringerOfficial: Happy Thanksgiving, Groot.

Me: Groot? Really? When did I become a talking tree trunk?

NateStringerOfficial: Come on. You're a Guardian, like *Guardians of the Galaxy*.

ME: GOD, THAT'S BAD. BESIDES, WHY COULDN'T I BE CHRIS PRATT'S GUY, STAR LORD? THAT EVEN SOUNDS COOL IN A TEXT.

NateStringerOfficial: ONE, CHRIS PRATT IS F'N HOT. TWO, YOU AREN'T EVEN CLOSE TO BEING COOL. THREE, I THOUGHT IT WAS FUNNY TO TURN THE GUY WHO GOT KICKED OFF HIS TEAM FOR BEING GAY INTO A GIANT PIECE OF WOOD.

ME: OUCH. THAT'S ME, A WALKING WOODY.

NateStringerOfficial: I'M HERE FOR YOU, BROTHER, EVEN IF IT MEANS TOUGH LOVE.

ME: THANKS, I THINK. WHY DID YOU TEXT AGAIN?

NateStringerOfficial: IT'S TURKEY DAY. JUST MAKING THE FAMILY ROUNDS.

I stared a moment at the words on the screen. To that point, we'd been two guys giving each other shit, as we always did. I hadn't seen Nate in months, maybe a year or more, not since moving up to the majors. We didn't talk or text often. We weren't really close.

But he was "making the family rounds."

He thought of me as family?

> **ME**: UH, OKAY. THAT'S COOL. YOU GUYS COOK AND SHIT?

> **NATESTRINGEROFFICIAL**: COOK AND SHIT? LOOK AT YOU INVOKING TRADITION AND CULTURAL RESPECT FOR THE HOLIDAY.

> **ME**: I'M A JOCK, NOT A HISTORIAN.

> **NATESTRINGEROFFICIAL**: I'M A MANGO. FRUIT TRUMPS ... WHATEVER THE FUCK A GUARDIAN IS.

> **ME**: I'M NOT TOUCHING YOUR FRUIT.

NateStringerOfficial: And there he is!

NateStringerOfficial: Anyway, Coop is dragging me into something, so I only have a second. We're doing a cruise … no idea where yet … but the whole gang is going. Sam, Miguel, Nate, Cooper, Tyler, Gabe, even Annie. You guys should join. It'll be fun.

I stared again. A cruise? With his whole *gang*.

We'd met some of the guys a while back, but again, we weren't close. They were more like friends of a friend than actual family to us.

A mishmash of emotions I couldn't identify suddenly warred within my gut.

My departure from Nashville had been sudden—and painful. I got along with most of my teammates, especially Nate and a few others, but virtually no one had stood up for me when the taunting and harassment had begun. Management barely blinked when they shipped me off to another city, despite my league-leading batting average and strong defensive stats. None of that mattered. I was the gay guy on a team whose management was old school—and in a city so steeped in tradition their Bible Belt actually had a buckle.

In the end, the move to Columbus had been the best turn my life could've taken. I became part of a team who represented the concept of family more than any I'd ever known. I'd met

Zack and Kervin, the best friends I could have hoped for. Most importantly, I'd met André and Ethan, my true family, the loves of my life who powered my every hope and dream.

I'd gotten over the pain and abandonment of Nashville. It was in the past, where it belonged. All those feelings were … they had no power … they didn't—

The phone chirped again.

NateStringerOfficial: Dude, talk to Frenchie. Ty and Gabe are bringing Ben. He's Ethan's age, right? They'd have a blast.

NateStringerOfficial: Gotta jet. Let me know. We're booking this week.

Chapter Nine

Nate (and Cooper)

THE IDEA OF WEARING a bathing suit around Sam, Miguel, and the others in our group accomplished something no amount of self-shaming in the mirror could achieve: it got my lazy, off-season, holiday-fattened ass back into the gym.

A smart player would never stop his workout routine. A smart player would take his profession so seriously that no amount of Thanksgiving, Christmas, Hannukah, Festivus, or other holiday involving eating entirely too much would ever force him to loosen his belt a notch. Or three.

Fuck.

I looked down at my poor belt. The little metal flappy thing had never been in the hole it now poked through, and I seriously doubted that was as exciting as my eight-year-old dirty-boy brain thought as I snickered at my own silliness.

Then I untucked my shirt, and there it was. No, not my sculpted abs. Not even one sculpted ab. There were no abs, sculpted or otherwise.

I had a muffin top.

Why, Jesus, why?

I'd gone from studly professional sportsman to a walking, talking confection. All I needed was powdered sugar on my nose to complete the image. I might as well have been on a Dunkin' poster, sitting merrily beside a steaming cup of java with lettering at the bottom that read, "Come eat me. I'm muffiny goodness."

Two guys chatted loudly as they entered the locker room and sat on the bench beside me. I changed faster than a penis at a bris then tossed my clothes into a locker and jetted onto the rubber-covered floor where the torture devices waited.

For some insane reason, I decided to start my glorious return with leg day. The proud pro baller in me refused to accept that I'd taken months off. He refused to do the logical thing and ease back into a routine. He refused to lower the weight from where he'd left it at the end of the season.

Three sets of leg presses nearly brought me to tears.

Why did I ever stop? I groaned.

By the time I stepped away from the last machine, my legs felt more like limp linguine, and I had to grab each successive machine to brace myself.

"Lactic acid is from the devil," a muscle head passing as I entered the locker room grinned.

"Fuckin' devil is right." I tried to straighten and recover my pride but with nothing to grab, I nearly toppled over.

Thick Neck grabbed my elbow and held me upright. "You okay, buddy?" There was no concern in his voice, only amusement, as he walked me into the locker room like some elderly grandma needing help to cross a busy street.

"I didn't need legs anyway."

He laughed and slapped me on the back. "Time for chest. Have fun driving with those sticks."

I wobbled and fell onto the bench.

Ice baths were our preferred recovery method at the Guardians' training center. We had state-of-the-art equipment and a staff of highly skilled professionals to help with every step of our development. Unfortunately, I wasn't in my vaunted work gym. I sat in a public gym where metal tubs filled with icy relief weren't a thing.

So, I decided to do the next best thing: soak in the hot tub.

I stripped out of my tighty-whities and wrapped an oversized towel around my waist, grousing at the pudge I encountered when tying it off, but before I could hobble across the locker room, through the bathroom, and into the men's sauna, my phone chirped.

Moving suddenly lost its appeal.

I sat back on the bench, reopened my locker, and grabbed my phone.

HawkeyeBB: Hey, babe. I know you're working out and probably really focused because you're a studly baseball player and all, but I'm really excited and couldn't wait to talk to you. I have a plan!

I stared a moment, waiting for details. Cooper had never been one to hold back … anything … but the dots never danced. That worried me. Coop had a plan he *wasn't* spilling. This couldn't be good.

Me: Okay. I'll bite. What's the plan?

HawkeyeBB: So, you know how we've been talking about doing a cruise with the boys for the holidays?

Me: Yeah.

HawkeyeBB: Well, I got to thinking, which is important when making a plan because making plans without thinking would just be a spontaneous act, and a plan requires, well, planning, which means thinking, so I thought.

I stared ... and waited.

HawkeyeBB: There were three-day cruises to the Caribbean, but none were on a cruise line the group liked, and we want to do more than three days, don't we? Of course we do. We need a real vacation. So I widened the search.

ME: SOUNDS GOOD.

My stomach was beginning to rumble. He was building toward something.

HawkeyeBB: THEN I GOT TO THINKING, BECAUSE, AGAIN, PLANNING … AND THINKING. SOME OF THE GUYS MIGHT NOT BE ABLE TO AFFORD A BIG CRUISE, AND WE CAN'T LEAVE ANYBODY OUT, NOT WHEN THIS WILL BE THE FIRST TIME OUR WHOLE FAMILY GETS TOGETHER FOR A VACATION, AND WE REALLY WANT THIS TO BE SPECIAL AND MEMORABLE, AND THE LAST THING WE WANT IS FOR ANYONE TO WORRY ABOUT MONEY WHILE THEY'RE GETTING AWAY FROM THEIR LIVES THAT TOO OFTEN REVOLVE AROUND MAKING AND SPENDING MONEY. RIGHT?

ME: UH, YES? I THINK.

HawkeyeBB: I KNEW YOU'D APPRECIATE THAT. YOU WERE A POOR, STRUGGLING MINOR LEAGUE PLAYER WHO COULD BARELY AFFORD DINNER, MUCH LESS AN EXTRAVAGANT TRIP TO THE

MEDITERRANEAN ... FOR TEN DAYS ... ALL
INCLUSIVE ... FOR EVERYONE.

ME: COOP, WHAT DID YOU DO?

HawkeyeBB: GRAMMY WOULD WANT US TO
DO THIS, BABE. I KNOW SHE WOULD.

ME: COOP, YOU DIDN'T.

HawkeyeBB: I DID. FOR EVERYONE. ISN'T IT
AMAZING?

Dear God.

There were ten of us. No, eleven.

How much had he just spent? My mind couldn't process the numbers. Then I remembered the night Coop told me how much money Grammy had left him, and my mind again failed to process a number with so many zeros ... and commas.

Us affording the trip wasn't an issue. Those who couldn't afford it might become one though.

What would Miguel think? Would he be pissed? He and Sam did okay, but neither of them was rich. They were proud though. Would Coop going overboard stomp all over their sense of honor? Ty and Gabe weren't wealthy either, but I doubted they would be upset by his generosity in the same way as Mom and Dad.

Then there was Nick and André.

I didn't know Nick *that* well. We'd played together, but he'd mostly kept to himself. From what I remembered, he was a good enough guy, but he played in the majors now. He could afford his own vacation.

The whole thing made my head feel like my legs had moments earlier.

I leaned back against the lockers, closed my eyes, and groaned. Then my phone chirped again.

HawkeyeBB: Anyway, I know you're working out, and I need to finish shopping. God knows you need new clothes for this trip. I already got you three new Speedos so you can show off your big, juicy mango. You look so hot in a mango hammock.

HawkeyeBB: See you at home. Love you.

Fucking muffin top.

Chapter Ten

Sam (and Miguel)

MIGUEL TOSSED A PAIR of knee-length swim trunks onto the bed. They bore a pattern of pea green palm trees and turd-colored coconuts at random intervals.

"When did you turn eighty?" I asked, snatching the vile fabric up before it could rub off on anything with a hint of class. "Put those back in the drawer. Better yet, let's burn them later. We can have a funeral. You can cry. It'll be good for you to get it out."

Without letting his annoyingly chipper smile droop, Miguel's hands flew to his hips in his best sugar bowl pose, and his head cocked sharply. "I'll have you know, those are quite the rage in The Villages."

I shook my head. "Have you seen the guys in our group? Ty will probably have Prada sunglasses and whatever brand thong is hot this year. We'll be lucky if tourists don't stop snapping pics of the sights and turn toward him." Miguel's smile turned smirky. "At least we have a decoy. The paparazzi usually ruins my vacations. It's so tiresome."

I snorted. "Okay, Prince Regent, or whatever the fuck you would be in a clearly dysfunctional royal household."

He gave me a mocking bow, then straightened and smoothed his face. "Shouldn't it be *you* bowing to me? I am a royal, after all."

I wadded a pair of undies I was packing and hurled them into his chest.

He laughed. "Why do you care anyway? You think Wrangler is high-end fashion. I doubt you'd know Prada if it leapt out of the water and bit your toe."

"Did you just call world-class fashion a bone-chewing fish?"

He shrugged and smiled ... again. "You're an old married woman now. Nobody's going to notice you anyway."

"Hey! I may be married, but I'm far from old, and I plan to look damn good on this cruise. I'd like for my hot husband to turn a few heads too. Let's make everybody jealous."

"Fine," he said, blowing out a long sigh, then turning and rummaging through his chest of drawers. "Will this work?"

He held up a tiny neon yellow Speedo I was fairly certain he hadn't worn once in the five years we'd been together. I felt a stirring below deck just imagining his bulge shoved into that all-too-small package.

"Yeah." I gulped back my desire to jump him. "That'll do."

He wiggled his brows, then tossed the sliver of silk across the bed.

"I still can't believe we're doing this," I said after a moment of silent packing.

"What? Have you seen my body lately? I'll look—"

"I meant the whole thing. The cruise. All of us getting together for nearly two weeks." I laid a pair of shorts on top of a pile in the suitcase, sat on the edge of the bed, and faced Miguel. "And Cooper, can you believe he just bought everything? We really shouldn't let him do this."

Miguel shrugged. "It's not like Marjorie didn't leave him enough to handle it. He could probably buy the Memphis Mangoes if they ever drop Nate."

"Come on. You know what I mean. It's not about affording anything. It just feels ... I don't know ... weird."

"Did you talk to any of the others?"

I nodded. "Ty and Gabe couldn't have afforded the trip without the help. Ty said it felt a little awkward, but they were grateful, especially since they get to bring Ben. He said Ben's come out of his shell a lot but still struggles when he's around unfamiliar people. They're hoping the trip will be good for him."

"That sounds like a thumbs-up."

I shrugged. "Yeah, I guess. Annie's stoked. She has this grand plan of getting the performers on the ship to let her steal their stage. I'm not sure if she'll be headlining or getting thrown overboard."

Miguel shook his head. "That sounds like Annie. Knowing her, they'll probably beg her to perform before she even asks."

"Did Coop tell you they invited one of the Mango players too?"

"No. Who?"

"His name is something with an S ...Stephen? Stephan? Yeah, that's it. Stephan. Nate called him Steph, I think. Pretty sure that's right."

"Huh. Okay. What of it?"

I scratched my scalp, struggling to put thoughts into words. "Like you said, it's not about the money, but still … It was already a lot, now he's including someone we don't know, a guy who isn't even part of our family. Do you really think he's thought all this through?"

"When have you ever shied away from new people?"

"Come on, babe. You know what I mean."

Miguel rounded the bed and sat next to me, his hand covering mine in my lap.

"Sam, you know Coop. He has a heart big enough to fill the whole world. He thrives on doing things for other people, especially people he cares about. He will probably get more satisfaction out of seeing us have fun together, knowing he made it all possible, than he ever would doing this himself. That's just who he is."

"I know, but still, it's just … it's a lot. I hope this wasn't some crazy impulse thing he'll regret later."

"Cooper is an odd duck, but he's smarter than all of us combined. Except maybe for André. He's another level. Kind of scary, actually."

"Babe? What's your point?"

"Right. Sorry." He scratched his scruff. "Coop doesn't do anything without thinking of the eighty-three ways it could go wrong. He probably built a spreadsheet with linked tables or whatever you do in a monster Excel file to map out a nuclear weapon. Shit, I doubt he made breakfast without researching where the eggs came from and the lineage of the chicken they popped out of."

I chuckled. "I could see him doing that actually. He'd name the chickens too. Poor Nate."

"Poor Nate? I'm pretty sure Nate loves him for it. Did you see how he looked at Coop the last time they were here? He's whipped harder than a meringue." Miguel reached up and gripped my shoulder. "We *all* love him for it—for his goodness, for his innocence, for the man he makes us want to be."

Now it was my turn to cock my head. "We're supposed to be mentoring him, remember?"

A father's pride stole his features. "A teacher can learn a lot from a student, especially one like Coop."

"Fuck. You're going full fortune cookie on me now."

He laughed and shoved me back. "Asshole."

"Last time I checked, you loved my asshole."

"Don't get my engine purring. We need to finish packing. Our flight leaves in three hours."

❧

As we settled into our wide leather seats, a flight attendant promptly appeared. "Would you gentlemen like something to drink before we take off?"

"Coffee, please," Miguel said.

"And you, sir?"

"How about a Screwdriver?" I asked.

"Of course." She smiled and moved to the row behind us.

Miguel leaned over and whispered, "She called you 'sir,' you old fart."

"Fuck off."

My displeasure only made his grin widen.

"First class?" I asked with a raised brow, my fingers roaming the buttons on the armrest between us. "Coop really went all out."

Miguel's head turned toward me. "Get it all out of your system now, okay? When we see the guys, we need to just be thankful to be together. No beating Coop up."

I started to defend myself, but bit my lip and nodded. "You're right. Sorry. It's just—"

"I know. It's a lot." He reached across and gripped my hand. "We may never get to travel like this again. Let's pretend it's just you and me doing this. Call it a second honeymoon."

"Second? When was our first?"

He squeezed my hand into a submission. "Your life with me *is* a honeymoon, *honey*."

The flight attendant appeared in time to hear the last part of our conversation. She leaned across and set a fancy glass tumbler on my tray table.

"You two are adorable," she said, then turned to hand Miguel his coffee. "Sir."

He glowered up as she winked in my direction, then continued with her service.

We sat in silence, enjoying our drinks and trying not to get caught eyeing each passenger as they strode past us toward their less-plush seats. The plan was for everyone to fly to New York, spend the night in a fancy hotel, then fly to Barcelona, where we would board our ship. As the boarding doors slammed shut, I realized something.

"Did you see Ty and Gabe board?" I asked.

"What? Ty?" He glanced around the cabin. "Huh. No, now that you mention it. Were they on our flight?"

I shrugged. "I just assumed they would be. Never thought to ask."

"There was a flight to New York pretty much every hour on the big board. They might already be there. Traveling with a kid can't be easy."

"Yeah, guess so."

Chapter Eleven

Tyler (and Gabe)

We packed the night before our flight. Gabe was a whirlwind, throwing virtually every piece of clothing he owned into our oversized suitcase, then racing to the store to buy another because he'd run out of room. I was fairly certain we'd packed enough clothes for the entire group, but there was no stopping Hurricane Gabriel. I hadn't seen him so excited all year.

We rose early and drove to our favorite breakfast spot, a small diner a few blocks from our house. Its metal roof looked like it was about to collapse, and most of the paint on the wooden siding was flaking worse than a guy in a dandruff commercial, but the breakfast food, which was served all day, was the best in town.

On the way home, Gabe insisted we stop at Target to grab travel-sized mouthwash and toothpaste. I suggested we just chuck all our toiletries in the big bags, but he wanted a backup in case the airplane somehow ate our luggage. We made one last pit stop at the grocery store to grab our favorite sliced honey ham so I could make a quick lunch before we headed to the airport.

As we pulled into the driveway, I glanced at the fuel gauge and grimaced. "Why don't you go on and start lunch. I forgot to get gas while we were out, and the airport's a good forty minutes away."

Gabe nodded and gave me a peck on the cheek, then grabbed the bags from the back seat and headed inside.

Ten minutes later, I stepped through our front door.

"TY!" Gabe screamed from our bedroom at the back of the house. "Ty ... oh, God ... come here, quick!"

I ran through the house and into the bedroom to find Gabe on his knees with Domino standing before him. Gabe's eyes were red, and tears fell freely down his cheeks. Nearby, Audie paced and whimpered, her tail firmly tucked between her legs and her ears pinned to her head.

"Something's wrong with Dom. He won't respond or move or anything. Ty, I don't know what to do. What do we do?"

I threw myself onto the floor and pressed a hand to Dom's back, something that usually set his tail wagging and his tongue flying.

He didn't flinch.

I scooted around to face him. His eyes were glassy, staring forward but seemingly unseeing. His breathing sounded labored, and his chest heaved with the effort.

I grabbed my phone and punched the vet's contact. They answered in two rings.

"Nashville Pet Hospital. How can we help your pet?"

"This is Tyler Hyatt. Domino is my dog. He's not breathing right. Something is seriously wrong. I need to bring him in right away."

"I'm sorry, sir, we don't have any—"

"Please, help me. I'm begging you. Something is really wrong."

"Sir, you need to take him to the Emergency Hospital on Mill.""That's all the way across town. I don't think ... I don't think we have time for that. Please, help me. Help Dom."

I could barely speak through the sobs. My hands shifted between stroking Dom's fur and wiping tears. Gabe, in no better shape, reached up and clutched my shoulder.

There was a muffled conversation on the other end, then the woman returned. "Bring him in. We'll be waiting. How fast can you get here?"

"Five minutes. We're on the way."

I scooped up Dom, pressing his body into my chest and burying my face in his fur, breathing him in, willing my life into his. I could barely see as we raced to the car. I climbed into the back seat with Dom, while Gabe sat Audie in the passenger's side then sprinted around to start the car. I kissed Dom's head and whispered to him the entire drive to the vet, hoping his dad's soothing voice might offer some healing comfort. Audie continued whining from the front seat.

The moment the automatic doors flew open and we raced through, an army of vets and techs barged forward and stole Domino from my arms. It felt like they'd reached into my chest and ripped out my soul.

"Tyler, why don't you come back here while the vet helps Domino?" a kind-faced woman at the front desk said as she stood, took my arm, and ushered us into a break room at the end of a row of exam rooms. There was a couch, a table with a few chairs, and a water cooler in the corner. Gabe sat on the couch, while I stalked the room like a caged lion.

"Gabe, I can't lose him. I can't. I love him so much."

Gabe tried to grab me, to wrap me in his arms, but I threw him off and continued pacing.

I closed my eyes and watched in my mind as eight-week-old Domino climbed atop his littermates in the puppy pen the breeder had erected. He was so small I could fold a bath cloth over him and still have fabric to spare. The moment I'd entered the room, the determined little fur ball had fixated on me. None of the other pups stood a chance.

I grabbed him and pulled him to my chest. He immediately peed all over my shirt.

The breeder laughed and said, "Well, that's easy. He just claimed you. Time for paperwork."

We'd been inseparable ever since. Hell, when he was a puppy, he slept on my pillow curled around the top of my head. I tried to move him the first night, but he refused to sit still, tottering back up each time to rest with his fur pressed against mine.

Dom wasn't just a dog. He was part of me. Over the next half-dozen years, when I'd lost my way in the party scene, drinking and getting high more nights than I was sober, Dom was the only thing that grounded me. He depended on me—no, he *needed* me.

More than that, I was his world too.

He looked at me as if nothing—and no one—had ever existed before we'd met, and that no one could ever exist as long as we were together.

Now his existence hung by a thread. *My* existence.

Five, maybe ten minutes later ... I'd lost track ... a woman in a sky blue lab coat entered through a door that led to the interior of the office, the place where vets and techs treated patients without humans interfering. Gabe shot to his feet. I turned and became numb when I saw the somber expression on the doctor's face.

"Tyler?" She looked between us.

"That's me."

She sucked in a breath. "I'm sorry. Domino's lungs are failing, and he's struggling to breathe. He doesn't have long now. It's time we discussed easing him on."

"Easing him ... Doc, no. What are you—"

"Tyler," her voice lowered. "I can treat him, give him another week, maybe two, but that's all. He would be in pain most of that time, struggling to get air into his lungs."

Her words rang in my ears, but nothing made sense. He was fine yesterday. He played and . . .

"Doc . . . why? I mean, he looks fine."

The vet's eyes softened. "Internal organs give can give out at a certain age. It's common in senior dogs. There's not always a warning sign or advanced symptoms. Their body just gives out."

"Is he in pain now?" I asked.

She hesitated, and her eyes darted to Dom then back to me.

"Yes, I believe he is."

I staggered back a step. Gabe's hand on the small of my back kept me from falling. My heart had clenched so tight in my chest, I could feel the ache in every part of my body. Tears washed down my cheeks.

Gabe's hand pressed into my back.

Dom stared at nothing.

Dom was in pain.

"No," I said.

She waited.

"No, I won't let him live in pain," came out more firmly. "What do we need to do?"

The vet nodded once. "We will give him a shot. He won't feel anything. It will be like drifting off to sleep."

"And it won't hurt him? He won't hurt anymore?" I could barely get the words out.

"No, he won't hurt anymore."

I paused only a heartbeat. "Do it."

She eyed me, then nodded again. "We'll be back in a few minutes so you can say goodbye."

When the door closed behind her, Gabe spun me toward him. "Are you sure about this? We could go to the emergency hospital, see if they can help him."

"Babe, I can't let him hurt anymore. I could feel it when I held him. I just can't—" Sobs racked my whole body, and I dropped to the cold tile floor. Gabe kneeled beside me, holding my head to his chest as I completely lost control, howling louder than the dogs in the nearby rooms, aching for the dog who'd been my family for nearly a decade.

When the door opened again, Domino bounded into the room. His eyes were bright, his teeth wide, his tail flying. My eyes widened as he fell into my arms and licked my face.

"Buddy, are you okay?" I could barely believe it. I scratched his ear and his slobbery tongue threatened to drown my face. A laugh laced with anguish leapt from my throat.

"No, Tyler. I gave him a shot of adrenaline so you could enjoy … so you could remember him this way."

The sobs slammed back into me. I scooted backward into the corner and clutched my knees to my chest, as Dom ran to Gabe.

I couldn't move. I could barely breathe. All I could do was watch as Gabe stroked Dom's head and offered a few last words.

It only took moments for the adrenaline to wear off and for Dom to settle back into his near-catatonic state. That's when I noticed the bandage on his right paw, and the tiny plastic tube where the vet would insert the needle.

My world tilted, and I began to wail again.

"Do you want to sit with him?" Gabe asked.

My breath caught. Sit with him? Watch him go? Everything in me seized, and my head shook.

"I can't. Gabe, I . . . just can't."

Guilt swelled within. Dom should see me as his last . . . but I couldn't . . . I couldn't move.

Through an ocean of sadness, I watched Gabe help Dom lay down, then kneel by his side. He never stopped talking to him or stroking his fur. The vet inserted a syringe, then stepped back. Dom's eyes grew heavy, but his ragged breathing smoothed.

Gabe grabbed Dom's face and held his gaze ... until he saw no more.

I gripped my legs, rocking forward, and wept.

"Take as long as you need," the vet said to Gabe. "I'll make sure no one disturbs you."

Chapter Twelve

Cooper (and Nate)

"I know. It was a little overkill getting here a day early, but I'm sort of the host of this trip, and I didn't want the guys to show up without being here first."

Nate shoved the orange wedge down the neck of his beer bottle and took a long draw.

"Need a tiny umbrella for that drink?" I teased.

When we first met, he preferred the bitterness of stout. Since joining the Mangoes, he'd flipped to the opposite end of the beer spectrum to drink exclusively Blue Moon—or anything else light that could be served with a citrus wedge. I tried not to tease him about how fruity he'd become, but some days restraint was impossible.

"Actually, that would be nice. I wouldn't want my beer to wilt under these lights." He held his hand up, as if shielding his eyes from fluorescent lights some hundred yards above us in the hotel's vaulted atrium.

"I think your beer is safe, but you do you, Boo Boo."

"Boo Boo? That is not going to stick." He scowled. "I will throw you overboard if you call me that on the ship. Don't think I won't."

"Egggggggcellent," I said with a sinister cartoon drawl while steepling my fingers. "Blackmail material suits you, Mr. Stringer."

He rolled his eyes and tipped his bottle again.

"I'll give it to you, it has been nice getting here early and not having to rush. When the team travels, it always feels like such a scramble. We've actually had time to relax a little," he said. "We slept in, had room service for breakfast, and now we're day drinking in a lush garden. I could get used to this."

"Gave us time to break in the hotel room too." I wiggled my brows.

"I'm pretty sure we could've done that without getting here early."

"Let's test that theory tonight, see if it's as hot when we know we have an early flight the next morning."

He saluted with his bottle. "I'll prove that to you right now."

My ass was still sore from the night before. Nate had been a beast; a very thick, very aggressive beast. My butt puckered painfully at the thought of a second round so soon.

"Uh, wow. You know I always want to, but we really should wait here in case some of the guys show up." I shifted uncomfortably in my seat.

"I drilled you pretty good, didn't I?" He chuckled, and I swear pride oozed out of his pores. Cocky fucker. Literally.

That thought made me laugh. Nate cocked a brow.

"Sorry, was kind of in my own head for a second. Trust me, you were funny in there too."

"I wasn't really going for funny when talking about ... never mind. I'll take funny."

I was about to keep the banter going when the lobby doors slid open and a rail-thin, toe-headed boy raced in.

"Uncle Cooper!" he screamed, loud enough for every head to turn. I'd barely stood before his spindly arms were squeezing my legs together, nearly knocking me off my feet.

"Hey, little buddy," I said, prying his hands loose and hefting him into the air. For a nine-year-old, he weighed nothing. "How's my favorite baseball player?"

"Uh, hello, I'm sitting right here," Nate said drolly.

"Ignore him," I whispered to Ethan. "He's a grumpy ole Mango."

The boy giggled, then squealed when I tossed him higher.

"We just got here and you're already abusing our child," Nick's tenor tones cut through Ethan's laughter. I squeezed Ethan to my chest long enough to glance up and see Nick walking toward us. André was dragging an overstuffed luggage cart a few feet behind.

"Oh, the abuse has yet to begin. This little man needs a good tickling. I can sense it."

"No! Papa, don't let him—"

His plea was cut off as my fingers dug mercilessly into his sides, and he fell to the floor, squalling and squirming.

"I believe this trip will be amazing. We have a built-in sitter." André smiled at Nick, then turned to the now-standing Nate. "And how is our favorite Mango? We watch your videos on TikTok all the time. Ethan loves them."

Nate stepped forward and wrapped André and Nick in warm hugs. "It's good to see you guys too."

I gave my victim a break, long enough to embrace the newcomers. Nick's arms tightened around me, as he whispered near my ear, "Are you sure I can't help with any of this?"

"It's already taken care of. You can buy me a drink or two, if it'll make you feel better."

He pulled back, his hands shifting to grip my arms. "You're not paying for one fucking drink this trip, you hear me?"

I chuckled and looked down. "You sound like Sam."

"I can't wait to hear the hell you catch from him," Nate added. "Mom can be a real bit—"

"Hello, child present," Nick said quickly.

"Aw, Dad. I know what a bitch is."

I nearly fell over.

André blanched, then schooled his features. "Really? Tell us. What is ... one of those?"

Ethan scrunched his brows, as if considering how to answer, then said, "It's that piece you put in a horse's mouth so you can steer it."

Four adults stared blankly, then Nate spat out, "A bit? Yes, Ethan, you're absolutely right. How did you get so smart?"

The other adults turned away to hide their amusement.

Ethan beamed. "I don't know. I just am, I guess." I couldn't take it anymore. "Smart *and* ticklish," I said, diving back to my knees and digging in my digits.

"Are we torturing kids today? How cool!"

I peeked over my shoulder to see Steph stepping into the expanding circle of boys. His hair testified to a restless night and lack of morning shower, curling and swirling in ways no stylist could ever conceive. The tiny curls on his forehead jiggled each time his head moved.

"About time you got your lazy butt out of bed," Nate said, bro-punching Steph on his shoulder.

"It takes a lot of sleep to look this good," Steph said, returning the jab.

There were three professional athletes, one almost Olympian, and an avid runner in our ring, and somehow, the bro-punches still managed to increase the testosterone drifting on the breeze.

"Guys, this is Steph. He's a Mango too," Nate said, motioning with a hand from Steph to Nick and André. "This is Nick and André. Nick is—"

"A fucking stud Guardian," Steph said, then realized Ethan was hanging on every word. "Sorry, little dude. Don't curse. That's a bad word."

André laughed. "I am sure he has heard worse back at the Ranch."

"Still, don't use that word. Got it?" Nick added, giving his adopted son a firm glare.

"Yes, Dad," Ethan said.

"Can we get back to me being a stud. Steph, forgive the interruption. Please continue praising me," Nick said, earning a round of jeers and another bro-punch from Nate.

"André, they're about to talk baseball. Nate and I already ate lunch, but I'd gladly escape with you and Ethan while they 'dude' each other to death."

"That sounds great." André grinned. "We still need to check in, and I could use some help with this cart. Do you think there is room for Ethan on here?"

Before I could answer, the boy had wedged himself onto the cart between two large suitcases. "Let's go, Papa!"

André shrugged at me, then gripped the cart and began pushing it toward the check-in counter.

Nick was busy answering Steph's questions about his transition into the majors as we wheeled away.

SAM, MIGUEL, AND ANNIE arrived a half-hour after André and I returned from depositing their bags in their room. Our ebullient Broadway babe flitted her way from one man to the next. Steph eyed her with curiosity, only to be swept away as Annie hooked her arm in the crook of his elbow and tugged him away from the group. She insisted she needed to "fully vet" all new applicants to the family, drawing a suspicious gaze from Steph and full-throated agreement from everyone else.

"Our dinner reservation isn't for another hour. Should we head into the bar?" Nate asked no one in particular.

No one answered, but the herd began moving in that direction.

Sam draped an arm over my shoulder. "You didn't have to do all this, but I'm glad you did. There won't be many times we can get this entire group together. This should be pretty special."

I blushed beneath his praise.

"Marjorie would be so proud of you, Coop."

That made me swallow a lump I hadn't known was there. We walked a few strides in silence before my mind raced in another direction.

"Have you heard from Ty and Gabe? Their flight landed a couple of hours ago."

"Oh shit. Sorry. I should've shown this to you before." He dug into his back pocket and flicked his phone to life. "Gabe texted a while ago."

He scrolled through his texts, then handed me the device.

GABE ROSSI: HEY, SAM. I'M REALLY SORRY TO DO THIS, BUT WE'RE NOT GOING TO MAKE THE TRIP. TY HAD TO PUT DOM DOWN LAST NIGHT, AND HE'S IN PRETTY BAD SHAPE.

ME: AW, MAN. I'M SORRY. HE'S HAD DOM FOR AS LONG AS I'VE KNOWN HIM.

GABE ROSSI: YEAH. HE WAS TEN, BUT STILL …

ME: I WISH WE COULD BE THERE FOR HIM. IF YOU GUYS WERE HERE, WE'D WRAP HIM IN THE BIGGEST BEAR HUG EVER.

GABE ROSSI: I WOULD HOPE THE TRIP WOULD BE GOOD FOR HIM, BUT I THINK HE NEEDS TO GRIEVE FIRST.

ME: I GET THAT. 100%. TELL HIM WE LOVE HIM AND ARE SO SORRY.

GABE ROSSI: I WILL ... AND THANKS. PLEASE TELL COOP HOW SORRY WE ARE. WE'LL PAY HIM BACK FOR WHATEVER HE CAN'T GET REFUNDED.

ME: I'LL TELL HIM, BUT I'D BET MY GARAGE HE WON'T LET YOU.

GABE ROSSI: WE'LL FIGURE IT OUT. YOU GUYS HAVE FUN.

ME: YOU BET. GIVE TY A SQUEEZE FOR ME.

"That really sucks," I said, staring blankly at the phone.

"Yeah, I know they were both really looking forward to this trip."

I looked up. "I meant about Dom. Ty loves that dog almost as much as he loves Gabe. I can't imagine having to ... make that decision."

"Yeah, would be hard." Sam looked across the lobby toward the hotel bar where the others stood, drinks already in hand. "The others don't know this, but Ty and Gabe have been talking about adopting."

"A kid?" My jaw fell open.

"Yeah, a kid." Sam grunted. "They'd been talking to some overseas organizations, were getting pretty close. Ty's always told me everything, but he's been tight-lipped lately. I think he's been afraid talking about it would jinx things."

"How long have they been together? Two years? Three? Wasn't Ty—"

"A total party boy? A circuit queen? Yep. Guilty as charged."

"I know he's settled down, but a kid?"

Sam smiled, and I swear I saw Grammy in his eyes. "If you'd asked me a few years ago about Ty adopting—hell, about him having sheets that lasted longer than a night—I'd say you were nuts. But Gabe ... Gabe was his miracle."

"He's changed that much?"

He nodded slowly. "I've never seen anything like it. Don't get me wrong, it didn't happen overnight, but it *did* happen. Ty is so protective of Gabe, I think he'd die before he hurt him."

"What about the whole 'sleeping his way through the phone book' thing?"

Sam actually laughed at that. "That's the craziest part. I used to joke that he needed a chiropractor just to fix the whiplash he got every time a hot guy walked by. His head was on more of a swivel than a periscope."

"And now?"

"I can't remember the last time I caught him give a guy a second glance. His world revolves around their relationship, around loving and supporting Gabe. It's the most beautiful thing I've ever seen."

My brows rose.

"I see that look, Coop. Don't go thinking I've gone all soft. I'm still the bend-you-over-the-couch mechanic guy."

"Ew. Mom. Stop."

He laughed. "I can describe—"

"No! You can't. Ever. Seriously, not ever."

He took a step back and waved his hand up and down his body like a gay Vanna White. "Are you telling me you've never looked at all this goodness and wondered—"

"No!" I said, a little too quickly. He crossed his arms, and his darn bicep bulged to perfection. "Okay, maybe—before I knew you and Miguel well. A little. I might've thought you were hot back then, when I came to deliver the news of Grammy's will and you were in your office and Ty walked in looking like a model and you looked like the biker dude every guy dreams of in their dirtiest dreams. You know, the ones where a plumber comes over to fix your sink, but he's super-hot and for some reason he has to take his shirt off to get under the sink and you can see his package tearing at the fabric of his jeans and his abs clench every time he stretches out and he starts to sweat, and before you know it, the radio is playing porn music and you're riding his wrench."

Sam blinked. Then blinked again. "Should we, um, drink ... I mean, join the others, you know ... for a drink?"

"So much for my fantasy." I grinned. "Lead the way, Mom."

Chapter Thirteen

Steph

I SPENT MOST OF my days surrounded by muscular, hot, sweaty guys. They're athletic, clever, funny, and about as shy as a heart attack. If I had a dollar for every time one of them walked past me on the way to the shower, dick and balls slapping happily in the breeze, I'd be a rich man—and a lot less horny.

On top of everything (no pun intended), almost all of these men were straight. Painfully straight.

After four years of baseball at the collegiate level, another three in the minors, and the past two as a Mango, one might think I'd become desensitized to the constant stream of abs and lats and pecs ... and butts ... and ...

Okay, maybe I wasn't desensitized. What twenty-five-year-old, testosterone-filled man was? In fact, science might argue that we were at our most sensitive ... sensual ... sensation-oriented ...

Whatever.

We were horny all the time, and being stuck in a locker room, day after day, with some of the most delicious slices of beef anywhere this side of the Mississippi (yeah, it runs by Memphis) did things to a self-respecting gay man's perpetually revved engines.

What am I saying? I have no self-respect. I would turn our often raucous shower scenes into a slippery-when-wet porn so fast the team logo would have to change from mangoes to bananas.

But, while I might have little self-respect, I have immense respect for my teammates, our mission to make baseball accessible and fun, and our collective desire to continue getting paid to play the game we all love. I would never put their careers—or mine—at risk just to get my rocks off.

The off-season was a perfect time to recharge and get images of our first baseman bending me over the dugout railing out of my mind, or to flush away dreams of Rusty, our Dominican shortstop, whose arms were nearly as thick as my thighs. The other night, I could practically feel him flexing while he took both my balls in his mouth.

Which left my balls a perpetually odd shade of cerulean ... or would that be aqua?

God, I needed to get laid.

So, to escape the torture of the man-market that was our team, I accepted Cooper and Nate's invitation to join them on a cruise. The pair of them were hot enough to fry bacon, but they're also so googly-eyed toward each other that I knew better than to suggest anything. I honestly thought this trip would be an escape, a chance to see some cool places, experience different cultures, and meet some new people. Heck, along the way, I might even find another guy to help relieve some of this pent-up tension.

Then I walked into the lobby and met our cruise mates.

Holy bananas, Batman.

Did these people have ugly friends? Was there some requirement to be cover-ready to get accepted into their group?

Sam looked like the nasty fuck the angel on my shoulder warned me about when I was a teenager, all muscly and stubbly, with gravel in his voice and heat drifting off his skin. His partner, Miguel, was a whole different kind of hotness. He was a mountain of a man, but his smile, and the ease with which he made everyone around him feel ... I don't know ... like they were *special* ... that made him dreamy in a way I wasn't sure I'd ever seen before. Nick, the baller whose rapid climb from minors to the bigs I'd followed from afar, had that whole don't-hate-me-because-I'm-hot-and-brooding thing going on, with his floppy curls and chocolate eyes, like some sexy, pouty goldendoodle with abs.

Don't get me wrong, I'm a pretty good-looking guy. I'm tall, lean, have really good hair most days; but crap, even the old man of the group, Doc André, had a smile that could melt an iceberg. I wasn't usually into gray hair, but his swooped back and fluttered in the wind like some male Marilyn Monroe. And his eyes were so ... kind. When he stared—and he always stared when he listened to someone—it felt like he saw into my soul. That was creepy at first, I'll admit. Now, knowing him a little, it made my chest warm.

On top of all that hot-out-of-the-oven, sugar-coated Krispy Kreme hotness, every single one of them was nice. I'd dreaded the whole "he's not part of our family" routine, the one every new in-law experienced when attending a family holiday for the first time. But there was none of that. They'd opened their arms and embraced me as one of them from the moment we'd met. We joked and jabbed like teammates, but I could easily see that everything was in a spirit of fun and companionship. These guys really were a family—and they'd taken me in.

How was I supposed to make it ten days on the open ocean with a pack of certified hotties without tripping over my own dick?

I'm a good guy. I would never cheat or hook up with some guy's boyfriend or husband. I wouldn't be opposed to squeezing in between a pair of hotties, if they were into it, but that would be adding to a pair, not subtracting from one.

Math *can* be fun, kids.

So why was my mind spinning out of control? I wasn't worried about one of them tripping and accidentally falling inside my asshole.

Although ... accidents *can* happen.

No, *that* wouldn't happen.

My fear was that I would spend ten days drooling over these guys, and the overheated engine already roaring inside me might combust, leaving tiny pieces of Steph guts all over the freshly cleaned boat.

That would not be pretty.

"Hey, Steph."

Nate nearly startled me out of a year of life. He and Sam strode up, each dragging a rolling suitcase.

"Oh, hey."

"We've got so much luggage, our car's full. Mind riding with Sam and Miguel?"

Riding Sam and Miguel. I know that wasn't what he said, but it's what I heard. The thought conjured images that stirred—

"Sure, man. That's cool," I said, my voice cracking like some prepubescent boy looking at his first *Penthouse*.

"Sounds like you're with us." Sam gripped my arm, and I swear he squeezed my bicep.

Great. My mind was now playing tricks, assuming every simple touch was sexual or intimate—or designed to get me naked and pin my legs over my head.

I shook the latest pulse-pounding mental image free. Sam and Miguel had been true gentlemen in the fourteen hours since we'd met. Nothing about them said they had any desire to play with others. Nate talked a lot about Miguel, about how he'd mentored him when he was at Vandy, about their friendship that continued after college. He'd talked about how Coop met the guys, and how he'd become an almost instant part of their lives. He painted a picture of the perfect marriage between two kind, caring men who couldn't even dream about anyone else.

What did therapists call what I was doing? Projecting? Yeah, that's it. I was projecting a shaken Coke can of lust onto them.

God, I wanted someone to pop my cap so badly.

"So, uh, how long have you and Miguel been together?" I asked, desperate for an ice bath.

"It'll be five years soon, but we've been married a little over two."

"He seems like a really good dude."

Sam's face brightened. "He's the best man I've ever known."

God, why did these guys have to be so perfect—and perfectly matched?

Then I realized something that might have frightened me more than excited: what I craved in *that* moment wasn't Sam's hard, naked body shoving me down on the back seat of our taxi (despite how good that sounded when I thought about it). No, what I craved was the companionship, respect, and boundless love I saw in Sam's eyes when he spoke of Miguel. Five years later, Sam was so in love with Miguel I could feel it when he spoke. It was palpable and real. It was overpowering and …

It was exquisite.

Dude, grab your sack and stop whining. You need sex, not your Disney soulmate, I chided myself.

But it didn't help.

No one had ever looked at me like that, not even once.

Then Miguel appeared, his smile almost reaching both ears, and their eyes met.

They'd been apart for what? Fifteen minutes? Probably less.

Apparently, time didn't exist in their world. A casual observer might've thought they'd been separated by an ocean through decades of a great war and were only now being reunited … with *Titanic* music playing in the background … and doves flying overhead.

Man, I *really* needed to get laid.

"Ready to go?" Miguel asked, giving Sam a peck on the cheek.

"Let's do this," Sam replied, grabbing Miguel's ass as he bent to fold his tall frame into the car.

I walked around and climbed in the back seat with Miguel, thinking Sam would ride shotgun up front, but no—oh no—Sam climbed in on my side, shoving me into the middle seat where I nearly had to cross my legs just to fit. Sam wasn't as tall as Miguel and me, but his shoulders were broad and his legs were thick as tree trunks. Miguel was my height, six three, but with a solid thirty pounds more muscle. Between our eternal legs and Miguel's massive chest, the two of us would've filled the back seat to capacity on our own. Add Sam, and there was barely room for oxygen, much less the men needing it to breathe.

We were sardines in a can, shoulder on top of shoulder, leg pressed firmly against leg.

I popped a boner.

Please don't notice. Please don't notice. Please don't notice.

"Somebody's happy to see us," Sam singsonged, pointing toward my crotch with his gaze.

A tidal wave of heat slammed into my face.

"Who knew the new guy had a thing for cops? You like handcuffs too?" Miguel asked, his voice chipper as ever but his eyes roaming my tented shorts.

"Uh, yeah, cops, I like them fine. And handcuffs. They're great for … coppish things … you know, like keeping people in place and stuff." I could barely form sentences.

Miguel's laughter traveled from his chest, through our shoulders, and into me.

"Coppish things? Really?"

"At least he's pretty," Sam said, earning another bout of laughter.

My crimson deepened.

Sam and Miguel shared a grin. The next thing I knew, they were leaning across my lap to give each other a kiss—inches from my face. And dammit, they pulled back and let their tongues linger, teasing, circling, touching.

My hard-on raged.

Sam's arm brushed against it, then his weight pressed down.

"Ah!" I called out, squirming beneath his pressure.

They parted and resumed their positions on either side. Neither acknowledged the evil, tawdry dance they'd just performed within a ball's hair of my mouth.

Neither of them was breathing heavily. Neither appeared to have a boner.

Then I realized I was looking from Sam's crotch to Miguel's. I snapped my gaze to the windshield and tried not to move.

"I like the rookie. He looks good in blush. Or is that more rouge?" Miguel teased.

"Looks more maroon to me. See, around his cheeks, it's darker there." Sam grinned, and I swear his leg rubbed against mine. "He's got potential."

Chapter Fourteen

Nate (and Cooper)

"Sir, would you like some champagne?"

That might've been the most shocking question I'd been asked in a while; possibly ever.

First, the purple-and-gold-clad child called me "sir," and there was only one setting where tagging me with that age-dependent honorific was appropriate. That required boots, a leather harness or chaps, perhaps chains and cuffs. The only way boarding a plane factored into that scenario would've been if we'd ushered into the back bathroom a mile above the ground with no one nearby to hear the door rattle and bang. Stepping on board and turning toward our plush first-class seats was clearly not that scene.

I tried to hide my offense.

Second, the woman offered me freaking champagne ... in a glass flute ... from a silver tray.

What airline does that? Seriously?

My head whipped back to Coop, and his already toothy grin widened to impossible proportions. He'd refused to tell me anything of the arrangements he'd made for this journey, though our first night at the Ritz Carlton hinted at a vacation more attuned to caviar than burgers.

But champagne? On a plane?

It even rhymed. Holy hell.

"Babe, take your glass and move it. Everyone's waiting." Coop's hand pressed into the small of my back, urging me forward.

"My name is Jack. I'll be your personal attendant on this flight if you need anything." Jack's jet-black hair curled, one lock falling just above his left eye. Chocolate flavored … I mean, colored … eyes stared back, and I swear his biceps bulged through his white uniform shirt. Had Coop brought in the stud of the skies just for our flight?

"Uh, thanks Jack," I said, unsure if personal attendants were a thing on planes these days. I hadn't flown in a while.

I stepped into a section of wide leather seats with armrests filled with buttons. Unlike the wide cabin behind us with rows of seats crammed together, there was only one seat by each window and two in the center, eliminating that uncomfortable middle space between sharp-pointed-elbow-wielding passengers I'd come to dread on each flight with my teammates. Behind the seatback of each was a tube-looking thing with a glass section, like some sort of space suit with a view hole. As I reached D3, my seat in the middle section, I noticed what appeared to be a travel kit in each seat. The pack was about the size of two palms held flat beside each other. On the face, embossed in a slightly lighter shade of navy, was the name Delta One.

"Would you like anything other than champagne, sir?" a second attendant asked as I bent to take my seat.

"Uh, no, thanks. I'm good."

"Excellent. Get settled in. We'll serve an amuse-bouche for you before takeoff."

Coop settled into the seat beside me, all gums and giddiness. He unzipped his pack and began rummaging. "Nice! There's an eye mask in here. Did you see that, babe?"

I took a sip and set my flute on the table thing wedged between our seats. "Coop, what have you done? This is insane."

Before he could answer, Miguel's head appeared from the seat in front of Coop. Thanks to the tube, he had to sit up on his knees like a kid about to bounce on his bed despite his parents' repeated scolding for doing so. His goofy grin was even wider than Cooper's.

"This is so freakin' awesome, Coop," Miguel said.

"We raised you right, kid." Sam's bristly head popped up beside him. "But what's an amuse-bouche?"

Sam slaughtered any elegance the French phrase might've once possessed, which only made it more endearing.

"A snack," Coop said. "I hear they feed us a lot, so loosen your belts now."

"You've never flown first class?" Sam asked.

Coop snorted. "This isn't first class. This is Delta One."

"Hear that, Sam? We're in Delta One," Miguel said proudly, though, by the look on his face, I doubted he had any idea what it meant.

Stephan stumbled by, boarding pass in hand.

"Just sit anywhere, Steph," Coop said. "We have the entire section."

Steph nodded, then leaned over and whispered, "Did you guys see Jack? Holy crap, his chest is popping out of that shirt."

"Go for it, single boy. You have seven hours to join the Mile High Club," I teased.

"I'm usually a good boy, but Jesus." Steph flopped into the window seat directly across the aisle from Miguel and began exploring the panel of buttons on his armrest.

Sam and Miguel's eyes snapped to mine. "Seriously? You bought the entire Delta One section?"

"There's twelve of us—there *were* twelve, counting Ty and Gabe—and there's twelve seats in this section. It's not like I had a choice." I grinned and nodded. "Besides, a minute ago, you didn't even know what Delta One was."

"I still don't, but it sounds really ... expensive," Miguel said, scanning the cabin.

"Yeah, I doubt the folks behind us are about to enjoy a pre-takeoff amuse-bouche," Sam added.

"Nope. They're not. They'll enjoy rubber chicken soon enough," Miguel chirped.

I was about to say something snappy, but a high-pitched squeal from behind cut me off.

"Uncle Cooper! This is awesome!" Ethan's willowy arms found Coop's neck, as the boy choked the life out of him. "Thank you so much."

"You're welcome, buddy," Coop said, pulling him back so he could look in his eyes. "Are you ready to see some crazy fun stuff?"

His eyes widened as he nodded. "Like what?"

"Have your dads not told you where we're going? What we're about to see?"

He shook his head. "They won't tell me anything."

"That's because we don't know anything. Uncle Cooper is good at keeping secrets," Nick said, raising his champagne flute and sticking his tongue out at Cooper.

Ethan giggled.

"Well," Coop said, lowering his voice to a conspiratorial whisper. "We're going to see where real gladiators fought against each other."

"No way!" Ethan's eyes widened.

"And I hear the ship we're on has an entire section just for kids."

"Papa, did you hear that?" Ethan said, spinning in the aisle to bump into André.

"It is all very exciting," André said. "This is a long flight. You will have plenty of time to ask Uncle Cooper about our plans. Go, find our seats."

The boy scurried forward as Nick and André passed our row.

"You've really outdone yourself, Cooper," André said. "Ethan will never forget this Christmas."

I don't think I'd ever seen Coop smile so wide. His joy filled my chest with such tenderness, I thought my heart might burst out at any moment. Before I realized what I was doing, my palm was cupping Coop's cheek.

"Aw, look at that, Miguel. Your little mentee is totally dick-whipped. That's the cutest little thing I've ever seen."

I looked up to find Sam, the burly mechanic, with his elbows on his seatback, chin resting in his palms, batting his eyes like a dramatic, love-struck schoolgirl.

Miguel chuckled and quickly mirrored Sam's posture, cocking his head to one side. "It's so sweet. My baby caterpillar finally grew wings."

I glanced up the aisle. Ethan was still in earshot, so I flicked the guys a bird and a scowl rather than responding with words.

"Oh, there he is. Still my little boy," Miguel teased.

Sam leaned his head so it pressed into Miguel's. "Isn't it fun, watching our kids grow up?"

"They grow so fast," Miguel sighed.

As the last of the guys settled into their seats, the entire cabin, including the two flight attendants in the forward compartment, turned and stared. Annie's crystal voice sliced through the usual boarding chatter.

I'm grabbin' my hat and coat

I'm leavin' the cat a note

I'm shinin' my travelin' shoes

Big scoop in the Daily News

"Who's sayin' his toodle-oos?"

Gettin' out of town.

We're leavin' the boys in style

We're linin' 'em up in file

And givin' them each a smile

I'm leavin' the cat a note

Quick, call me a ferry-boat

Gettin' out of town . . .

As she reached the crescendo, the point in the show where I assumed every actor on stage had their hands in the air and voices turned to full volume, even more passengers—and one of our flight attendants—added their full-throated voices.

Not on the OCR

I'm wearin' my hat and coat

I'm leavin' the cat a note

Quick, call me a ferry-boat

Gettin' out of town.

My tickets are in my hand

Gosh, isn't the feelin' grand

Good gracious, they've sent a band!

Gettin' out of town.

A round of applause and wild cheers thundered from the cockpit to the back cabin, as Annie beamed and raised her hand to nearly scrape the ceiling in a princess wave, first toward us, then toward her adoring fans behind.

"What was that?" Steph asked, a dumbstruck look in his eyes.

"That," Miguel said, his teeth bright in the plane's blue accent lights, "is Annie."

"Yep," Sam added, "that sums it up."

As the applause died and Annie finally took her seat, Jack returned and served the amuse-bouche, which consisted of a round cut of crusty bread topped with a thin slice of salmon, cream cheese, a wedge of cucumber, and a dollop of caviar.

"Where's the rest of it?" I heard Sam ask.

Coop stood and leaned over his seatback. "It's a one-bite dish. You get all the flavors in one tasting."

"What's the point of that? If I'm hungry, I want more than one bite."

Coop grinned. "There's more food coming. Think of this as a tease. That's a loose translation of the French: a tease for the mouth."

Miguel couldn't hold back any longer. "Sam is more into leather rod than feather teases."

"Dude, really?" Steph leaned across the aisle. "I never pegged you guys for—"

"We're not," Sam snapped. "Miguel's using a metaphor. A simile? A comparison? Fuck, he's being an idiot."

"Sounded hot to me," Steph said, sitting back.

Coop flopped down, a smile teasing his lips as he tossed the bite into his mouth.

An hour later, Jack served an appetizer, offering a different selection of wine because, apparently, the champagne we had as we boarded wasn't good enough for the poached shrimp with spring pea hummus, romaine Caesar salad, and spring carrot soup.

"Three appetizers? I thought we were going to pick from the menu," I said.

Coop shrugged as he took another bite of salad. "It's good, isn't it?"

I nodded and sipped my wine, which did, in fact, blend well with the rich notes of the soup, like a cold beer just goes with pizza.

I'd barely finished the last of my salad before Jack arrived to snatch my tray and replace it with another filled with sides of green beans, roasted potatoes, and a blend of cabbage and something else I couldn't identify.

"Which fish would you prefer," the attendant asked. "The snapper, salmon, sea bass, or cod?"

"Uh"—I looked from my plate to Coop then up at the attendant—"sea bass, I guess."

"Great choice, Nate. Would you prefer a chardonnay or pinot grigio with your sea bass?"

I startled at his use of my name, then glanced back at Coop, desperate to avoid eye contact with the attendant.

"We'll both have the pinot grigio with our sea bass," Coop said, like he'd been born in a wine barrel.

Jack smiled. "Good call, Coop." He nodded and shuffled on to the next row, where he greeted each member of our party by name.

"Holy shit, Jack learned our names already," I whispered.

"Guess he's more than tits and arms," Coop said with a smirk. "He might be too much for surfer dude to handle."

I snorted, nearly spitting wine.

The sound of Annie's smile drifted forward as she clapped her hands and giggled. If I hadn't known her to be in her seventh decade, I would've sworn we'd brought a small girl with us. Ethan's voice bounced from the opposite end of the cabin as Nick and André wrestled to keep the excited child in his seat.

I reached over and raised Cooper's hand to my lips.

He cocked his head, a warm smile reaching his eyes. "What's that for?"

"For all this." I glanced around. "And for being you."

His eyes sparkled. "I love you so much," he said.

I kissed his hand again. "You too, babe."

A throat clearing pulled us apart.

"Pinot grigio and sea bass," Jack announced, presenting a new tray with plates loaded with a massive slice of perfectly seared fish.

"How are we supposed to keep eating?" I asked. "Don't all planes serve crappy food?"

Jack tsked, as though I'd cursed in church. "This isn't a plane. It's Delta One."

I made it through most of my sea bass before surrendering. Jack's hand was on the edge of my tray almost before my fork hit the plate.

"Would you like more wine?" Jack asked.

I glanced at my nearly empty glass and nodded. Coop's was still half full, but I pointed and said, "Fill him up too. He needs it."

Jack grinned, then vanished.

The next course arrived a dozen minutes later, and included not one but two pasta dishes: a jumbo shrimp scampi and a roasted vegetable ravioli. Of course, Jack insisted we switch to a different wine, offering a selection of three pinot noirs he swore would serve as a palate bridge between the pasta and meat courses.

"There's a meat course after this?" I asked, staring at the twin bowls of pasta.

"Then a palate cleanse, then dessert, then a night cap with—"

"Dear God, I'm going to be fat *and* drunk."

Jack chuckled, then placed a hand on my shoulder. "Small bites, deep breaths, take your time. We have seven hours, and a lot more food to go. Trust me, I'm a professional."

We'd been eating for nearly an hour and a half when Jack arrived with two more plates for each of us, one containing a seasoned ribeye and another with a braised duck breast.

"That's a big piece of meat," I said, groaning and clutching my swollen belly.

"I've heard that before," Jack said, winking as he dashed away.

Coop laughed, then dove into his steak like he hadn't eaten in days.

"Where do you put it?" I asked.

Half-chewed steak grinned back. "I'm a growing boy."

"And I'm a hurting boy," I said, reluctantly grabbing my fork and knife, determined to try everything my dear one had bought.

I barely made a dent this time.

"Giving up so easily?" Jack said as he reached for my tray. "And here I thought you were impressed with my meat."

I gaped up.

Coop snorted.

Jack winked again.

"I like him. He's funny," Coop said.

"He's flirting."

"Oh, babe. He's just reading the room and being friendly. Did you hear the conversation he had with Sam and Miguel? I swear I could see Sam's blush rising above his seat—and it takes a lot to make that man blush. Miguel was practically vibrating."

"Huh," was all my food-induced-coma brain could muster.

"I might've—"I groaned. "You might've what?"Coop's grin turned mischievous. "I might've told the airline a little about our group and requested a, um, *member of the team* be assigned to us."

My head fell to the rest. "And by *member of the team*, you didn't mean Delta's flight team?"

"No, think rainbow, not blue. And—"

"Oh no, there's an and."

"And I *may* have asked for a hunky gay guy, and may have actually selected from a menu of options that included several men who looked like they walked off the cover of *Men's Fitness*, one who offered to wear a Delta-colored Lycra suit, and a drag queen whose boobs would barely fit through the cabin doors. The airline normally wouldn't entertain requests like this, especially calling out an employee's sexual orientation, but the supervisor, whose flame burned so brightly you could see it from space, happens to be a friend and was very accommodating. I went with option one."

"Oh, Coop."

"And—"

"There's more?"

He steepled his fingers and released a faux evil villain laugh.

"You're not going to tell me, are you?"

"Nope," he beamed. "Surprises are my jam."

"Speaking of jam," Jack's voice startled me again. "For your first dessert—"

"*First?*"

"We have a chocolate cake. Between the three layers is milk chocolate mousse, white chocolate mousse, and raspberry coulis, all of which is topped in a chocolate ganache."

The mountain of sweetness landed with a thunk on my tray.

"This dessert should really be paired with—"

"More wine?" I grumbled.

"Jack, we trust you. Bring whatever you would choose," Cooper said with a sugary smile almost as sweet as the death-by-chocolate sitting before me.

"Back in a flash," Jack said.

I was truly miserable by the time Jack arrived to describe the second dessert. He kindly agreed to hold that course until we'd had time to recover, say, in a week or so.

The last thing I remember before the cabin lights dimmed and the tube hood thing slid over my head to shut out the last of the plane's noises was Cooper leaning over and kissing my cheek, then stealing the last of my uneaten chocolate cake.

Chapter Fifteen

Cooper (and Nate)

Jack had been everything my friend at Delta had
promised. He was friendly, incredibly efficient, attentive, and
ridiculously easy on the eyes. He teased the couples and
flirted shamelessly with Steph, played games with Ethan while
his daddies slept, and let Annie drool over him as only a
seventy-plus-year-old woman could. The rebellious hair that fell
to his forehead made me want to reach up and flick it back
every time he walked by. Whoever landed this fish would spend
a lifetime battling that curl.

"You sure you won't join us on our cruise? It's only eleven
days." Steph leaned against the bathroom door. Jack stood
inside the galley where the crew prepared our endless meals, his
hand a hair's breadth from where Steph's rested on the metal
counter. Every one of us—including Ethan—watched in rapt
silence.

I couldn't hear Jack's reply, but our entire group erupted in cheers when the dreamy flight attendant stuffed a folded paper into Steph's pocket.

Our resident surfer dude's ears were crimson by the time he made it back to his seat.

"Well," Miguel said, leaning across the aisle with Sam perched over his shoulder. "What happened? We saw the note. What's it say?"

Steph's blush deepened. "Come on, guys. Don't I get a little privacy?"

Sam barked a laugh. "You don't know our little family yet, do you? There's no such thing. Now, out with it. What did Sky Captain over there slip into your jeans? And what did he promise to slip—"

"Sam!" Steph protested.

"Don't tell me you weren't thinking about it. I could practically name his religion by how tight his pants were. That thing looks huge." Sam pantomimed a two-foot fish.

"I thought you two were the adults in the group," Steph said.

"Sam and Miguel? Adults?" I leaned in. "Who do you think corrupted the rest of us?"

Miguel laughed. "That was all Sam. I'm sunshine and rainbows."

Nate tossed his eye mask into the back of Miguel's head. "Keep tellin' yourself that, sensei. You're the dirtiest old man of the bunch."

"Who you callin' old?" Miguel shot back.

"Ladies, please," Sam said. "Steph still hasn't spilled the beans."

Steph looked to me for help. I shook my head. "You're on your own here, soldier."

"He gave me his number. He lives in Atlanta. We might do something when we get home. We'll see."

Sam and Miguel high-fived, then the rest of us joined in, all palms leading to Steph, who reluctantly returned the gesture.

"Did I miss something worth celebrating?" Jack's voice cut in from the aisle.

Steph looked like he wanted to crawl under his seat.

I looked at Jack, and, with a sincere tone, said, "We were just talking about how much we like Atlanta."

Sam, Miguel, and Nate burst out laughing. Steph covered his face with a blanket.

Jack, to his credit, didn't miss a beat. "Bet you won't like it nearly as much as Steph will when he visits me. He'll be surfing bowlegged by the time I'm done with him, bless his heart."

Everyone howled as Jack turned, smacked his own ass, and strode back toward the galley.

I turned to Nate when he came up for air. "We only have a few hours in Barcelona before we need to board the ship."

"When does it leave?"

"Not until four or five, I think, but the tickets all said to get there several hours ahead. The website talked about long lines checking in, that sort of thing."

"Makes sense, I guess," he said. "Gives us just enough time to eat lunch."

He glared when I laughed. "What?"

"I seem to remember someone telling me he never wanted to eat again. About five hours ago."

"A lot can change in five hours."

I grinned. "Apparently."

The plane rocked as its wheels touched down, then the crew lead welcomed us to Barcelona and offered tips to the non-Spanish travelers on how best to navigate customs in the airport. The buzz racing through our section was electric. Ethan's face was plastered to the window, both palms pressed into the plastic. Nick mussed his hair, and André stood to collect their carry-on bags from the overhead bin. I glanced around to find each of the couples chatting excitedly about what was to come. It was especially heartening to see Steph and Miguel bantering as Sam made his way back to where Annie sat.

The warmth of Nate's hand pressing into my forearm turned my head.

"You really are amazing, you know that?"

My brows furrowed. "Why?"

"Look around. You did this. You brought our family together. I don't think even Sam and Miguel could've pulled this off—and I'm not talking about the money either. This is a lot of cats to herd."

I leaned my head to press against his. "Thanks, babe. This is going to be so much fun."

The whoosh of the door opening brought everyone to their feet, and, in moments, our feet touched down on Spanish soil.

We wound through the glass-walled airport, following other passengers like a line of lemmings, until signs directed us to the customs area. A lone man in a red Delta coat stood holding an iPad with the name "Mr. Hawk" glowing on its screen.

Nate chuckled behind me as I waved at the man and stepped forward. "I'm Cooper Hawk."

"Welcome, Mr. Hawk. If you and your guests would follow me, I will show you to the diplomatic corridor." The man's smile was warm and the Spanish flavoring his words was swoon-worthy. His dimples didn't hurt either.

"Thank you," I said, turning back to my wide-eyed companions. "Come on, this shouldn't take long."

"Coop," Nate whispered as we began walking. "Diplomatic corridor? How did you—"

"Remember Sam's old hookup, Joe Gibson? He's the one married to our congressman."

"Oh, right, the SEAL who ran for governor."

I nodded. "Yeah, that one. I tried to get them to come, but David—Congressman Reese—had some kind of commitment. But he offered to make a few calls to smooth our entry into Spain. I didn't even know that was possible."

"Guess anything's possible if you know the right people." Nate was silent a few strides, then his whisper fell quieter. "Does Sam know you reached out to Joe? I'm not sure—"

"They patched things up a long time ago, babe. Sam and Miguel have even had them over to their house for dinner a few times." I turned and hooked my arm around Nate's. "It's all good. But no, I didn't tell anyone about this. I didn't even ask David to do it. He just offered."

We rounded a corner, where our dimpled Delta guide waved a badge at an unmarked door, then punched in a code. When the light on the pad turned green, he opened the door, held it for us, and motioned with an upturned palm. "Right this way."

Inside the door was a more elegant version of the glass box normal people stood before to answer their customs questions. Rich wood polished to a mirrorlike sheen held golden letters that read in Spanish, "His Royal Majesty Welcomes You to Spain." Behind the desk, King Felipe VI, wearing his regal navy uniform with golden epaulets and a sky blue sash, stared down from his gilded frame.

A woman in a military dress uniform rose from behind the desk and inclined her head. "Welcome to Spain. May I see your passports, please?"

Her English was flawless, and, where our guide's accent was thick like overcooked tomato sauce, hers carried the light touch of a Mediterranean breeze.

There were no questions. No one was grilled about the purpose of our visit or if we'd given our bags to a stranger. The officer simply flipped to a blank page and affixed a stamp, then handed the booklets back with a pleasant smile.

"Enjoy your stay in Barcelona. Come back when you have more than a few hours to spend," she said, then reached down, opened a drawer, and removed a sealed envelope, extending it toward me. Its golden seal glittered in the room's bright lights. "Oh, and please extend His Majesty's greeting to Congressman Reese when you return home."

"Of course. Thank you," I said.

When the last of us received the stamp, our guide led us through another series of back hallways, and then out a door that emptied directly before the escalator to baggage claim.

"If there is no other way I might assist, enjoy your stay." The Delta man bobbed his head as the customs woman had done. He waited until we were all descending the escalator, then vanished back down the private hallway.

A line of black-suited men stood in a row at the foot of the escalator. Each held a sign, iPhone, or iPad with the name of their customer. Again, one of the screens read, "Mr. Hawk."

"I don't think I'll ever get used to this," Nate murmured behind me.

I chuckled and strode forward, greeting the man with my name. "We just need to gather our bags."

He nodded and raced off, returning moments later with a young boy, each of them pulling two baggage carts. Retrieving our luggage took nearly three times as long as passing through customs, but forty minutes after descending the not-so-golden escalator, we were piling into a black minibus, chatting and laughing like teenagers going on a school field trip.

We drove away from the airport with downtown Barcelona looming in the distance to our right, past a slew of farms and fields, before commercial buildings and warehouses came into view. A moment later, industrial parks were replaced by the tightly packed, red-tiled roofs of houses, apartments, and small businesses. We rolled to a stop before a sprawling one-story house with a wide circular drive. A small, neatly painted sign in the center of the perfectly groomed grass circle read, "El Restaurant de Dalt."

We were escorted through the restaurant to a patio whose deck emptied onto a grassy lawn. Tables draped with white linen spread before us, water glasses already filled. Beyond the yard, sunlight glittered on the water of the nearby river.

"This looks like a postcard," Annie said, wonder lacing her words.

In moments, we were seated, our glasses were filled with sangria, and bowls of rich soup steamed before us. Platters of tortillas held together by tiny clothes pins arrived next, some stuffed with shrimp, others with seasoned beef or pork.

Miguel began to protest his swelling belly when the servers arrived with savory chicken resting on a bed of spinach and mushrooms, smothered in tomato sauce and melted cheese, but his resistance failed the moment he put the first bite into his mouth.

"I take back every bad thing Sam has ever said about you," Miguel quipped.

I gasped. "What has Sam said bad about me? I'm pure as the driven snow."

"*Driven* is the key word there. Right, Nate?" Sam jabbed to the hoots of our nearby friends.

"Uh, guys, kid," Steph said, nodding toward where Ethan sat a table away.

Nick waved him off. "Don't worry about us. Ethan's heard a lot worse than that. Just keep the body parts vague and we're good."

"Dad, why is driven snow dirty?" Ethan asked.

André chuckled and shot Sam a glare as he spoke. "Because when people drive their car on it, it gets slushy, isn't that right, Uncle Sam?"

"Uncle Sam!" Steph hooted. "That's priceless. We should totally get him one of those tall hats, maybe the full suit with the sequined tails."

"Who invited Surfer Boy?" Sam growled.

I raised my hand. "I did. Got a problem with it? You can swim home."

Miguel nearly lost his chicken. "You tell him, Coop. Uncle Sam needs to learn respect."

I started to fire back, but our driver strode up behind me and whispered, "Sir, we need to get you to the port."

"Alright, everyone. I know you want to sit here because the tablecloths are nice and the food is amazing and the wind on the river makes this feel like a dream you never want to wake up from, even though you know waking up lets you experience a new day, and new days are filled with fresh beginnings, which means you get to do something new and exciting like go on a cruise—"

"Coop!" Sam barked.

"Sorry, Mom. Time to load up. Dessert's on the ship," I said, standing.

The last thing I heard as I walked into the restaurant was Miguel muttering to Sam, "He said *load*."

Their laughter followed me all the way onto the bus.

Chapter Sixteen

Nick (and André and Ethan)

Ethan's chattering was ceaseless on the bus ride from the restaurant to the port. He practically vibrated as we stood in line to check our bags onto the ship and receive our boarding passes. When we stepped up to the edge of the ship where the captain and several officers stood to greet us, I thought he might jump out of his shorts.

"Welcome aboard, sirs," the captain said to André and me, then kneeled before Ethan. "Little man, would you like to drive the ship?"

For the first time since I'd met the tiny monster, Ethan couldn't speak. It wasn't like back in the beginning, when there was a psychological block keeping him from talking. In that moment, his excitement overloaded his brain and commands to his tongue simply didn't make it. He tried a few times, croaking out sounds that approximated ill-formed words, but failed to communicate anything meaningful. The captain glanced up at us with a knowing grin, then back to Ethan.

"I'll take that as an affirmative. Tell your dads to bring you to the bridge at nineteen hundred—that's seven o'clock for you land-lovers."

"Yes, sir," Ethan forced out.

The captain patted his arm, then straightened and gave André and me a wink.

"Hello, gentlemen. I am Catalina. Mind if I show you to your cabin?" A woman in a crisply pressed uniform held out her hand for our boarding passes. Her voice was as rich as the hair that fell like an onyx waterfall past her shoulders. "Oh, excellent, you're in one of our aft-facing club suites."

André and I exchanged a confused glance.

Catalina smiled at Ethan as she spoke. "Your suite accommodates four, so you have plenty of room for the little guy and both of you to spread out comfortably. Plus, you have a wide balcony that looks over the rear of the ship. These suites are quieter than those in the forward part of the ship. You're on deck nine."

"The rest of our group is behind. Can we wait and see if our cabins are close to each other?" I asked.

Catalina nodded. "Of course, though I doubt—"

"Hello, boys," Sam's gravelly tones cut her off. He fumbled with the satchel strap on his shoulder, then handed Catalina his boarding pass. "Mind pointing us in that direction?"

Before she could answer, Annie, Steph, Coop, and Nate stepped up.

"Mind if I see your boarding passes? I'll take each of you to your cabins so you can settle in." She shuffled through the papers, her eyes widening. "You're all in the same section. That *never* happens with large groups."

I laughed.

Catalina looked up and cocked her head.

"That's Cooper." I pointed. "He booked everything. If I've learned anything so far on this trip, it's that Coop can make the impossible possible."

Cooper beamed. Nate elbowed him, pride scrawled across his face. Sam and Miguel shared a moment of their own parental pride, despite being no one's parents.

Catalina checked the papers one last time, then her eyes snapped up to Cooper's. "Mr. Hawk, welcome aboard. Your butler is standing by to make you comfortable. Right this way."

Coop and Nate followed Catalina as she strode purposefully toward a bank of elevators. Sam turned to Miguel, brows raised, and muttered, "Butler?"

Miguel shrugged as we all trailed behind.

"THIS IS DECK EIGHT," Catalina said as we disembarked from the elevator. "We have to walk the length of the ship to get to the aft section, so I thought this would be an excellent opportunity to help orient you to some of the ship's amenities."

"Where's the ping-pong table?" Ethan shouted from the back of the pack.

Catalina smiled. "That's top side near one of the pools."

"How many pools are there?" Miguel asked, surprised.

"Three—two adults-only and one for families with children," Catalina explained.

We passed a couple dozen cabin doors before the walkway opened into an atrium with a tall glass ceiling that made it appear one could reach up and touch the puffy clouds as they drifted by in the crystal sky.

"Most of the shops on this level are restaurants," Catalina said as we passed a door with a giant green shamrock carved into its face. "They are ordered from casual to formal, starting with O'Shay's Irish Pub and The Pour House, which is a traditional English pub."

"We really don't need to see any other restaurants," Sam quipped.

"Ignore him," Cooper said, glancing over his shoulder with a mock scowl. "He's a barbarian. The rest of us would like to know where napkins and tablecloths replace peanut shells on the floor."

"Of course, Mr. Hawk." Catalina grinned. "But I do suggest keeping the barbarians happy. Otherwise, they won't give you a moment's peace to enjoy the finer dining."

"Damn straight," Miguel barked.

"Nothing straight about you, Dad," Nate teased.

"Thank God," Sam said, earning a round of playful jeers.

Catalina didn't miss a beat. "This middle section contains seven restaurants. There's everything from Mexican to Peruvian to Italian or Chinese. These dining rooms are like Chili's or, on the upper end, Outback."

"Hmm. Bloomin' Onion," Sam groaned.

"Pipe down back there," Coop chided. "Some of us want to hear what Catalina has to say without fatty food references."

"That's *your* son," Sam said to Miguel. "I don't know what you did to him. I raised an angel."

A chuckle flowed through the group.

"Is there a piano bar? Somewhere with live music?" Annie asked.

Nate put his hand over his heart. "God, no. Don't tell her, Catalina. Whatever you do—"

"Absolutely. Deck ten is where you'll find the casino and bar area. It's designed to look like Bourbon Street in New Orleans. Do you enjoy live music?" Catalina asked Annie.

A collective groan rose from the group.

"Ignore them. They're all barbarians, no matter what that puppy up front says." Annie grinned toward Coop. "I performed on Broadway for nearly thirty years; still return from time to time."

Catalina's brows rose. "I'll have to introduce you to our entertainment director, then. I'm sure he'll find a stage with your name on it before the cruise ends."

"Did you not read the sign, Catalina? It clearly stated, 'Please do not feed the animals.' What about that was unclear?" Sam quipped.

Annie stepped up and punched Sam's shoulder. "You behave before I bend you over my knee and—"

"Uh, Annie, he really likes a good spanking," Miguel said.

Annie and Catalina's faces turned the same bright red as the rest of the group burst into laughter.

"I don't get it," Ethan said, his face scrunched in confusion. "Why would Uncle Sam like a spanking? Does he get in trouble a lot?"

I looked to André, but he just tossed his hands in the air and shook his head, clamping his lips tight.

"Buddy, the boys are just being silly. No one likes getting spanked," I said, patting his back.

"Um-hm," Sam grunted a little too loudly.

Catalina cleared her throat and tried to regain control. "Alrighty then, here we have the formal dining rooms. Stevenson's is our American steakhouse, La Fromage is French fine dining, and Dominico's is Italian fare. Oh, and Moderno is a classic Brazilian restaurant where they slice meats at the table. I would suggest making reservations quickly, as all of these restaurants book to capacity each night."

"Is there a limit on how many times we can eat in each restaurant?" Coop asked.

Catalina shook her head. "Not for our Club and Haven guests. You have unlimited dining privileges throughout the ship."

"I think I just fell in love with Catalina," Miguel said.

Sam elbowed him in the ribs.

Catalina grinned. "There are also two cafeterias, one on deck seven and another on deck nine. The one on deck nine is open twenty-four hours a day."

The walkway ended at another bank of elevators. Catalina walked to one marked "Private" and inserted her badge. "You may use any elevator, but this one is reserved for the exclusive use of our Haven passengers and their guests. Your passes indicate Mr. Hawk had each of you included in this feature."

"Aw, Coop, didn't want to keep the fancy elevator all to yourself? That's so sweet," Sam teased.

Cooper flicked him a bird. "There wasn't a 'Barbarians Only' elevator."

Miguel snorted, earning a sharp look from Sam. "What? The kid's funny," Miguel said.

When the elevator doors opened, everything changed.

The carpet was thick and lush, its pattern no longer whimsical but elegant and refined. The walls of the walkway were paneled with cherry-stained wood, and actual paintings hung in thick frames. Even the lighting was different, casting a warm yellow glow rather than the blaring white lights of the other sections.

"Your badges are required to enter this section, whether you take the private elevator or enter through one of the doors from the rest of this deck." Catalina pointed to a pair of doors I assumed led to walkways and more cabins. She then stepped up to a set of double doors whose wood was darker and richer than the paneling, inserted her badge, and flung the doors open with a dramatic flair.

A fit young man stood just inside the door, facing us, as if he'd magically known we were about to enter. Brown curls flew in every direction, yet somehow looked perfectly in order. Stunningly white teeth gleamed as he smiled and said, "Mr. Hawk, Mr. Stringer, welcome to The Haven."

Chapter Seventeen

Nate (and Cooper)

Coop and I stepped through. As the door swung closed, he turned back toward the group and called out, "We have a dinner reservation tonight at seven at Moderno."

The door clicked shut before anyone could respond.

"Uh, hi," I said to the hottie with the curls, unsure how one greeted his butler on a cruise ship.

"Mr. Stringer, please call me Dario."

Coop turned, eyed Dario up and down, then asked, "Dario, what does a butler do? I've been on cruises, but have never stayed in a suite like this."

"There is only one other suite like this, the fore-facing Haven, which is slightly smaller than your suite." Dario smiled. "And to answer your question, a butler does whatever you require. If you like breakfast in bed, I will bring it to you. If you need linens or anything for your suite, just ask. If you need reservations, entertainment, or anything else, I will do my best. You need not call the general lines. Simply press the button by that intercom and I will answer."

Coop blinked a few times.

I hardly knew what to say—or ask.

"How many suites do you, um, work with?" Coop asked.

"Only yours."

More blinks.

Dario smiled knowingly. Apparently, our stunned reaction was common.

"Why don't I give you a tour?"

I glanced around. The cabin was nice, much larger than what I'd seen online for the average room, but it hardly required a tour.

"This is your living quarters," Dario began. "The sitting area seats six. Your television has full satellite channel capability and includes all the premium movie and sporting channels you may be accustomed to at home. Through this door," he said, stepping through an open doorway to his right, "is your bedroom."

A king-sized bed held court at the room's center, flanked by a pair of side tables. Another television hung on the wall opposite the headboard.

"Your restroom is through there"—he pointed through another open door—"and there is a sliding door to your balcony from every room in your suite, but the Aviary is only accessible through the seating area."

"Aviary?" I mouthed to Coop. He shrugged ... and blinked.

Dario's grin widened; his impossibly white teeth sparkled like he was in a toothpaste commercial.

We followed him through a door just beyond the television in the sitting area, stunned to step into a glass-roofed space similar to the atrium with all the restaurants. Palm trees and other plants rose nearly to the roof from massive planters. Patio tables and padded lounge chairs that could lay flat were scattered about, and at the center was an oval hot tub, already bubbling and steaming.

"You will forgive us. There are no birds in your Aviary. It is simply the name of the room." Dario paused, as if expecting some reaction to his joke that wasn't really a joke. "That door leads to the next cabin. I believe Mr. Nuñez and Mr. Prescott are in that suite. Their key cards have been programmed to allow entry into the Aviary, but not into your living quarters."

"What about the others?" Cooper asked.

Dario nodded. "Every member of your party should have access. If anyone has trouble, please call me. I will have it corrected immediately."

"This is … a lot," I said as my eyes roamed the surrounding luxury. Between our cabin and the Aviary, our combined space on the ship was nearly as large as our downstairs back area at home. From everything I'd heard about cruising, I'd expected to be cramped on board.

Dario guided us back into our suite. "Mr. Hawk, porters will deliver your luggage shortly. I will accompany them to ensure there are no issues."

"You really have to stop making us feel old. I'm Nate, and he's Cooper, please."

Dario inclined his head. "Yes, sir. Nate."

I tried not to flinch at getting "sir-ed."

"Was there anything you wanted to do straight away?" Dario asked.

Coop and I exchanged a glance, our blank expressions mirroring each other.

"When do we take off?" Coop asked.

Dario nearly chuckled, but caught himself. "We set sail in"—he checked his watch—"thirty-two minutes. May I suggest you head to the upper deck to enjoy the launch? Barcelona is beautiful this time of day, especially when seen from sea."

"Uh, sure. That sounds great," I said. "Thanks, Dario."

Chapter Eighteen

Nick (and André and Ethan)

Sam and Miguel vanished into their suite, then Catalina turned and bent to eye level with Ethan. "Are you ready to see your room, little man?"

His head bobbed. "Yes, please."

We walked back up the hallway, past Coop and Nate's double doors, to the next numbered suite.

"Here we are," Catalina said. "Before we scatter, there are a few things each of you should know. First, your key cards work on the doors to this section, in all the passenger elevators throughout the ship, and on the doors of the Aviary."

"The Aviary?" Steph asked.

"It's that door." She pointed to an unmarked door a few feet down from Coop and Nate's entryway. "It's a common area for your group to enjoy."

She turned toward André and me. "The children's section is on deck ten, fore, and it's staffed from eight in the morning until ten at night. You can sign Ethan in and feel comfortable he will be well tended until you return."

"Is there ping-pong there?" Ethan asked.

Catalina's laugh was a tenor bell tinkling in the ocean breeze. "Of course there is. You will also find tables on every deck at the fore of the ship."

"That's so cool!" Ethan beamed up at me.

I mussed his hair and smiled. "You think you can take your dad down?"

"You're so goin' down," he said.

Steph bent down. "Bet you can't beat me."

"Oh, Steph," André said, a hint of warning in his voice. "You don't know what you are starting."

"I think I do," Steph said, grinning at the boy. "We might have to play a lot on this trip, you know, like a ping-pong World Series."

Ethan poked a finger toward Steph. "That's gonna be awesome."

"Last thing," Catalina continued. "We set sail a half-hour from now. You do not need to wait for your luggage to arrive. I recommend you go up top and enjoy the launch, or watch from your balcony, whichever you prefer. Any questions?"

Everyone shook their head, so she swiped her badge and opened the door to our suite.

We stepped in to find a simple cabin with a queen-sized bed, with a small couch facing a television mounted to the wall above a writing desk that doubled as a coffee nook. In the far corner, a door led into a tiny bathroom and even tinier shower.

Ethan leapt onto the bed and bounced up and down.

Catalina didn't flinch. "The couch folds out to make a bed for Ethan, unless you'd prefer—"

"Oh no. We love him dearly, but we prefer to do it from a distance," André said with a smirk.

I nodded. "He kicks."

Catalina looked past me to Ethan and grinned. "Do you have any questions before I move on with the others?"

"No," I said. "I think we'll take our little monster up top. Thank you for the tour."

"It was my pleasure," she said, backing out of the room and closing the door.

THE SHIP'S CITY-BLOCK-SIZED TUBA roared, as the crowd of gathered passengers leaned over the railing and waved to onlookers. I'm not sure what I expected from the launch of a cruise ship, but it moved so slowly from the dock I barely felt it.

"Was that it?" I asked as we watched the people of Barcelona shrink, millimeter by millimeter.

André chuckled. "What did you expect? Fireworks and plumes of seawater shooting out of the back of the boat?"

I rolled my eyes. "Not exactly, but I also didn't expect the ship to move slower than the people walking back to their cars. Catalina made it sound like some glorious event we needed to witness."

"Dad," Ethan's voice carried an irritated tone known only to preteen boys. "We're floating on the ocean. That *is* cool."

"That's right, little man," André said, placing a hand on Ethan's head. "Don't let your downer dad take a moment of fun away from you on this trip."

"Downer dad?" I said, far poutier than intended.

"Exactly." André grinned at me, then looked down at Ethan, his tiny hands still clutching the silver banister. "I think we should head to the front of this ship and check out the children's section. I bet they have some really fun things up there."

"Ping-pong!" Ethan squealed.

André laughed. "Yes, ping-pong, and perhaps other fun things too. Let's go find out."

Chapter Nineteen

Steph

My cabin was nice enough: a queen-sized bed, a large-screen television, a walk-in shower almost large enough to turn around in, and a balcony with two lounge chairs and a small table. I sat on the edge of the bed and flipped on the television. The ship's announcement channel flared to life with a message of welcome and a note about luggage delivery. The guide revealed an insane number of channels, including dozens in Spanish, French, German, Italian, Chinese, and a couple of other languages I couldn't identify. A beach volleyball tournament playing somewhere in Brazil caught my eye, so I tossed the remote onto the bed, dug out every pillow I could reach, and settled against the headboard.

As soon as I'd gotten comfortable, someone banged on the door.

"Mr. Breeden, your luggage is here," a youthful male voice called.

I hopped up, opened the door, and let the twelve-year-old-looking porter struggle in with my bags. Road trips with baseball teams had taught me to pack light, but Cooper made it sound like I'd need a different outfit for every hour, so I brought nearly everything I owned. The poor kid could barely move my largest piece.

"Here, let me help with that," I said, taking mercy on the boy.

He smiled weakly, stepping back. "Thanks, that's a heavy one. Got a dead body in there?"

"Nope. I might take one of those home as a souvenir though," I joked.

He was a slow one, chuckling nervously and taking far too long to realize I was kidding.

With my bags securely shoved in the corner and the skittish child-attendant gone, I threw myself back onto the bed and resumed watching scantily clad men slapping a ball over a net. The score was almost as tight as one of the guy's shorts. I adjusted the pillows and cranked up the volume.

Another knock came at the door.

"Good grief," I muttered, then grabbed the remote to search for a pause button. "Shit, no DVR. Oh well."

I hopped up and opened the door to find Cooper, Nate, and Annie standing in the hallway.

"Dude, you're not sitting here in your cabin like some loner. Get that pretty ass of yours into your trunks and come up top with us. The ship's about to take off," Nate said.

Cooper poked his ribs. "Launch or set sail. Ships don't take off unless there are rockets attached to the belly."

"Yes, dear," he said, then turned back to me and mouthed, "Save me. Now."

I grinned and started to shut the door. "Alright. Give me a minute."

"Aw, I wanted to watch you change. I bet those trunks barely hold everything you've got, big boy."

I hadn't seen Annie's cougar fangs until that moment, and it nearly bowled me over.

"Look at that," Cooper spat. "He's blushing and speechless. Annie, you're the best."

"I know," she said, flicking her hair dramatically. "But I wasn't joking. Have you looked at—"

"Annie!" I protested.

"What?" She gestured with a palm toward my shorts. "Prosecution rests. That thing's a python. Good thing I'm a professional snake handler."

Cooper doubled over. Nate could barely breathe. I slammed the door and tried to regain a shred of composure and dignity after being eye-fucked by a septuagenarian. Oddly, my python had wiggled at his invocation, and I did, indeed, have to shove him down as I wriggled into my swim trunks.

When I opened the door, the trio of troublemakers hadn't moved.

Annie's eyes licked up and down my body as she tsked. "I'm buying you the tiniest Speedos this ship has. Those trunks simply won't do. Let's go, boys."

Without warning, she stepped between Cooper and Nate, hooked her arm around mine, and hauled me toward the elevator, humming some show tune I didn't recognize. Coop and Nate laughed as they closed my cabin door and followed a few strides behind.

"We need to get up top or we'll miss the launch, but you're mine after that. We're getting you that thong," Annie said as we waited for the elevator to deposit us on the upper deck, her arm clutching mine as though she was lost at sea and I was her life raft.

"Thong? When did we go from Speedo to thong?" I asked, ignoring the catcalls from Cooper and Nate.

"Honey, if I can wrap you in mesh with dental floss up that pretty butt, I'll do it. There's no need for you to cover up any more than is required. Mama needs to see the goods, you know."

My face burned brighter than the elevator's lights, and Cooper howled as the doors opened.

Annie finally released my arm when we reached the railing. She leaned over and waved at the well-wishing crowd standing on the dock.

I turned to scan the water ahead of the ship. It stretched forever, an endless canvas of brilliant blue.

"I'm more used to riding the waves up close than on a ship like this. It feels weird to be so high up," I said, imagining myself atop my board.

"Think of the ship as a huge board, with restaurants and shops and a kids' area and bars and clubs and massage tables and balconies and thousands of people ... oh, and three swimming pools and ... oh, look, a hottie in a thong." Cooper's eyes never settled, bouncing from one barely clothed passenger to the next.

"I'm not sure that's how surfing works, but I'll take it," I said, grinning toward Nate.

He was staring adoringly at Cooper, as though the guy had just declared his undying love rather than rattled off a nonsensical comparison.

Annie reclaimed the stage. "I love it when my people come to send me off. Isn't it wonderful?" she said in a faux English accent, as her hand did a perfect imitation of the late Queen Elizabeth II's wave from her Buckingham balcony.

"We are all your people, Your Majesty," Nate said, sticking a foot forward and bowing.

"I don't care about you two anymore. You're all married and happy. But this one"—she poked a bony finger toward me—"is all mine."

Cooper leaned over and whispered so we all could hear, "You know he's on *our* team, right?"

Annie waved a hand in the air. "Oh, honey, I played Broadway for more years than you've been alive. The gays love me. Besides, I'm too old to do anything with his massive slab of meat, even though I can tell he's dying to give it to me."

I blanched again, and Nate had to turn away, he was laughing so hard.

"Annie, you might be the most amazing woman I've ever met," Cooper said as a tear trickled down his cheek.

"I know. It's my curse," she said, then, without pausing a beat, hooked our arms again. "Time for that butt floss, my dear."

Chapter Twenty

SAM (AND MIGUEL)

THE FIRST DAY ABOARD was relaxing. The ship inched lazily from the Spanish coast to the vaunted French Riviera. There were no port calls that first evening, so our group, scattered throughout the day, gathered for dinner as per Coop's previously announced reservation at Moderno, the Brazilian steakhouse.

Meat fell from endless skewers. Wine flowed freely. Annie held court and kept everyone in stitches. Poor Steph squirmed. Miguel's hand spent more time gently stroking my leg than it did above the table.

It was a great night.

"So, Mr. Hawk," Miguel said, his voice slightly slurred. "What do you have planned for us tomorrow?"

Coop grinned from across the table where Nate's arm lay draped about his shoulders. "Nothing."

Even Annie fell silent at that pronouncement.

"Really? Nothing?" Miguel asked.

"Well, the ship docks in Cannes," Coop explained. "There aren't really any excursions or activities. It's basically a shopping stop. In case you haven't noticed, the tastes in clothing and fashion at this table are about as widely varied as exhibits at a zoo. You and Dad have worn the same jeans since the eighties. André might've lived in the States for decades, but he still has European sensibilities, regardless of the poor influence of our dear Nick. And Annie—well—Annie is in a league all her own. It's as likely she'll come back with a designer ball gown as a blouse."

"Screw ball gowns," Annie said, sloshing her glass over the table wildly enough to make Steph lean away. "The shops on this damn boat didn't have anything worthy of Mr. Snuffleupagus over here, so the two of us are going banana hammock shopping."

"That's mango hammock, thank you very much," Nate shouted over the raucous table's roar.

"Honey"—Annie held up a finger—"no mango has ever grown so large. We might need a whole new fruit for this one."

She wrapped her wiry arm around Steph, only making his blush deepen and everyone else's laughter grow louder.

"Steph, we've been teammates for over a year, and I can't ever remember being all that impressed in the locker room. You get an adjustment? Or are you stuffing those shorts to fool Annie?"

"Come on, dude. You're supposed to protect your teammates," Steph protested. "Besides, it's freakin' cold in that locker room."

Steph's pleas fanned the flames. I almost felt sorry for him in that moment.

Almost.

Then Miguel threw him a lifeline. "Actually, Annie, I hate to ruin your plans to turn Steph into a bathing suit model, but Sam and I have him reserved for the day."

Miguel's hand squeezing my leg was the only urging I needed to roll with him.

"Yeah, we haven't had a chance to get to know him, and, as the parental units of this highly dysfunctional family, we need to assess our newest applicant."

Annie stuck out her lower lip. "Fine. I'll just have to guess your size."

Her hand vanished below the table, causing Steph to jump up so quickly he nearly upended the table.

"You can feed the animals, but this isn't a petting zoo," Nick called out.

Annie shot him a glare. "Reptiles aren't animals. Neither are fruits. I'll grab any papaya that swings nearby!"

Napkins flew onto the table in surrender as Nick and André stood.

"Little man's bedtime was probably a few grabs ago. Time for us to turn in," Nick said, pulling Ethan's sleepy head into his side.

"Who's up for a night cap?" Annie bellowed.

"We're in," Cooper said, as Nate raised his empty glass.

"Steph? Sam, Miguel?" Annie asked, a drunken brow raised.

Miguel waved a hand. "Not us. We have a date with a balcony."

"Me too," Steph said.

Annie's other brow shot up. "And what are you doing on Miguel and Sam's balcony?"

"Uh ... I didn't mean ... not their ... my own balcony. I meant my own ... Guys, help me," Steph stammered, his eyes pleading toward Miguel.

"I was planning to bend him over the balcony, since you asked," I said.

Miguel's head spun around, a question in his eyes.

Steph's gaze flared almost as bright as his cheeks, then he looked down.

Annie's jaw dropped.

"Just kidding," I said, and Steph let out a deep sigh, as his shoulders relaxed. Then I added, "Although, all this talk about what's in his shorts has me curious—"

"Oh, man," Nate said, stretching his arms above his head. "I'm so tired. Annie, we'd better get that drink before I fall asleep."

Steph mouthed, "Thanks, dude," to Nate.

Miguel clapped Steph on the shoulder and whispered, "Sam's harmless. Just roll with him and you'll be fine."

Steph, the only one of us able to meet Miguel's gaze without looking up, nodded tentatively, but let Miguel's grip remain on his shoulder as we left the restaurant.

ANNIE, COOPER, AND NATE peeled off from the group as we left Moderno. The trio skipped, arm in arm, like Dorothy, the Tin Man, and the Lion, singing "We're Off to See the Wizard," as they skipped toward the Irish pub at the opposite end of the atrium. I couldn't help laughing at Coop's pitiful attempt at skipping in time with the others, as Annie's soprano rose above the men's worse efforts at singing.

It hadn't been that long ago that Cooper had been a sad, nearly broken shell of a boy.

I chuckled thinking of him as a boy. He was only four years younger than me, but there was an innocence to Cooper that made me want to wrap my arms around him and keep the world away. He only saw the good in people, and had the most generous, honest spirit of anyone I'd ever met, with the possible exception of his grandmother, Marjorie. She'd been a spitfire, and she adored him more than anything in the world. I guess that's why her request for Miguel and me to take Coop under our wing surprised me so. We were good guys, but we were no parents. Hell, neither of us even had nephews or nieces of our own. We didn't know the first thing about raising kids—or whatever it was she wanted us to do with her precious boy. Who were we to help guide another person?

Cooper had never really had parents in his life. He'd thrown himself into taekwondo, an individual sport that spotlighted how alone he was, in the center of a large white circle. He was a dedicated and gifted athlete, but no medal or trophy could ease the solitude he felt in his heart.

When we met Coop, Marjorie had just died. He painted on a smile and pretended to be strong but was alone and about as down as anyone I'd ever seen.

Watching Coop skip down the center of a cruise ship with the love of his life and one of our dearest friends, never giving the passing crowd a second thought (despite their stares), I couldn't help but marvel at how far he'd come.

A strange feeling pricked at my chest. Pride? Was that what parents felt when they saw their child grow?

I shook my head. Coop was a grown-ass man, not some wayward teen. I was being ridiculous.

"You did great, Dad," Miguel's voice smiled nearly as wide as his lips.

"Huh? What?" I looked up, then followed his gaze back to Cooper.

"He *is* our son, I don't care what biology or age or anything else has to say about it. Marjorie asked us to take care of him, to watch out for him, and we've done a damn fine job—especially you. He's grown into himself, allowed himself to be free, and he loves you like ... like the father he never knew."

My eyes fell to my feet and heat clawed at my neck. A lump lodged in my throat, and I swear the ship's air filtration was failing, because my eyes were watering. I tried to rub the blaze racing into my face away, but my palm only made it grow hotter.

"I'm proud of you—and him, babe," Miguel said.

My mouth opened, but nothing came out.

"You guys should hear how Coop talks about you." Steph's voice was like a punch in my already delicate gut. "Especially you, Sam."

An emotional monster gripped my shoulders and began to shake. I grappled and fought, but he was too strong.

Dammit, tears began to fall. I was a fucking mechanic, not some weepy—

"Feels good to be a dad, doesn't it?" Steph said.

And that stole the last of my reserve. Miguel had to wrap me in his arms and guide me down the hallway toward our suite as a well of emotions I'd not even known were hidden beneath the surface poured out. Steph's hand found my back and stayed there until we reached the door to our cabin.

"I'm not a crier, Steph. Dammit. I'm not."

Miguel swiped his card and shoved our door open. "He totally is. Don't let his rough-around-the-edges act fool you. He falls apart at Kleenex commercials," Miguel teased.

"I do not."

"What about Coke commercials, especially around the holidays?" he asked.

"Those—" I jerked back. "Those are sentimental. They have bears and ... stuff."

Miguel glanced at Steph, then they both burst out laughing.

"Fuck off, both of you," I said, storming into our suite, desperate to hide the smile I knew would just egg them on.

"We're going to relax on the balcony, watch the water go by, maybe open a bottle of wine. Want to join us?" Miguel asked Steph.

I turned back and watched Steph hesitate, then say, "Uh, sure, sounds good."

Miguel clapped him on the shoulder, then turned and strode toward the writing desk where Cooper's butler had left several bottles of wine.

"Can you believe Coop has a butler?" Miguel asked as he fumbled with the corkscrew. "I mean, I know he inherited a shit-ton of money, but still ... a butler? On a cruise?"

"We're gonna be old one day. Our boy's gotta take care of us," I said, finally getting my feet under me again.

"Well, as long as the dude keeps bringing wine, I'm good with him having a little help," Steph said.

"A little help," Miguel snorted. The cork came free with a loud pop, and he began filling glasses. "Vino, gentlemen?"

Wine in hand, I slid our balcony door open and we plopped into the cushioned chairs. Countless stars twinkled in the cloudless sky, like millions of fireflies trapped in some celestial spider's web.

Autumn's kiss sent a chill across my skin as a constant stream of air blew by with our ship's passage across the sea. The bottle or so of wine I'd drunk at dinner was the only thing keeping me warm enough to sit outside without warmer clothing.

Moonlight reflected off tiny ripples, then exploded in the frothy wake that trailed our massive vessel. Oddly, though we were surrounded by thousands of souls, the stirring of the Mediterranean by the ship's systems was the only sound to be heard.

I sucked in the tangy air and relished the peace of the moment.

"Where's home, Steph? All Nate told us is you're from California," Miguel's voice cut through the silent roar.

"I grew up in San Diego, but my folks moved us to Huntington Beach when I was eight. My dad had just retired and decided to open a surf shop on the beach."

"Huh. Sounds like a midlife crisis to me," I said.

Steph grunted. "It was more my mom's dream than his. She'd been talking about getting back to the ocean for as long as I could remember. She was a competitive surfer before she met my dad and started popping out kids."

"Kids crush dreams," I quipped.

"Damn straight." Steph raised his glass.

A heartbeat passed before Miguel rose to the defense of urchins everywhere. "I doubt Nick and André would agree with that."

"Why do you always have to be such a good guy? Can't you wallow in the mud with Steph and me, just for a minute?" I nudged him with my elbow.

He chuckled. "Nope. Gotta keep my smile. It's one of the things you always say makes you want to rip my clothes off."

I reached over and rubbed a thumb over his dimpled cheek, and he leaned into my touch. "You've got that right, Smiley," I growled, low and wanting.

Steph cleared his throat and shifted in his seat. Miguel's amusement at Steph's discomfort flowed into my palm.

"You miss the ocean?" Miguel asked, reclaiming his face from my hand.

Steph's gaze remained fixed on the water beyond. "Always. There's nothing like riding a wave, feeling the power of the ocean under my feet and knowing it could crush me anytime but doesn't."

"Sounds like a death wish," I muttered.

Steph chuckled. "More like a thrill ride. It's a rush, flirting with danger and coming out the other side soaked and exhausted. There's nothing like it."

"Oh, I know something *exactly* like that," I said.

Steph turned with one brow raised.

"Riding Miguel. Have you seen all that muscle? Talk about power. It's like straddling a volcano as its lava roils and writhes beneath, howling to be released in a massive burst of—"

"Alright, alright. I get it. Miguel's a stud and all." The light of the moon and stars might've been dim, but no night could hide the color that flared across Steph's cheeks in that moment.

Miguel didn't miss a beat, reaching over and rubbing his palm across Steph's chest. "You aren't too bad yourself there, Surfer Boy. Firm chest, nice arms, and I bet there's a rack of abs under that shirt, just begging to be licked."

Steph squirmed so hard, he nearly dropped his wine. "Uh, thanks ... yeah ... abs are good and shit, I guess."

I couldn't hold back a laugh. "And shit. Here's to that."

Miguel and I clinked glasses and tossed back the last of our wine.

"Refill?" Miguel asked, bracing himself on the chair's arms and rising unsteadily to his feet.

"Yes, please," I said without hesitation.

"Uh, I'd better … you know … get back to my room … I mean, cabin. It's kind of late and—"

"Steph," I said, reaching across Miguel's empty seat to grip Steph's forearm. "You're on vacation. Take a breath." Steph's eyes dropped to my arm faster than when the last unbroken egg slips free of the carton when you need it for the recipe you're almost done making.

I rubbed my thumb across his skin and could practically feel his pulse quicken.

"Uh, Sam, damn. What are you … I mean, you two—" He looked up to Miguel.

"Easy, tiger. Sam growls a lot, but he's friendly, especially when he's had wine. We've never done anything outside the two of us. You're safe here," Miguel said, stepping past without realizing his crotch was eye level with Steph and nearly smacking him in the face.

Steph sucked in air. "Oh, God, you smell …"

Miguel stopped and turned. "Yes?"

"Like musk and shit."

"There you go with the 'and shit' again." I squeezed his forearm, then released him and leaned back. "You're going to have to explain what the 'and shit' is about. We need things spelled out clearly. We're not that bright."

"Speak for yourself, grease monkey. I'm a brilliant investigator ... and shit," Miguel said, a smart-ass smirk playing on his lips.

I couldn't stifle the laugh that flew out.

Steph's gaze flitted between Miguel and me, finally settling back on the passing sea once more.

As Miguel popped another cork and refilled our glasses, I asked, "Why no boyfriend? You're hot, nice, reasonably smart ... for a Mango, at least."

"Thanks, I think." Steph let out his first relaxed laugh since we'd sat on the balcony. "I don't know. Memphis isn't exactly the greatest dating city in the world. I mean, it's okay, I guess, but baseball takes up so many of my evenings. You know how that is, right, Miguel?"

Miguel nodded. "Yeah, I remember. Even when you have a free night, the single guys want to hang out together. Most of us were from other cities and didn't have many friends outside our brothers in uniform."

"Exactly," Steph said, nodding. "I spend more time with Nate and Coop than anyone I've ever dated. They're like family now."

Miguel and I shared a look, then I asked, "And you've never—"

"God, no," Steph said emphatically. "Have you met them? They're like superhuman magnets that the world's strongest machine couldn't rip apart."

"Not sure I'd put it that way, but I get it. They are pretty special," Miguel said. "Coop is ... he's something."

Steph and I chuckled in unison.

"That's for damn sure," Steph said. "Half the time, I don't know what he's saying. Hell, I don't even think *he* knows what he's saying until it spills all over the floor."

Miguel grunted a laugh. "That's for sure, but you know, it makes him Cooper. It's part of him, part of what I love so much about him."

"I can see that," Steph said. "He's definitely not like anybody I've ever met."

"He's good for Nate too," Miguel said.

Steph cocked his head. "You think?""Oh yeah," Miguel nodded. "Nate was a mess after Nashville dropped him. I don't think he would've made it through without ...."

When he spoke again, Miguel's voice was soft and distant. "Nate's like a little brother to me, and I couldn't reach him. For the first time in years, I couldn't help. All I could do was watch as he spiraled into ... as he slipped further away."

Miguel sipped his wine.

"Cooper found a way to reach him. He brought him back. That goofy, innocent, ridiculous boy brought Nate back to us, and I don't think I could love him more for it."

The gurgling of the water behind the ship filled the silence that followed, as we sat, our eyes fixed on everything and nothing.

"That sounds like the Coop I know," Steph finally said. "It also makes sense. I mean, how close they are makes more sense now. It sounds like they saved each other."

I turned, as if seeing Steph for the first time, and smiled. "They sure did."

Chapter Twenty-One

Steph

IF I HADN'T KNOWN we were moving across the Mediterranean toward Cannes, I might never have known the ship was even moving. I'd envisioned two weeks of vomit-inducing rocking, but the sea barely stood a chance against our behemoth bobber. I stared up at the ceiling, willing the light fixture to sway or give some indication we were no longer on dry land, but it simply stared back, indifferent to my insomnia.

I'd probably drunk a bottle and a half of wine since we sat down to dinner. Sam and Miguel's extra glasses should've finished me off.

Why couldn't I fall asleep?

My mind kept wandering back to our conversation on the balcony. Sam and Miguel were so proud of Cooper. I could hear the love and admiration in their voices when they spoke about him.

And Nate …

Miguel still seemed to view him as a mentee, a college kid who needed a seasoned hand's guidance. Knowing my bestie the way I did, that wasn't terribly far off the mark, but still, he was a grown man. Miguel's protectiveness should've bothered me—or, at least, felt out of place—but it didn't. In fact, it felt almost as natural as the banter between the two of them.

They were a matched set if I'd ever seen one.

And the way they looked at each other ... I'd only seen that with my parents. And between Cooper and Nate.

Come to think of it, André and Nick shared that same effortless, utterly smitten gaze too.

Then my mind recalled the group crammed around the table in Barcelona. The servers had set two tables with plenty of elbow room; but no, this group of a dozen largely broad-shouldered friends insisted on squeezing into a space made for eight. My mind replayed the conversation, the constant teasing and playful chatter. It saw the glances, knowing and questioning. Their touches were familiar, intimate even, their smiles easy and free.

Then I realized something.

They looked at each other with that same affectionate gaze. Every one of them.

It wasn't the gaze of a lover like that of Sam and Miguel, but their eyes brimmed with a boundlessness that left no room for doubt, no question of their commitment to one another—and their love for each other.

I'd seen that between a few players over the years. When guys practiced and played for endless hours, friendships naturally developed.

But these weren't friends. This was a family in every sense of the word that mattered.

And they'd welcomed me into it with open arms and sincere hearts.

I rolled over, hoping a new position might calm my restless mind. It didn't.

My hand unwound from beneath the pillow and rubbed into my chest ... almost the same way Miguel had.

Heat flooded through me. Miguel's eyes were more than welcoming in that moment. He wasn't flirting, but there was fire in his gaze. And his palm felt so good—

Stop that! I chided. *Sam and Miguel are the dream couple. They said it themselves—they've never done anything outside their marriage. There was no invitation to fool around or play or whatever. Miguel was drunk and being friendly. The big guy was affectionate like that and there was nothing more to it.*

Then my forearm flared where Sam's fingers had gripped it, so firm and rough, just like everything about him. God, he was hot.

Before I knew what was happening, my other hand wormed its way beneath the covers and gripped my shaft as it rose.

Sam's growl rang in my ears.

My cock pulsed in my hand as I imagined those fingers belonged to Sam. The pillow pressed against my neck, and I craned back at Miguel's kiss.

I threw the covers back and stroked myself, feeling Miguel's beefy arms wrapped around me, pulling me into him, while Sam took my dick in his mouth.

Pre-cum dribbled from my head, slickening my fingers and making my abs clench.

"Fuck!" I groaned.

My butt quivered, imagining Miguel's cock sliding between my cheeks, teasing my hole, begging for entry.

Sam's one hand gripped my balls and pulled them down while his other squeezed the base of my cock, forcing its length to stretch taut against its skin.

My back arched.

Miguel slid inside me. His teeth sank into my neck, while Sam's head bobbed faster.

I could barely breathe.

Miguel drove deeper, slower, longer. His hand kneaded my chest. His tongue drank in my skin.

Sam squeezed my balls.

My whole body shook.

Miguel shoved harder.

Sam jerked and sucked.

Stars filled my eyes.

Then my cock filled Sam's mouth, and Miguel filled my soul.

"Shit, I need to get laid," I muttered aloud, as the last spurts of cum leaked out, making me shiver with pleasure.

Chapter Twenty-Two

STEPH

THE PHONE RANG, JARRING me awake. I rolled over, prying the sheets from where they'd stuck and dried to my stomach. For the briefest moment, I gave thanks to having no hair to be pulled, though I'd always wanted to have fur. My head swam, as hungover awareness kicked like an ass refusing to climb a mountain.

"There'd better be coffee with this phone call." That wasn't the traditional "hello" greeting, but a friendly welcome to the day was beyond me in my present condition.

"Breakfast in the Aviary in ten," Miguel's too-cheery voice said.

"Uh, fuck, okay."

"Did I wake you, precious?" he teased.

"My head hates you," I groaned. "In fact, my whole body hates you."

Miguel chuckled. "Not your whole body. I saw your shorts before you left."

Seriously? These guys were going to kill me.

"Oh, that, sorry. He hasn't seen much action lately. Guess all the wine and—"

Miguel laughed again. "You're apologizing for your dick thinking we're hot? Please."

I tried to respond, but what was I supposed to say to that?

"Clean up your sticky ass and get over here. I know you jerked off thinking about us. Many men do. We're irresistible."

How did he know I was sticky? My eyes scanned the room for cameras. Then I let my head fall back on the pillow. He was giving me grief, despite hitting ridiculously close to the bullseye. I was being stupid.

Miguel barely took a breath. "Hurry up. Eggs will get cold, and that pisses Sam off. He can be a little bitch about things like that."

My head swam from a lot more than wine in that moment.

"Okay. Be there in a minute."

When I walked into the Aviary, the entire gang was sitting at three small tables scattered about. Sam, Cooper, and Annie ate quietly at one, while Ethan chattered away at the other with his two dads. Miguel sat alone across from an empty place setting.

"Steph, over here," Miguel waved as I entered.

Annie leapt to her feet and wrapped herself around my waist before I made it to the safety of Miguel's table.

"Did I do something?" I asked.

She pulled back, her hands still gripping my sides. "No, I'm just happy to see you. Besides, given how tall you are and how short I am, my boobs wanted to poke around your junk, get a morning feel before we start the day." She rubbed her chest against my crotch like she meant to sandwich my cock between her breasts.

The peace of the Aviary erupted in laughter. Even little Ethan was howling at the mention of boobs, though I doubted he understood what Annie had really said. I tried desperately to avoid blushing, but was sure I'd turned redder than the tomatoes on André's plate.

"Annie, leave the poor boy alone," Miguel finally said between gasps. "Come on, Steph, they just brought a fresh pot of coffee."

"Can you ask Coop's butler for an IV bag? I'll just plug it in," I said, flopping into the chair across from him and reaching for a piece of toast. "This looks great."

"Yeah, I doubt the common folk in the rest of the ship are enjoying a custom breakfast. Coop did us right," Miguel said.

A half-hour later, I'd eaten my fill and was still nursing a mug of coffee when the loudspeaker crackled.

"Ladies and gentlemen, we have arrived in Cannes, France. You may now proceed to the gangway to enjoy your day. If you still need help arranging excursions or shopping, tents have been raised just beyond the ramp on the docks. The gangway will retract and the ship will depart precisely at six o'clock. Don't be late. The swim to Florence is a long one."

"You guys have fun today. Ethan talked Annie into joining us," Nick said above Ethan's excited babble and Annie's attempt at calming him by singing. It was like squirting lighter fluid on a grill. André gave up quieting the pair, hooked his arm around Nick's, and pulled him toward the door.

Nate stood next, with Coop rising to stretch his arms above his head, then crane to relieve tightness in his back.

"You planning to spar today?" Miguel teased.

Cooper grinned. "You never know. Besides, it's Christmas Eve, and we have a ton of shopping to do. Cannes is supposed to be one of the best places in the world to shop, and I've seen how you and Sam dress. Lord knows, you two need help… and before you object and say the cruise is enough and that I should never get you anything again even though you are like fathers and brothers and uncles and … everything else in between … to me, I'm going to do what I'm going to do because I'm a grown-ass man and Grammy left me a fuck-ton of money."

I gaped.

Sam blinked.

Miguel grinned. "Fuck-ton?"

Coop nodded. "I worked with numbers. That's a technical term. A ton of money is for petty thieves and criminals. A fuck-ton is for people who inherit so much they could never spend it all on themselves so they choose to share it with the people they love more than anything in the world and don't care if they catch shit for it, even a little … or a ton."

Sam shook his head.

Now I blinked.

Miguel chuckled. "We love you too, Coop. Knock yourself out. Sam might be a little bitch about you spending money on us, but I'm not. I deserve to be showered with gifts and praise. Bring it on."

Coop shot forward and slammed into Miguel, wrapping his arms around him and burying his face in the big man's neck. "Merry Christmas Eve, Mom. I love you."

Miguel's massive paw gripped the back of Coop's head, and I heard him whisper back, "I love you too, buddy. Now go buy me some good shit."

Coop gave him a peck on the cheek, then pulled back.

"Where's my hug?" Sam huffed.

Coop cocked his head, then barreled into Sam at precisely the same time as Nate hit him from behind. "We love you too, Dad."

"Can't ... breathe," Sam squeaked out.

The pair squeezed harder and laughed.

A moment later, Sam, Miguel, and I stood alone in the oddly quiet Aviary.

"I'm scared of what *your* son is doing to Christmas. He's already spent ungodly amounts of money getting us here," Miguel said.

"Don't look at me. He's *your* son. I didn't raise him to throw money around. That's all you," Sam snapped back, a smile teasing his lips.

"You two are ... something," was all I could think to say.

Miguel beamed. "Yes, we are. Isn't it great?"

"Don't encourage him. He's worse than when Annie finds a lonely piano," Sam said, placing a hand on his husband's shoulder. "We're not big shoppers, but it'll be nice to walk around, work off some of the food we've been eating. You game?"

"Totally," I said, a little more enthusiastically than necessary.

"There's our little surfer dude. I wondered when he'd pop his head up again," Miguel said, patting my chest in exactly the same place he'd rubbed the night before.

And darn it if my little head didn't pop up again too.

Cannes was exactly what I'd expected. And not.

Streets were filled with shops selling ridiculously expensive brands to tourists, as though they were passing out bread to a starving populace. Street-facing restaurants and cafés reminded me of Paris—well, the Paris I'd seen in the movies. I'd never actually visited.

What I hadn't expected was the heavy emphasis on the movie industry. Sure, I'd heard of the Cannes Film Festival. Who hadn't? But it took a long while to register that we were visiting *that* Cannes.

We were midway through a lazy morning of strolling when Sam stopped walking. Beaches nuzzling the Mediterranean sprawled to one side, while a row of stores filled the other. All the signs were in French, but most had English subtitles beneath the larger lettering for hapless foreigners wandering aimlessly with open wallets.

We were aimless, but our wallets were closed tighter than my ass's pucker around Miguel.

"Let's do a tour," Sam said suddenly.

Neither Sam nor Miguel had shown any interest in actually entering the shops, which was perfectly fine by me, but this was the first mention of doing anything remotely touristy.

"A tour?" Miguel asked.

"Yeah. One of those trolley things passed a while back, had a sign that said something about seeing where the stars did stuff."

I laughed. "You make it sound so exciting."

Miguel chuckled.

Sam planted fists on his hips. "We have five hours to kill. Unless you want to try on bikini bottoms with Annie, we have to do *something*."

"No!" I raised my palms. "Please no. A tour sounds amazing. Stars, actors, singers, and shit. Let's do it."

"Lions, tigers, and bears, oh my?" Miguel quipped.

Sam grinned, for once wider than Miguel.

Twenty minutes and another half-mile of walking later, we stepped onto a fire engine red trolley whose elegant sign read, "*Curiosités* (for English speakers)."

A woman with far too much rouge and electric red lips bounded onto the top step near the driver, snatched a microphone from its holder, and shouted for all the Riviera to hear, "Welcome to Cannes!"

She startled me so badly, I nearly leapt out of my seat.

"I am so happy you came to my city. Isn't she beautiful?" She waved her hand around like some French game show gal showing off the new car or boat a contestant might win. "And it is a perfect day for a tour. Look at the sun on the water. Sheer perfection, is it not?"

"Her accent is sexy, but if she stays this perky, I might have to kill her before this is over," I muttered to Sam.

"I want in on that," Miguel grunted. "They call me Smiley, but she's like caffeine laced with crack wrapped in cocaine."

The guide sucked in a deep breath that carried through the microphone, then began a clearly memorized speech:

"If you rewind Cannes's history all the way back to the tenth century, you'll find a town by the name of Canua, quite similar yet different from the name of Cannes, as you know the city by today. It is believed that Canua came from the term 'canna,' which means reed, or cane, named after its once-reedy shore. The name Cannes is first known to have appeared in 1030 in a deed of donation by Rodoard's son to the Abbot with the mention of '*De Portu Canue.*' The word 'canue' comes from a Ligurian word, which means height or peak, and this refers to the hill on which Le Suquet is on, and the watchtower built on it. The reason the tower was built by the monks on Le Suquet was in order to warn the island of invasion. When suspicious sails were seen on the horizon, the town was lit to signal to the island. Cannes was ruled by monks for hundreds of years before separating from them and becoming independent ..."

"Dear God, maybe you should kill me instead," Miguel groused. "Put me out of my misery."

"Come on, history is fun," Sam said, a wry grin twisting his lips.

"Since when have you *ever* liked history?" Miguel asked.

"I love it when it involves cars. Maybe there'll be some famous cars on this tour. You know, something a star once owned."

Miguel rolled his eyes. "Have you been dipping into her crack?"

"Nope. Your crack is the only one for me." Sam winked as Miguel shook his head.

I tried to keep the mental image from fully forming.

"I am sure you all know of the Cannes Film Festival, yes?" The guide finally said something to turn our heads. "Unfortunately for Jean Zay, the French education minister whose idea it was to host a festival to celebrate the world of film in France, World War II delayed plans for the first Cannes Film Festival. Even more terribly, Zay was later murdered by the French Vichy government in 1944 for being Jewish and a member of the French Resistance. As a result, the Cannes Film Festival was only able to begin in 1946 when the war was over. In 2014, President Hollande ordered that Zay's ashes be interred in the Panthéon in Paris as public recognition for his efforts toward improving education as well as in fighting the Nazis during the war."

"Well, isn't that cheerful?" Miguel grumbled.

"Shh. This is interesting," Sam said, surprising us both.

"Did you know, every festival goes through two kilometers' worth of red carpet? Amazing, no?"

"Whoa, that's cool," Sam said.

Miguel glanced back with a baffled expression. I shrugged.

"Cannes has a population of just over 70,000 people, but during the festival, the figure rises to 200,000. That's a lot of people walking on a red carpet, which soon gets very dirty, and it, therefore, has to be changed at least three times a day."

Sam's gaze was fixed on our guide.

Miguel stared blankly out the side of the trolley, where scantily clad beachgoers frolicked on the supple sand.

I was just struggling to stay awake.

The trolley trudged along at a snail's pace, while Perky Patty chatted about one star after another to attend the town's annual festival. Aside from shops and a few landmarks related to the film industry, there wasn't much to jar any of us out of our mind-numbed stupor. Still, the tour was a nice rest from all the walking we'd done earlier in the morning.

As we stepped off the bus, Miguel's meaty paw rested on my shoulder and stayed there until we'd ambled several paces down the sidewalk. There wasn't anything provocative in his touch, but it somehow felt … I don't know … intimate? I know that's ridiculous and was probably the last thing he was thinking, but it's how it felt. Sam didn't bat an eyelid at the gesture. In fact, I was pretty sure he turned and offered a smile of … approval?

I'd never been one to read between lines. Hell, I rarely even saw the lines to begin with, much less what was wedged in their midst, but everything about my time with Sam and Miguel felt like more than three new friends hanging out.

It was more than the occasional touch that lingered, it was the questions they asked too. They wanted to know me; like, really know me. We'd ticked all the usual boxes in our initial meeting. *Where are you from? Do you have any brothers or sisters? How do you like being a Mango?* They were the arm's-length questions one asked when they might or might not really care about the answer but feel obligated to feign interest in another person.

Sam and Miguel dove deeper.

Sam grilled me on what I wanted in life, what I wanted to become, who I wanted to be. Coming from the gruff mechanic, that was a surreal line of Dr. Phil questioning. Miguel wanted to know how I felt when I got dropped from the minors, something he understood in a very personal way, based on how he'd described his own journey.

That was another thing. They didn't just interrogate me; they opened up with their own stories too. I could feel the conflict in Miguel's voice when he talked about choosing between his baseball dream and the needs of his family all those years ago.

But more than the career choice, it was his description of the family dynamic that drove him in those days—the challenges his parents faced, their need for him to be an active part of their lives and to follow in their footsteps—that made his retelling so personal. It wasn't some proud cop talking about the glory of service and the power of his badge. Miguel's story was one of sacrifice, commitment, and a family legacy that was more important than any one member's desires.

Still, when he spoke of those days, his eyes drifted far away, like mine did every time I spoke about how close I came to wearing an MLB uniform—but how far out of reach it remained.

I was probably thinking too much, which again wasn't a problem I usually faced. Back home, if I ever got down or inside my own head, the ocean called, and I rode waves until my mind was clear and my heart was light. The surf was magic, medicinal, in that way. There was no deep thought required. In fact, thinking tended to mess with a surfer's instincts, so we avoided it at all costs.

I made a mental note to never tell Sam and Miguel any of that, lest the teasing about me avoiding thinking never end.

"Dude, where'd you go?" Sam's voice cut through the clatter as he draped his arm around my shoulders. His embrace felt so … safe.

"Oh, sorry, just got inside my noggin there for a minute."

"Anything you want to share?" Miguel asked.

I considered a moment. "You guys … you're not … you're different from what I expected."

Sam laughed and squeezed me closer. "What did you expect?"

Miguel threw his arm around me, on top of Sam's. It made walking awkward but was the most muscular, musky moving hug ever. I nearly missed a step.

"Well, I don't know. You're just … really cool."

Both of them laughed at that.

"From a surfer dude, I'll take that," Miguel said, and I felt him pat Sam's back over my shoulder.

Miguel then checked his watch. "The tour didn't kill nearly enough time. We should probably hit a shop or two. I have a feeling Coop has something ridiculous planned for Christmas."

Sam grunted. "Yeah, I got that feeling too. He's already given us too much."

"We could get something for Ethan, make tomorrow all about him," I said.

Sam and Miguel stopped walking and turned to look across me at each other. Mirroring smiles bloomed on their faces as

Miguel's hand left Sam and cupped the back of my head, his fingers diving deep beneath my hair.

"I knew I liked this guy," Miguel said.

Sam nodded, as his gaze shifted from Miguel to me. "Make Christmas special for the little guy. I like it," he said.

"Not bad for the Jewish guy, right?"

Miguel and Sam froze. Like two golden retrievers, both their heads cocked. I had to stifle a laugh.

"Missed that part?" I asked, reaching beneath my shirt to pull out the Star of David pendant I always wore. "Just one of the tribe."

They spoke at the same time, but Sam deferred to Miguel.

"Sorry, didn't mean to look shocked. Neither of us is particularly religious, so we don't care. I mean, we do care, especially if it's important to you. We just don't care about—"

"What the dumb cop is trying to say," Sam butted in, "is that we love all the little boys and girls."

"That just sounded creepy," Miguel said.

"You know what I mean." Sam rolled his eyes, then looked at me. No, he looked *into* me. "Coop really is going to make a big deal out of Christmas. Will you be okay with that?"

"Guys, my family celebrates Christmas. It's not a religious holiday for us, but I loved the whole getting-gifts-twice thing as a kid. I'm totally Team Santa." I laughed.

"Team Santa," Miguel barked. "That's priceless. Like Team Edward or—"

"Fuck no. Our house is Team Jake all the way. Keep that blood sucker out of it," Sam growled, nearly matching what I remembered from the movie's brilliantly wolfy dialogue.

"I'm good with Christmas. Let's do some shopping so Santa can throw up all over the ship and rock Ethan's world," I said.

Miguel's smile at that must've hurt because it nearly reached his ears. Then he did the last thing I expected: with his hand still on my head, he pulled me toward him and kissed my forehead.

I missed the next step and nearly fell face-forward.

"Whoa, I've got ya." Sam's other arm reached across in a soccer-mom-arm-save and caught me, pulling me upright into his chest.

"He can be a lot, I know," he rumbled into my ear.

Then Sam kissed my cheek.

Chapter Twenty-Three

André (and Nick and Ethan)

FOR A NINE-YEAR-OLD BOY, the idea of shopping, even in
a historic and stunningly beautiful town such as Cannes,
was akin to torture. Nick and I dragged him into one shop
before realizing our hopes of a peaceful day strolling from one
storefront to the next were in vain. The gremlin that was our
son would not allow it, at least not without perpetual whining
and repeated attempts to escape.

Thirty minutes into our shore leave, we surrendered,
purchased a beach towel and new swim trunks, and made our
way to the sandy shores that spread just across the road from the
row of glitzy shops we'd hoped to visit.

"Papa, look." Ethan pointed excitedly at a gathering of boys
and girls around his age playing with a beach ball near the
waterline. "Can I go play? Please?"

"Okay, but stay where we can see you," I said.

He hopped once in celebration, then darted away to meet his new best friends.

"It wasn't that long ago he wouldn't even speak to strangers," Nick said, dropping onto the towel and handing me a tall glass with far too many fruit wedges clinging to the rim.

"He would not speak to *anyone*, remember?"

Nick smirked and cocked a brow. "He spoke to me."

I shook my head. "Yes, he did, and I will forever be grateful that a dumb jock outwitted an entire staff of professionals."

"Dumb jock?" he said in mock offense. "I'll have you know, I'm a remarkable, intelligent jock, thank you very much."

I grunted. "Perhaps mildly intelligent. I will agree to that."

"I was going to kiss you, right here in front of everyone in France, but you blew that, monsieur."

I rolled onto my side to face him and propped myself on an elbow. "You say that like anyone would notice. We French do not have the same … sensitivity … to such things."

His eyes grew wide as a topless woman strode by, her well-endowed chest bouncing with each step across the sand.

"Uh … yeah. I see that."

I reached across the towel, took his hand, and raised it to my lips.

December days in Cannes rarely saw temperatures warm enough to enjoy the beach, but the mercury on this Christmas Eve day was nearly reaching seventy degrees. The brilliant sun in her cloudless sky made it feel even warmer. Nick stripped off his shirt, his tan skin instantly soaking up rays in ways my pasty shell never would.

Nick fell asleep while I alternated between watching Ethan play with new friends and reading a trashy romance novel I'd bought in one of the shops earlier in the morning.

"Whatcha reading?" Nick asked, an hour after dozing off.

"You do not want to know. It would offend your not-so-dumb jock sensibilities."

He snorted. "Try me."

"It is called *Deep Dive*."

He reached across and snatched the book out of my hands, a broad smile crawling across his face as he stared at the scantily clad men on the cover.

"And here I thought you were reading something educational about scuba."

I grabbed my book back. "It is educational, but about a very different type of diving. You might actually enjoy what I learn … later."

His brows rose. "Oh really?"Before I could explain, Ethan raced up, kicking sand everywhere. "Oh good, you're awake," he said to Nick, then looked at me. "I'm hungry. Can we get lunch?"

"Me too," Nick said.

"Alright. Help us pack up. What would you like to eat?" I asked.

"Pizza," Ethan said. "No, chicken nuggets."

"We are in Cannes, France, and you want chicken nuggets?" I tried to hide the offense from my voice.

"Pizza sounds amazing. And beer, there needs to be beer," Nick echoed my barbarian son.

"We are in the South of France and you demand the drink of German monks?" I scoffed as I rose and brushed sand off my shirt. "Very well, bring your heathen child. We will find pizza and beer."

"You hear that, little man? Papa gave in. We get pizza," Nick said, scooping Ethan up and tossing him into the air. The boy's giggles could surely be heard half a beach away.

At nine, Ethan was still only the size of an average six-year-old. His doctors refused to predict how tall he might become, but warned that his stunted growth early in life would be nearly impossible for his body to overcome, despite how we pumped him full of vegetables and vitamins. He might never reach the size or strength of others his age, but his spirit had already surpassed that of many adults I knew. Long gone was the sullen boy who refused to speak. The lad before us smiled as easily as he breathed, and his laugh ... there wasn't a sound in all the world that filled my soul like the little man's enjoyment.

I watched a moment as Nick tossed him a few more times, both their faces painted with unbridled joy, and my heart soared as high as my son's flailing arms with each throw. Nick's face mirrored Ethan's, dimples forming at the corners of his tooth-filled grin. He'd yet to don his T-shirt again, and the lean, corded muscles of a professional athlete rippled through a slick coating of sweat with his every movement.

My chest swelled with pride as I caught a group of women walking by and pointing, shy giggles emanating from their midst as one loudly commented on how hot my husband was.

"Come on, you two," I said, folding the beach towel. "We have just enough time for pizza and to help Santa with a Christmas gift or two."

WE RETURNED TO THE ship a few hours later. Nick walked with a sleeping boy draped over one shoulder and a couple shopping bags dangling from his other hand. I, meanwhile, looked like Julia Roberts in *Pretty Woman* as she returned from her day of much-needed "attention over here" on Rodeo Drive, struggling under the weight of a half-dozen more shopping bags and our beach kit.

Dario stood in the hallway between Cooper's cabin door and the entrance to the Aviary.

"Gentlemen, welcome back," the butler said. "Let me help you."

Dario shot forward and swiped his badge on the reader, unlocking our cabin door, then snatched the bags from Nick's hand. Once inside, Nick carefully laid Ethan on his fold-out bed, while I littered ours with the shopping bags.

Dario cleared his throat and extended his hand. "I have a note for you from Mr. Hawk."

As I took the proffered envelope, Dario nodded crisply and said, "If you need anything else, I'll be in the hallway until Mr. Hawk returns."

"That's so bizarre," Nick said after the door clicked shut.

"What?"

"Coop has a butler who waits for his return. Feels a little too Victorian romance novel-y to me."

I laughed and ripped open the envelope. "Novel-y? English is my second language, but I am fairly certain that is not a word."

"And I'm just a dumb jock, remember?" He smirked and pecked my cheek then fled to the bathroom. "What's the note say?"

"Cooper suggests we visit the Aviary this evening. He has a tree set up and apparently he took the liberty of playing Santa this year."

"That scares me. Coop's already spent a small fortune on all of us," Nick groaned from the throne. "Does it say anything about dinner tonight? Any Christmas Eve plans?"

"Everyone is on their own tonight."

"I like the sound of that," Nick said. He emerged from the bathroom and stepped toward the door. "Be right back."

Before I could ask where he was going, he vanished, returning only minutes later with a sly grin on his face and something in his hand.

"Where did you go? And why do you look like you just pulled a prank?" I asked.

"I'm a cheerful guy. What can I say?" He shrugged, batting his eyelashes innocently. Then his gaze fell to the bed. "We need to wrap the little bug's presents while he's asleep. Think Dario can get us some paper and tape?"I chuckled. "I doubt there's much Dario cannot procure if *Mr. Hawk* insists."

Nick grunted. "This is so weird."

ETHAN DEMANDED CHICKEN NUGGETS for Christmas Eve dinner.

"He is clearly your son. No self-respecting Frenchman would—"

Ethan crossed his arms. "I'm not a Frenchman. I'm a boy."

"Yes," I said, biting back a laugh. "You most certainly are, as is your dad."

"Hey! Don't drag me into this," Nick said.

"Oh, but you are in this, *mon petit ami*."

Nick leaned down and pretended to whisper, loudly, in Ethan's ear, "See what Dad has to deal with? French people are so stuck up."

The boy giggled.

I dropped to one knee and grabbed him, digging my fingers into his ribs. "How dare you side with the barbarian. You must be punished."

Ethan's squeals could probably be heard a continent away.

"You two, knock it off. I'm hungry. We can teach him the glories of France later," Nick said as he rested a hand on the door handle, a not-so-subtle hint.

"Fine," I said, sneaking in one last jab to Ethan's ribs. "But we will eat proper chicken tonight, not nuggets. This is Christmas Eve, not McChristmas."

Ethan giggled and began chanting, "McChristmas," then, "McSanta," then, "McRudolf," a refrain we heard on our entire walk to the restaurant. By the time we reached the All-American Bistro, our dinner destination whose chicken was most definitely not breaded and fried, Ethan had Mc-ed every member of Santa's band, as well as any Christmas-themed cartoon character he could think of.

Nick squeezed my hand and mouthed, "That's *your* son," as we entered the restaurant.

The excitement of the day, combined with a carb-laden fried dinner, drained the last of Ethan's energy, and I almost had to drag him back to our stateroom. His little body limped forward with each step, like a zombie in *The Walking Dead*. Nick laced his finger with mine and laid his head on my shoulder.

I could scarcely remember dreaming of a more perfect moment, much less experiencing one.

As Nick swiped his key card, I noticed a sealed envelope shoved in the seam of the door.

"What's that?" Nick asked.

I shrugged and tugged the envelope loose before Ethan could push the door open. Scrawled in elegant script on the outside was "Nick and André." I removed a card bearing the ship's logo and more equally elegant writing. A key card I hadn't noticed dropped to the floor before I could catch it.

Messrs. Martin and Dunlap,

Mr. Hawk thought you might enjoy the privacy of the suite reserved for Messrs. Hyatt and Rossi, since they were unable to join your voyage.

Dario

"Privacy? We are married with a child. Why would we require privacy?" I asked, perplexed.

Nick's eyes blazed, as he leaned over and nipped my ear. "Because you might like to do adult things without you-know-who watching."

My eyes widened and my mouth formed a very French O.

"For such a smart doc, you sure are slow sometimes," Nick teased. "It's a good thing you're so darn hot."

A flutter tickled my ribcage. I glanced to where Ethan had already climbed into his bed and passed out, fully clothed. "Did you bring—"

Nick nodded and stepped into the tiny bathroom, retrieving a small kit then shaking it, as though the rattle told me everything I needed to know.

And it did.

"Let's go before the monster wakes up and ruins our chance," Nick said with a head tilt toward Ethan.

We crept from our room and pulled the door closed, both of us cringing at the mechanical click that sounded when the electronic lock engaged. We waited a few heartbeats in case Ethan woke, then strode two doors down to the empty suite.

Nick turned as I chuckled. "What?" he asked.

"Cooper thinks of everything."

Nick smiled and nodded. "Yeah, he's something else. Now, get that pretty ass inside and stop thinking about Cooper."

"You are so bossy tonight."

His only reply was to slap my butt and shove me inside.

The flutter erupted into a torrent of flapping wings, and other parts of my body began to rise.

The moment the door closed behind Nick, his hand flew to my arm and he spun me to face him. I reached up for my glasses, but his other hand stilled me.

"Leave them on. I love how smart you look in them."

I didn't mean to laugh. It just slipped out.

He cocked a brow.

"Sorry, you said I look smart. You know I actually *am* smart, right?"

He rolled his eyes and smirked. "You're convincing me otherwise right now."

Then, without another word, he shot forward and our lips met, tasting of fried chicken, barbecue sauce, tater tots ... and unbridled hunger.

Nick's hand left my arm and his fingers tangled in my thick hair, massaging my scalp as we kissed. His tongue danced against mine, teasing and swirling, just light enough to make me crave it more fully before disappearing back behind his lips.

Time evaporated as we stood in that cabin, an identical suite to ours, held each other close and kissed like lovers reunited after years apart. Nick's touch was heady, his caress sensual yet tender. The hardness of his body pressed into mine, and the timpani of my heart thrummed through every part of me.

This was my man. My partner. My husband. We'd grown together, lived together, adopted a child together. This man wanted *me*, and only me, for this day, and every day. He craved me.

In my soul, I knew it to be true, but the small boy inside still stood in awe of his desire.

"Stop," he breathed.

"What?"

"You're thinking."

I couldn't hide a smile.

"Just 'cause you're wearing those glasses, looking all hot and professor-like, doesn't mean you get to think. I want you to forget everything and just be present—with me—right now."

I stared into his eyes, again struck dumb by how much he loved and wanted me. I reached up and traced the lines of his cheek with my fingers and nodded. "No more thinking."

His eyes closed, our lips met again, and all thought fled.

Moments, perhaps days, later—I'd lost track—he laid me on my back, lifting my head and gently stuffing a pillow beneath it. Starting with the top button, he slowly unfastened my shirt, kissing the skin revealed each time the fabric opened wider.

I watched, his eyes rarely leaving mine, unable to suppress an excited shiver as his fingers wound through the thick hair of my now exposed chest.

"I love your hair," he said, leaning forward and kissing a nipple. "And your nipples." He kissed the other. "And your stomach." He kissed the top of my lean torso. "And your belly button." His tongue speared inside, and a wave of ticklishness shook my frame.

He grinned up and wiggled his brows. "And how ticklish you are."

His teeth dug into my side where ribs offered easy targets, and I folded over in a laugh-fueled squirm, desperate to escape his touch. He grabbed both my wrists and slammed them into the bed by my head, his body hovering above mine.

"You're all mine, André Luis Adolfo Martin. All. Mine."

He punctuated his last words with a kiss more passionate and ravenous than any before, as the weight of his body pressed against mine and I felt just how much he longed for me in the hardness of his cock.

I moaned through the kiss.

His hands released my wrists and made to sit me up, to remove my shirt. I reached out to lift his, but he beat me to it, grabbing it by the bottom and yanking it over his head. I pressed my hand to his beautifully tanned skin stretched taut over hardened muscles, feeling the strength of his chest, then tracing the lines of his unfairly perfect abs.

"They are like tiny baguettes, lined up for sale in the market."

He snorted, and his abs flexed. "Did you just call my abs bread?"

I nodded, not looking up from the feast laid before me. Then my fingers were on his jeans button. A moment later, he towered on his knees above me, naked and hard, a tiny pearl of excitement beaded on the tip of his cock.

"Someone is happy tonight," I said, scooping up the bead with a finger and dabbing it on my tongue.

"You're wearing too many clothes," he growled, scooting off me and unbuttoning my pants in one easy motion. With a few yanks and a hip-raise assist, my slacks crumpled to the floor and Nick again sat above me.

"You're so damn sexy," he said.

I looked away.

His fingers gripped my chin and turned me toward him. "Don't look away. You *are* fucking hot, André."

I didn't mean to blush, but color rushed to my face unbidden.

Nick pressed his naked weight onto me and cupped my cheek. "You are the most beautiful man in the world to me. You know that, right?"

I nodded tentatively, though I still couldn't fully understand what this man saw.

He pressed his lips to mine again, and his sincerity poured through the touch. The muscles of his chest ground into my own as our cocks slid together, sending a wave of pleasure up my spine and stilling my silly insecurities.

He ground himself against me, rutting, dribbling more pre-cum across my skin.

My fingers dug into the meat of his shoulders as he grabbed the sides of my head and kissed me harder, sending his tongue deeper.

I could barely catch a breath as he released my lips and dove to wrap his mouth around my cock. My whole body spasmed at his touch. Fire bloomed where slick heat had trailed before.

He wasn't gentle. He wasn't tender.

He devoured me.

His hand gripped the base of my shaft, pulling my balls down and the skin taut, as his head bobbed, taking my entire length so his lips hit pubes before rising.

Again and again.

My hands gripped the pillows. Fingers dug into the sheets. My toes bent and knees buckled. Lust and love and fire and ice welled inside me, begging to burst free, yearning to explode.

And he stopped.

I gasped as his lips left my skin. I needed him to keep going, to free me, to let me—

Then the tiny hairs around my hole sent a tickling sensation to my brain and another spasm of pleasure rocked my senses. His tongue teased back and forth, circling my hole, threatening to breach but never entering.

I grabbed his head, gripped his curls. Any other time, I might've worried how hard I pulled—but not then. I couldn't think. All I could do was feel, and I wanted him to feel with me.

So I dug into him, pulled against him, bent my back and offered myself up to him.

His tongue slipped inside.

Stars danced before my eyes.

His hands gripped my cheeks and pulled them apart, and he speared deeper into me.

"Oh, *merde*. Nick!" I called.

He rammed in again, faster and deeper, harder.

His hand reached up and gripped my cock, already so hard I thought it might break, and began to stroke. With each thrust of his tongue, his hand squeezed and slid.

My body shook. My hands left his head and gripped the headboard, stretching my body as far as it would go.

He spread my cheeks wider, shoved and stroked.

The welling returned, this time a greater need, like my whole body might turn inside out if he didn't stop.

But he did. Again.

The fucker.

I dared a glance down, and hunger burned in his eyes as he lifted my legs above his shoulders.

"You didn't think I'd let you finish without me, did you?"

I tried to speak, to say something pithy, but words died on my raspy breath.

I don't know when he dug the lube out of the kit, but he squirted some into his palm, then rubbed his hands together to warm it before coating my hole in a rich layer of liquid. It took all the control I had not to erupt at his touch.

A moment later, his head pressed against my hole, and my whole body reflexively flinched.

He grinned. "I like it when you tense. Makes you tighter."

I tried to relax, but my ass was being snarky.

His dick didn't care. It slipped inside, and sparks seared my mind.

"God, it's good to be home," he said, though my eyes were closed too tight to see his toothy grin.

My body resisted but quickly relented, as he slid deeper inside, slowly filling me until his hips pressed into mine.

He sat there, fully inside, and didn't move. My eyes opened. Only then did he slide out and back in, even slower than the first time.

My back arched, as the thrill of him consumed me.

Out and in again. Even slower.

His hand cupped my cheek.

Out. In.

He leaned down and pressed his lips to mine.

Out. In.

I grabbed his hips and pulled him toward me. His body flexed.

Out … then he slammed into me, hard and rough, nearly knocking my head into the headboard.

"Oh, God!" I cried.

He sat up on his knees and began apace, ramming in and out as fast and hard as he could.

His breathing was now loud and ragged, mirroring my own.

His cock throbbed inside me, as my body shook.

I reached down to stroke myself, but he slapped me away, gripping my cock in his slickened palm, yanking and squeezing as roughly as his cock tore into my ass.

His breathing sped up.

His thrust quickened.

He pumped me faster, gripping tighter.

"Nick, fuck, I can't stop," I yelled.

He redoubled his effort, bracing himself and shoving somehow deeper than before.

The waves slammed into me so hard this time, there was no turning back, no pausing, no stopping. When the first shot fired and cum spattered across my chest, it felt like my whole being was fired from a cannon, over and over, again and again.

Still, Nick pressed into me.

His abs flexed and the muscles in his arms tensed. I could feel how close he was. Then he craned back, his hair flopping behind him, and roared so loud the entire ship might wake. A welcome heat struck inside me as he released himself deep within, filling me in every way I'd ever dreamed. I finally opened my eyes as his thrusts slowed, and marveled at his sweat-slicked body …

And his eyes that were fixed on mine.

"I love you so damn much, André," he said, through gasps for air.

"I love you too, babe," I said, cupping his cheek and wishing he could live inside me forever.

Chapter Twenty-Four

Cooper (and Nate)

Glass globes shimmered in the sunlight streaming
through the glass roof of the Aviary, giving the massive
Christmas tree a life all its own as dots of light danced about
the space. Cheerful music, rich with bells and drums, played
in the background. The lounge chairs were draped with white
faux fur, and the glass-top tables, normally bearing fruity drinks
and fluffy towels, were covered in red and green velvet cloth
and bowls of holiday-themed finger foods. Tinsel and giant,
sparkling plastic snowflakes hung from the rafters, above the
doorways, and anywhere else Dario could find purchase for
such decorations. He'd even unfurled red carpets, creating
walkways along the sides of the giant hot tub and between each
doorway.

"Holy shit," Nate said, resting his chin on my shoulder as I
stood in our suite's doorway admiring Dario's work. "It looks
like Santa pooped a big one everywhere. It's red, green, and
glitter-covered turds all over the place."

I nudged his head with my own. "Yeah, Santa pooped a big one, alright. Ethan won't know what hit him when he wakes up."

He wrapped his arms around my waist and squeezed me tight. "You really are amazing. You know that, right?"

As he kissed my neck, I said, "Yeah, I know. Amazing, wonderful, articulate, brilliant, unmatched, unique, unequaled, incomparable, benevolent—"

His teeth bit into my skin. "Are you just rattling off words now? Are we still describing *my* Cooper?"

I huffed. "All of those words describe me perfectly—maybe not all in the same moment, but if you take the many moments of my existence and our time together and all the time I've had together with all the people I've known over the years, then yes, each of those words, and all of them collectively, paint a fluid image on the canvas of my life, like a Mona Lisa, except where she's actually smiling and not smirking, and where her eyes don't follow in that creepy way that says she wants to bite your wiener off."

A heartbeat passed, then a second.

"Why would the Mona Lisa want to bite your wiener?" Nate asked slowly.

"Have you looked into her eyes?" I said.

"Uh, no. I don't think I have actually."

"She's a wiener biter, I tell you. Sharp, pointy teeth, like the bunny in Monty Python—"

He snorted and his forehead dug into my shoulder.

"Did you just compare the Mona Lisa to a Monty Python sketch?"

I wheeled to face him and tried to maintain a defiant posture. "Absolutely."

He shook his head and laughed, but before he could respond, the door to the hallway opened and Dario entered, two porters trailing behind pushing carts filled with food, plates, and utensils.

"Merry Christmas, Mr. Hawk, Mr. Stringer," Dario said with a broad smile and Elizabethan bow.

"And to you, good sir," Nate said in a miserable British accent.

Dario's eyes sparkled. "We should have breakfast set up in a few minutes. Do you expect everyone this morning?"

I nodded. "I was about to go wake them. I really want everyone in here before we let Ethan in."

Dario glanced toward the Christmas tree and the colorfully wrapped boxes spilling out beneath it. "Make yourself comfortable. Perhaps pour a cup of coffee. I will rouse the others," he said before bowing again and shuffling out of the room.

"I could get used to this," I muttered under my breath. Nate pinched my butt, and I squealed in the least manly way possible.

The younger of the porters glanced up and grinned.

"Where's that coffee?" Nate asked. "I could drink a gallon myself."

"Right here, sir." The young porter pointed to a silver urn he'd just set up on a side table.

Moments later, Sam and Miguel entered, each wearing long-sleeved pajamas printed with cartoon reindeer in risqué poses. A bare-chested, hunky Santa adorned Sam's chest, while Mrs. Claus, pouring out of a glittery string bikini, stared out from Miguel's.

"Ho, ho, ho," Miguel said.

"Yeah, I heard we could find hos here, and look, there's Coop and Nate," Sam added.

The porters nearly spat as they tried to stifle their laughter.

"Aw, Mom and Dad, it's so good to see you made it up this morning," Nate snarked. "I was worried Dario might need to fetch a walker or wheelchair."

Sam planted his fists on his hips, making Santa flex. "We're not that much older than you, sonny, and Miguel could kick your ass in ten directions without breaking a sweat."

Nate draped his arm around my shoulder. "And Coop here could do a spinning head-kick thing without lifting a foot."

Miguel and Sam's heads cocked in unison.

"Uh, babe, how am I supposed to kick without my foot?" I asked.

"Oh, whatever," Nate said, stepping forward to pull Sam into a hug. "Merry fucking Christmas."

Before he could let go to embrace Miguel, a chime sounded.

"You have pockets in those things?" Nate teased.

Sam reached into one of the reindeer heads and retrieved his phone. He glanced at it quickly, then looked up. "It's from Ty."

I stepped toward the coffee urn and grabbed a cup. "How's he doing?"

Sam flicked his phone to life and read aloud.

SexyBeastTy: Hey guys. Gabe and I wanted to wish you all a Merry Christmas and tell you how much we miss you. We wish we could be there but … well … you know what happened. It's been a tough few days, but we're making the most of our holidays now.

A few seconds passed and the phone *dinged* again.

SexyBeastTy: We have some news, a little Christmas miracle of our own to share, but want to wait until we can be together to tell you about it. I know, Sam, I'm such a tease. Some things never change. Ha ha. We love you guys and can't wait to see you all again. Tell everyone hi and merry Christmas for us, especially Ethan.

Sam slipped his phone back into the reindeer's head, then looked up at Miguel. "I wish they could've come. This trip would've done a lot for Ty after Dom ... after everything."

When Sam's voice caught, Miguel wrapped him in both arms and held him close, kissing his head. The giant cop was so strong and tough, yet the gentlest beast I'd ever met. The moment made me want to melt.

Then Nate spoke and shattered the mood. "Why's he SexyBeastTy in your phone?"

Sam laughed and buried his head in Miguel's chest, mumbling something I couldn't understand.

"Uh, we can't understand when you talk into Miguel's cleavage. As nice as his man boobs are, they don't carry sound well."

Sam's shoulders shook with laughter, as his head rose. "I said, it was a joke from when we first met and he was trying to make it as a model."

"Oh," Nate said. "Guess that makes sense. He is pretty sexy.""Fucking hot," Miguel chimed in.

Sam punched Miguel's arm.

"Hey!" Miguel protested.

"I'm the only man you get to think is sexy. Got it?" Sam growled.

Miguel leaned down and kissed his forehead like one might a small child. "Yes, dear one."

Nate spat coffee across the deck.

I stayed by the urn, safely out of the line of fire. "What do you think he meant by their Christmas miracle?"Sam shrugged. "Probably got another puppy. I can't imagine Gabe would want Audie to be their only dog."

The sound of music stilled our conversation. Literally *The Sound of Music.*

Annie's voice drowned out everything else:

Edelweiss, edelweiss

Every morning you greet me

Small and white, clean and bright

You look happy to meet me.

Blossom of snow, may you bloom and grow

Bloom and grow forever

Edelweiss, edelweiss

Bless my homeland forever.

The porters had stopped their preparations and were staring at Annie as she flitted about the room, her voice ebbing and flowing with effortless grace. Her red, green, and gold pajamas, complete with padded footies, belied her elegant entrance, but was quickly dismissed as she began the second verse.

Edelweiss, edelweiss

Every morning you greet me

Small and white, clean and bright
You look happy to meet me.
Blossom of snow, may you bloom and grow
Bloom and grow forever
Edelweiss, edelweiss
Bless my homeland forever.

The Aviary exploded in applause.

"Does *Edelweiss* have something to do with Christmas I'm not aware of?" Nate asked Sam.

Annie charged forward, thrusting her aged frame between the beefy men and stabbing a bony finger into Nate's chest.

"I will have you know, young man, that *The Sound of Music* is a holiday classic, played in my family's home each year on Christmas Eve for as long as I can remember."

He grinned down at her. "Uh, okay, but—"

"No buts, not even for you gay boys—and I know that's a lot to resist." She turned and smacked her ass, stunning Nate and sending the rest of us into fits of laughter.

Steph strode in as Annie snatched a cup and began filling it with coffee from the urn.

"What did I miss? Is Annie acting out again?" he asked.

Annie gasped dramatically. "I never!"

The laughter and jeers grew louder, as any mercy our circle might've shown one another for the holiday vanished into bacon-scented air.

"Merry Christmas!" Ethan's squeaky voice cut through the din, and everyone turned and cheered at the little man's entrance. He beamed in the spotlight, then noticed the tree and all the presents. In a flash, the boy dashed across the deck and slid to his knees, pulling box after box, his eyes widening as he learned each tag bore his name.

André and Nick stepped in.

"Cooper Hawk, what have you done now?" the Frenchman boomed.

"You know exactly what I've done," I said, a gleam in my eye. "You helped me put it all together."

André grinned and shoved a finger to his lips. "No one is supposed to know that part."

"Papa, can I open them? They're all for me! Every one of them. Oh. My. Gosh. Oh my gosh. OH MY GOSH!" The boy's words burbled out faster and faster as he dug more and more boxes from beneath the pine needles and silver bells.

"Your breakfast is ready when you are, Mr. Hawk," Dario said, appearing from thin air without so much as a tinkling bell. I nearly tossed my coffee, he startled me so badly.

"Thanks, Dario."

"If you need anything, please call. We disembark in Florence at eleven o'clock local time."

Without another word, the butler spun and led his troops from the Aviary, where the order of our morning had descended into a familial festival of epic proportions.

By the time the last fork rested on the edge of a plate, our band of misfits had eaten several pounds of bacon, immeasurable stacks of pancakes, and enough eggs to make hens give up whatever they do to get pregnant with the orbs in the first place.

Ethan had scored—big time.

The area around the tree had transformed from a festive postcard into a torn-wrapping-strewn present graveyard, where

Transformers, toy cars, baseball bats, and catcher's mitts held court. I'd made sure he received enough Lego to build a fully functional space shuttle, while Nate had insisted on more sporting equipment. The boy was still gangly and uncoordinated, but Nate insisted we give him the chance to love sports—or not—on his own.

Sam and Miguel merged their professions, giving the child a remote-controlled police cruiser whose lights flashed and siren blared. I chuckled at how often Nick and André would soon curse them for that gift.

Steph had bought a few puzzles and games at shops in Cannes, and Annie, not to be outdone by her gay sons, provided a robot whose vocabulary exceeded a thousand words.

André filled a lull in the commotion, retrieving a small gift from behind a plant where he'd hidden it the night before. Nick unwrapped the box, quickly strapping a golden watch to his wrist and holding it up for all to see.

When no one else offered surprises of their own, I sucked in a breath and stood. "Everyone, can I have your attention please? Just for a moment."

I waited as eyes turned and conversations died.

Just as I was about to speak, a phone chimed. All eyes turned to Steph. The stunned look on his face made it clear he hadn't expected anyone to text or call. He glanced down, then back up, his eyes dancing with ... something.

"What was that?" Sam growled in his direction.

Steph tried to act casual. "Nothing, just a text."

Miguel piled on. "Oh no you don't. You look like someone just offered you Santa's cock for Christmas.""Miguel, *child*," Nick hissed.

"Sorry," Miguel mouthed, glancing toward Ethan, who was fully distracted by one of his many new toys.

"Well?" Sam asked, undeterred. "Let me see before Mom over there loses her mind." Sam glanced meaningfully toward Miguel. A round of chuckles acknowledged the common reference.

When Steph didn't respond, Sam stuck out his hand.

Steph huffed in annoyance, then reluctantly handed him his phone.

Sam read aloud.

DeltaOne: Hey, Stephan. Just wanted to wish you a merry Christmas. It's been really great getting to know you these past few days, even if it's just been in text messages. I can't wait to use my flight privileges to see you for real. Have fun in Italy (but not too much—ha).

"Delta One?" Sam mused aloud, then his eyes brightened in recognition. "Have you been texting with our hot flight attendant? What was his name? Jake?"

"Jack," Miguel corrected, his broad grin a mirror of Sam's.

"Holy shi—" Nate caught himself. "Sorry. Holy *cow*!"

"Yeah, yeah," Steph said, snatching his phone back. "We're just talking."

Sam nearly doubled over. "Your face matches Santa's coat right now. I'd say there's more than *talk* going on. Have you sexted? Seen a dick pic? How big is he?"

"Sam!" Annie, Miguel, and Nate called in unison.

"What? Don't tell me you aren't curious." He turned back to Steph. "Have you at least seen him shirtless? He looked ripped in that uniform."

Steph glanced around the group, then surrendered and held up an image of Jack standing in a shower with water dripping off his hard body. The frame cut off at his waist, but Greek god perfection was clear in every part of him we could see.

"Holy mother of fuckness," Sam said.

"Sam!" This time André joined in the choral rebuke.

"Oh shit, sorry," Sam said, then ducked his head. "Sorry for the shit. I mean ... sorry."

"Shit! Fuck! Fuckness! Yay!" Ethan shouted from the far side of the Aviary, holding up an action figure as if the toy had shouted the expletives.

Daggers bore into Sam from all directions before the entire group erupted in laughter.

When everyone had settled, I reclaimed the floor. "Guys, and lady"—I offered a respectful nod toward Annie. She beamed—"I, um, have a few things I'd like to say, if it's okay."

"Of course it is, Cooper," Annie said, her voice brooking no argument from the others. "You go on. I'll kick anyone who interrupts."

A murmur of chuckles rippled through the group, then I gathered myself and continued.

"This is such a special trip to me. I can't begin to tell you how much having each of you here means. My Grammy ... she wanted me to get to know Sam and Miguel. She loved you two so much, and knew we would become like a family."

"We *are* family, Coop," Miguel said.

I stared at Miguel, then nodded. "I guess we are. Grammy would've loved every minute of this trip."

"She would've been singing on stage with Annie," Sam called out, to everyone's chuckles and nods.

"Yeah, she probably would have," I agreed. "But I know she's happy for us. This is what she would've wanted, for us to be together, to celebrate together, to be … the family we were always meant to be." I looked around at my closest friends, those I loved more than anyone in the world, and my throat caught.

"But … I have a confession, and it's not going to be easy, so give me a minute, okay?"

The mood in the room sobered as everyone's attention sharpened in my direction.

I drew in a breath. "This trip was about something more than just getting everyone together. I mean, that's reason enough, and I love you guys … I mean, *we* love you guys." I glanced toward Nate and smiled. "We love you guys to the moon and back, and getting to see you and go on excursions and have dinners together and everything … and getting to see Ethan and all his presents and Santa … oh my gosh, I can't believe how big he's gotten … it's all amazing and wonderful and something we'll never forget." I sucked down another breath. "But it's not the only reason I did this. It's not what made me want to go overboard. Not literally overboard. That would be bad on a cruise because unless you grabbed a preserver you might drown and the ship would keep moving even though you were flailing in the water because no one would know you fell and there are sharks and whales and tiny fish with sharp teeth and stuff …"

I froze. Everyone's mouths were open.

"Um … anyway …" I glanced at my shoes, then looked up again. "None of this would be possible without … without the love and support of Nate."Miguel reached across and gave Nate a bro-punch.

"I don't know how we made it here. Not here, literally. I know how we got here. We were all on the same plane and boarded this ship together and ... never mind. I mean, Nate and me. We kind of ran into each other under the Nashville stadium and then at the Blue Bird and like, overnight, Nate was texting me and wanting to be with me and couldn't live without me and, somehow, we couldn't be apart. He was kind of a stalker, if I'm being honest. If he wasn't so hot, it would've been creepy."

Chuckles ran through the group, as Miguel patted Nate's shoulder.

"*You* stalked me on Insta, that's how it happened," Nate called out to a round of lighthearted jeers.

I nodded. "Yeah, I guess I did, didn't I? But you liked it."He groaned, but a smile filled his eyes.

I paused a moment and looked at him, then something strange happened.

The room fell silent. Everyone else faded into the background. There was only Nate and me.

"Nate, I love you with all my heart. When we met, I was such a mess. Grammy was my whole world, and losing her shattered me in ways I didn't even understand back then. You held me when I could barely stand on my own. You believed in me when I'd lost ... so much. You teach me, every day, how to hope and dream and never give up, no matter what life throws our way. You make me a better man simply by standing next to me."

I blinked the moisture from my eyes.

"Nate, I didn't do all this"—I waved around the Aviary—"just so our friends could enjoy a vacation, even though that's reason enough. I did all this because ... because I have something to ask you. Something bigger than any move or job or city or … bigger than *anything* … and I didn't know how or where …"I gulped in air.

"Nate, I can't stand the idea of spending a single day without you. You're *everything* I want in this life, everything I could ever hope for. I don't care if we have all of Grammy's money or live in a cardboard box under a bridge. I just want … no, I *need* to be with you. Every day, every moment, for the rest of my life." I dropped to one knee and pulled a box from my pocket. "Nate Stringer, will you marry me?"

Tears were streaming down my face by the time my fingers fumbled the box open to reveal a pair of golden bands.

Nate threw himself to the floor and gripped my shoulders, his gaze delving into me as tears fell from his eyes. "Of course I will, Coop."

He wrapped his arms around me and held me close as both our shoulders heaved and our friends applauded and cheered. Had I not been balling myself, I might've heard Annie's sobs as she leaned into Steph's chest.

A moment later, each of our adopted family had gathered around to join our embrace. Even tiny Ethan's arms clung to my legs.

Nate's lips found mine in the midst of the huddle, and he whispered, "This is so perfect. Merry Christmas, babe."

Chapter Twenty-Five

Miguel (and Sam)

"I can't believe we've been on this boat for a week," Sam said as he flopped onto his back on the bed.

"I know. It feels like we just boarded ... but somehow feels like we've been here forever too. Weird, right?" I tossed the stuffed dolphin we bought for Ethan in Corfu onto Sam's chest. "Swimming with the dolphins today was pretty cool."

"Yeah. They really are like big dogs."

"Except for all the swimming," I chuckled.

"Right, that too." Sam was quiet a moment while I stripped out of my swimming trunks and dirty shirt. "What's been your favorite thing so far?"

I tossed my shirt into the corner where our laundry had grown into an unruly pile. Dario would likely take care of it if we asked, but it still felt weird having someone waiting on us hand and foot.

"Hmm. That's a hard one. Every day, I think it's my favorite, then the next day comes, and we see or do something even better." I pulled on a loose pair of jogging shorts and thought a moment, replaying the past few days in my mind's eye. "Florence was probably the best food so far, but the bus ride from the ship to the city killed a lot of time. It felt like we'd just made it into town when we had to turn around and head back."

"Oh, right, that was a long bus trip," Sam groaned. "Is that where we had that fish with the head still on it? The eyes creeped me out, but it tasted great."

I laughed. "You're *such* a barbarian."

"Hey!" He smacked me with the dolphin, daring me into a pillow fight like the mature men we were.

I grabbed the fluffy fish and tossed it across the room, then nuzzled up next to him, draping my arm over his chest.

"Florence was beautiful. Everything was so old, and the architecture was just like I imagine it would be in some story from the ancient past. As the ship pulled out of the harbor, the sun set, and it was like a blanket of colors fell over everything, painting the stones in reds and oranges."

Sam rolled onto his side and propped himself up on an elbow. "Look at you getting all poetic and shit."

I snorted. "More shit than poetic."

"No. Poetic." His face straightened, and his hand reached over to caress my cheek. "I like it when you talk all smart and artsy."

I tried to keep a straight face. He was being sweet, but the mechanic in him made it impossible to take too seriously. Another snort escaped.

"Sorry," I said, genuinely regretting the laugh at his sincerity.

He leaned over and kissed my nose like I was a four-year-old. "It's okay. I know you're just a little kid."

I grunted agreement.

"What else?" he asked. "Florence was, what, three days ago? Four?"

"Yep. The next day was Naples. Again, food. God, the food. I could die happy here, knowing I'd eaten everything my stomach ever desired."

Sam grinned as his eyes glazed at the memory of handmade pasta and a grandmother's sauce to rival any meal, anywhere in the world.

"I can't wait to print out our pictures from Valetta. Florence was amazing, but Valetta felt like walking back in time. You know I'm not big into churches, but St. John's was crazy."

"Anything built in the 1500s would be nuts, but the inside of that place ..."

"I know. I got stuck in the doorway looking up at the ceiling," I said.

Sam chuckled. "I remember. I had to push you out of the way so the rest of the tour could keep moving."

"The whole city felt like that though. I mean, everything wasn't that old, but it had that feeling, like we'd stepped through a mirror and walked into another time and place."

We lay there a long moment in silence, each flipping through memories.

"I think today was my favorite so far," Sam said suddenly.

It was my turn to roll over and prop up. "Why's that? Corfu's nothing like Florence or Valetta. It's just an island, kind of like a big Florida Key."

"First of all, it's nothing like the Florida Keys, even though it is an island. I'll give you that much, my brilliant one." Sam rolled his eyes. "I don't know. Today was the first time we got to do stuff. The whole dolphin thing was awesome. I could've stayed in the water with them all day. Then the ATVs, bouncing all over the island, in this perfect weather? Hell, I could do a ten-day vacation of just this and be happy. Coop could keep the ship and butler."

I cleared my throat.

"What?"

"Can we keep the butler?"

"Huh?"

"Just think about it, never having to cook or clean or do laundry again."

Sam grunted. "And a creepy old guy lurking around to see if 'sir' needs anything? No, thank you."

"Wait, you're still talking about the butler, not me, right?"

He laughed and shoved me back. "Asshole."

"I think tomorrow's going to top them all," I said.

Sam's grin widened. "You inviting Steph in finally? We gonna make a surfer sandwich?"

Most days, the couples would explore the port city on their own, but Steph was always by our side. He talked like a surfer dude, but we'd come to know a far more layered guy than either of us expected. He held most people at arm's distance, but when he opened up, he allowed us in without reservation. Sam and I could be a lot to handle, with our snarky banter and teasing tones, but Steph blended in beautifully. His light humor and easy smile made him impossible to dislike, and our flirtation had only grown more open as we'd come to know him better.

I groaned. "You know I've just been playing with the boy, right? I don't want anyone in our bed but you and me. I mean, he's hot and sweet and all, but what we have—"

Sam leaned over and smothered my lips with his, and his hand found its way to the back of my head, pressing me into him harder.

A breathless moment later, he pulled back. "I only want *you*, Miguel, now and forever," Sam said.

I gulped back a lump as moisture flooded my eyes. We'd been together for years and still this man's smile filled my chest with the warmth of a thousand suns.

"Steph's a good guy. I really like him," Sam said. "And he's a good addition to our little cadre, but he needs his own Miguel, not the pair of us."

I grinned. "There's only one Miguel."

"Oh, I know," Sam said, his hand reaching down and cupping my crotch. "My big boy."

I tried not to wince as he squeezed my balls the wrong way, sending a jolt of nausea through my stomach and into my chest.

"Your big boy smells like dolphin poop," I said, desperate to free myself from his grip. "Tomorrow's a big day, and I'm kind of beat. Why don't we get cleaned up and order room service? We can catch up on *The Walking Dead*. We're on, what, season ten now?"

We'd fallen into the habit of binging Netflix shows in the evenings, and the eleven-season *Walking Dead* was taking forever to complete.

"Yeah, I think there's a few more to go before the final season," Sam said. "You go shower. I'll order food and get the laptop hooked up to the TV. Sounds like a perfect night."

I gave Sam another kiss, then rolled over and off the bed. I was about to step into the bathroom when a knock sounded at our door.

"Hello?" Sam called.

"Mr. Prescott?" Dario's voice answered. "I have a message for you and Mr. Nuñez."

Sam and I exchanged a glance, then he rose and opened the door. Dario handed him an envelope, then Sam closed the door and turned, ripping the paper.

You are summoned to an audience in the Red Keep tomorrow at noon. Do not be late unless you wish to face the King's justice.

Sam looked up at me, his brow scrunched.

"Tomorrow is the *Game of Thrones* excursion in Dubrovnik."

Sam nodded. "Sounds like Coop's grand gestures aren't stopping with his proposal."

Chapter Twenty-Six

Cooper (and Nate)

"You're nervous."

It was a statement, not a question.

I smiled, tight-lipped, up at Nate. "It's a big day. You know how much I love *Game of Thrones*. We've watched the series, what, six times now?"

"I'm pretty sure we're on our eighth." My laugh quivered. "Yeah, eight. Sounds right."

Nate kneeled in front of where I sat on the end of the bed and gripped my hands. "So, what's up? Why do you sound like you're expecting one of the dragons to scoop you up and drop you into the ocean later?"

Dammit. How did this man know me so well? He'd barely given me one glance as I was brushing my teeth and knew I was hiding something. How was I ever supposed to surprise him?

"Uh, no dragons, unfortunately. That would be really cool."

Nate didn't budge. If anything, his grip on my hands tightened.

"Coop." He dragged out the *oooooo* sound, like a mother questioning her son. "What are you hiding? You're a terrible liar. You know that, right?"

I looked down at our hands, at his hand, where a ring would soon rest, and a smile pried its way loose.

He followed my gaze, and his brows arched. "You're not—"

"No," I said, shaking my head. "I wouldn't spring that on you. I mean, I would. I totally would. Now that you mention it, I wish I had. How cool would it be to get married in the middle of the city where *Game of Thrones*—"

"Coop—"

"Think about it. We could hold hands ... I mean, do a handfasting ceremony ... *in the Throne Room*, and have the officiant sit on the Iron Throne. Who gets to do that? Right? The whole gang could be dressed in armor or whatever we could scrape together. If you didn't want to do the Throne Room, I'm sure there are a million places that overlook the bay that would be amazing—"

"Coop, you already said it's not a wedding," he said, a dog refusing to release a bone. "What do you have planned? I saw you give Dario all those envelopes."

Shit. I thought he'd been asleep.

"I ... uh ... crap ... you're not going to let me win this, are you?"

He shook his head, a determined set firming his jaw.

"Fine. I *may* have arranged for ... a special guest to fly in and surprise our party while we're on the *Game of Thrones* tour."

He leapt to his feet and began pacing. "Holy crap, Coop. Did you get one of the actors? That's totally something you would do. Is it Jamie Lannister? Queen Cersei? No, it's the big redhead. Tormund Giantsbane, isn't it?"

I wanted to laugh so hard, but he wouldn't stop guessing long enough for me to fully let loose.

Then he froze and his whole body tensed, his eyes flew even wider. "Wait. Jon Snow. It's Jon, isn't it? No fucking way. You got Jon Snow to fly in, didn't you? Is he going to be in costume? Will he have his sword? Sam will wet himself."

I raised my palms in surrender, but clamped my lips tight.

"Don't tell me. I want to be surprised too, even though I sort of know now." He darted about the room, gathering things to take with us without actually picking anything up, just releasing a burst of energy that *had* to go somewhere. "Babe, you're so freakin' amazing. I can't believe you did all this, then pulled off Jon freakin' Snow. Is he bringing his dire wolf? If he walks in with Ghost, I might pass out right there on the cold hard stones."

He was practically vibrating with excitement by the time the horn sounded and the "it's time to disembark" announcement crackled through the loudspeakers. Dario stood in the hallway outside our door as we stepped out.

"Mr. Hawk," he smiled conspiratorially. "All of your messages were delivered. Arrangements have been verified for your tour ... and your guests. The Red Keep is yours for the afternoon. All the arrangements will be made for your return."

"Thanks, Dario," I said. "I couldn't have done this without you. Please give the captain my thanks too.""Of course," he said, offering a respectful dip of his head.

"Captain?" Nate hissed in my ear. "What the hell did you need the captain for? And he said guests, not guest. How many did you manage to ... wait ... we have the Red Keep to ourselves? Seriously?"

I turned back and wiggled my brows, then raced down the hallway where a few of the others were leaving their rooms, where he couldn't continue his interrogation.

BY THE TIME OUR amoeba-shaped group made its way off the ship to a section of cobblestones where a large black minibus waited, Nate had lost any control over his mouth and had most of the gang worked into a frenzy over our impending meeting with Jon Snow and his famed wolf. Somehow, as often happens in the best game of Rumor, the tale had grown to include everyone's favorite snarky little person, Tyrion Lannister, along with a hoard of Night Walkers they were sure I'd shipped in just to enhance the background of the photo shoot that was sure to occur.

No one was even asking me if any of this was true. They latched onto Nate's excitement and swallowed his story hook, line, and sinker.

I had to admit, we'd barely set foot onto Croatian soil and the city already sent chills up my arms. Behind us, the Adriatic Sea stretched as far as we could see, its deep blue waters juxtaposed against the warm, terracotta rooftops that dominated Dubrovnik. The air was crisp, a tang of salt and sea tickling my nose as the sun blazed brightly overhead, highlighting the centuries-old architecture whose stones had withstood generations of time and history.

Beyond the walls, the landscape was lush with greenery, adding color and contrast to the stones of the walls and towers. A heartbeat of ceaseless waves crashing against the rocky shores and clifflike walls pulsed through the very foundations of the city's stones.

"You've really outdone yourself this time," Sam said, his grin nearly as wide as Miguel's for the first time since I'd known the pair.

I smiled coyly. "You don't know the half of it."

He waited. I clamped my mouth shut.

"Well, shit. It must be good if *you* can keep from spewing all over us. I never took you for one who could keep secrets."

I cocked a brow. "I'm good at a lot of things, thank you very much. You don't get to be an almost Olympian by wearing blinders, though I'm not sure why anyone would ever wear blinders since they're made for horses and people need their peripheral vision, especially when doing things like taekwondo, and at the elite level, that's even more important because guys are coming at you from every direction, and I'm not talking about how Ty would have guys coming at him … or all over him … back in the day before he met Gabe, because I'm sure Gabe is the only guy coming all over him now … not that I know their sexual habits or how messy Gabe might be or even if Ty would like that, because, you know, some guys don't like having that all over them, especially when their partner eats salty or spicy foods because that makes cum taste terrible … or so I've heard … I mean … God, I didn't just say that, did I?"

Sam was staring, his smile fully morphed into an open-jawed gape.

"I swear, we were talking about *Game of Thrones*," he said. "How the hell did we get cum in your mouth?"

"What's that? Someone shooting in Cooper's mouth while my back was turned?" Miguel butted in, teeth flashing in every direction.

"Uh, yeah, something like that. You might want to duck before—"

"Guys!" I barked. "No one's coming on anyone, or in anyone's mouth, unless this tour stops at Littlefinger's brothel, which is an actual possibility, and no, I did not arrange for Littlefinger to be on this tour. He's a disgusting, petty character who deserved what he got, and if you don't know what I'm talking about because you haven't seen that scene, then you need to watch the series."

Now both of them gaped.

Miguel slowly turned to Sam. "What did you do to press his button?"

Sam's hands shot into the air. "Don't look at me. He just started—"

"All aboard!" a man in khaki pants and a light blue shirt called. His nametag read "Josip."

"Come on. This is going to be fun," I said, grabbing both of them by the arm and pulling them toward the bus.

As the door slammed shut, Annie, who ended up squished between me and the window, asked over the clamor of the bubbling cauldron Nick had stirred up, "What's going on? Everyone's losing their minds over *Game of Thrones*."

I cocked my head. "What do you mean?"

She scrunched her brows. "I've never seen the show. Is it really that big of a deal? It's not like we're meeting Julie Andrews or anything."

I grinned. "No, it's not like that. She would be awesome, but this is pretty cool too. Nate and I have watched *GoT* four times all the way through. It's actually become a Christmas tradition. We start season one the week of Thanksgiving and race through to finish by New Year."

"Season one? How many seasons are there?"

"Eight."

She whistled. "You boys need to get out more."

"We love it," I chuckled. "It's one of the best shows ever made, really. Have you never seen any of it?"

She shook her head. "I tried watching once, but it was all blood and gore. I just couldn't do it."

"It can get pretty dark, that's for sure. The author tried to portray real life in a medieval setting. Guess it was pretty grim back then."

She didn't respond, just looked out the window.

"Lady and gentlemen," Josip's lilting accent magically quieted everyone. It reminded me of Russian, but if sunlight had replaced dark clouds and hard-packed snow. "If you will look to your left, we are passing the steps used in the scenes with the Sept of Baelor. The stairs are real and have lived here for centuries. The building in the television show was created using 3D computer modeling and green screens. As you can see, our real-life church at the top of the steps is not crowned with a dome, and very little of the facade made it into the show."

"I can almost see the crazy guys in brown robes lining those steps," Nate muttered as he leaned across me to peer out Annie's window.

Josip parked the bus and opened the door, then turned to face us. "This is where we begin. The rest of the tour is on your feet. Now, who will be doing the Walk of Shame?"

Pandemonium erupted as everyone pointed at a different victim they wanted to endure the ultimate punishment meted out to Queen Cersei.

"What's that all about?" Annie asked.

"One of the characters was stripped naked and made to walk from here to the Red Keep as a punishment. The entire city turned out and threw veggies and poop at her," I explained.

Annie tsked. "See, this is why—"

"This is so cool!" Sam's voice drowned out whatever she was about to say, as the burly man bounded out of the bus and onto the stairs where Josip waited.

Dozens of photos and a handful of questions later, the nine of us tittered behind Josip like a pack of besotted schoolkids, winding our way through the ancient city on exactly the path the abashed Queen of the Andals had trod. Josip chatted away, tossing out fun facts and reminding us of memorable scenes. Ten minutes later, we stood, slack-jawed, at the far end of the bridge that led to the Pile Gate.

"You will recognize this spot as the entrance to the Red Keep. This is where the authority of the Gold Cloaks ended and the crimson guards of House Lannister took over. Cersei fell into their care midway across this bridge."

"That's the Red Keep! Like, the real thing!" Sam shook Miguel's shoulder.

Josip laughed. "We call it Fort Lovrijenac, but yes, this is the Red Keep, the seat of power for the Seven Kingdoms. Come on, let's go inside."

Josip turned and walked slowly across the bridge. If they hadn't needed a guide, I was sure Sam, Miguel, and Nate would've darted past him and vanished beneath the stone archway, happy to explore their not-so-childhood dream on their own.

We crossed into the past as we entered the fort, rounding corners and descending stairs. Josip showed us the lower levels, where prisoners were held and tortured, then wound his way outside, into the brilliance of the gardens. Something about the dank gray cool of the stone made the luminous hues of the flowers even more dazzling.

Annie stepped forward and cupped a particularly yellow bloom. Her voice was a breath on the wind when she spoke, "I don't think I've ever seen such a beautiful place."

Josip smiled. "Many of the scenes were filmed out here for that very reason. Today, this is one of the more popular sites for local weddings."

Nate's head whipped around, and his gaze stabbed into me. I grinned and shook my head, then mouthed, "Nope."

His smile remained, but his shoulders drooped a tiny bit.

Huh. I hadn't expected that.

Josip led us to a stone half-wall that melded with the cliff's edge. Beyond, a sea of the bluest water shimmered in perpetual motion. Steph stepped back, insisting on taking pictures with each couple's cameras. As he started to turn, Sam grabbed his arm.

"Oh no you don't. Get over there and pose. I'm sure your sky mattress will appreciate a few pics."

Miguel nearly doubled over laughing as the rest of our heads whipped around.

Steph screw up his face. "Sky mattress?"

"You know," Sam said. "Your flight attendant. What's his name? Jace? Jam?" "Jack," Steph said, annoyance lacing his voice. "And he's not *my* anything. We've just been talking. That's all."

"Wait, Steph's hooking up with Jack, the hottie from the plane?" Nate asked loud enough to get everyone's attention.

Ethan raced up and began chanting, "Steph and Jack, sittin' in a tree, k-i-s-s-i-n-g ..."

Steph rolled his eyes and backed up to the stone facing us. "We're just talking."

"Uh-huh," Sam said, snapping several images before handing Steph's phone back. "Make sure you save those. You'll want to remember this spot for … you know."

Steph's eyes widened. "You're already marrying me off? We haven't even been on a date."

"Don't argue with your mother," Miguel said, his scolding tone earning a round of laughter from the others.

Steph grinned despite his annoyance. "Since when is *that* my mother?" He inclined his head toward Sam.

"Since we adopted you," Miguel said matter-of-factly, then turned and strode after Josip, leaving Steph staring, openmouthed, with the sea crashing behind him.

Josip made a show of checking his watch, then turned back without slowing his stride. "I believe it's time for your council meeting."

A nervous hum trickled through the group. They'd been anticipating a big reveal, and any hint or tease sent them spiraling out of control.

"Jon Snow. I really can't believe it. He's so freakin' hot," Sam said.

"For a pocket date," Miguel added.

I quirked my brow. "A pocket date?"

Miguel grinned. "A guy short enough I could stuff him in my pocket."

Groans echoed off the stone. Even Annie moaned and shoved Miguel's shoulder with her bony hand.

"Do you think he'll let me pet Ghost?" Ethan asked.

A pang of guilt pricked my chest, as I realized the boy had bought their fantasy too. Oh well, nothing to do about that now. They'd be happy soon enough, even if it wasn't for the reason they thought.

We stepped back inside the torch-lit castle, rounded two corners and entered an all-too-familiar chamber we'd seen dozens of times throughout our favorite TV show. I could picture Cersei or Tywin Lannister sitting at the head of the table, with their sycophantic band gathered around to screw up something else within the kingdoms. Before I could move toward the head of the table, Sam shoved Miguel out of the way and planted himself in the high-backed chair reserved for the King's Hand.

"Sit, everyone. We have much to discuss," he said with an impressive amount of medieval authority. Miguel had often teased Sam about how he liked to take charge, but I'd always thought it just playful banter. Now, though, I could see my rugged adopted momma slamming my hunky dad against the stones of the fort and doing naughty things while the palace guards listened.

I shook my head, desperate to get the image out of my mind's eye.

Josip gave us a brief history of the chamber, then allowed us a few moments to wander about, taking pictures of each other holding court around the table or sitting at the Hand's regal desk.

"One last stop," Josip announced.

"Here we go," Sam said, gripping Miguel's arm like a nine-year-old about to ride his first rollercoaster.

Josip turned and motioned toward a large wooden door banded with iron. "The Throne Room awaits."

We practically tumbled into the next room, one friend after another shoving backs and butts, eager to see the pièce de résistance of the Red Keep. Sam, who'd managed to elbow everyone else out of the way, froze a few strides into the vaulted chamber—but it wasn't the towering columns, elaborate staircase, or ridiculously cool Iron Throne that dropped his jaw. It was who stood at the foot of the dais, and what they held.

"Joe?"

Miguel stepped up beside Sam. "Is that the congressman and—"

Sam nodded slowly. "Yeah, and Joe, the guy I hooked up with before we met."

Congressman David Reese, a six-foot-three slab of deliciousness, in his light blue dress shirt that hugged his chest like it was made of Spandex, took a step forward. His dark brown hair was highlighted by a dusting of silver at his temples, but everything else about him screamed vitality and strength.

"Please, everyone, join us."

His voice was warm and welcoming, but commanded obedience. David's time as a Navy SEAL was well documented, but I'd never met him nor fully understood why people snapped to his call. Now it made sense. He was impossible to look away from and even harder to defy.

Joe, David's husband of six years, a few inches shorter and a decade and a half younger, stepped up and hooked his arm around David's. "It's good to see you again, Sam. Come on in. This place is amazing."

Miguel and Sam stepped forward and exchanged hugs and handshakes, then turned and introduced everyone else. Most of the others were too distracted by the majesty of the hall to worry too much about the newcomers, but a thread of curiosity wove through all their gazes when they fell on David and Joe.

"Josip, why don't you tell us about this room and let everyone do their pictures, then we can bring in our other guests," I said, smiling at how Sam now struggled between focusing on Joe and whatever surprise I was about to reveal.

Our guide regaled us with tales of filming in the room, scenes most of us remembered well, and a few fun facts about the original fort's use of the chamber that was never intended as a seat of power. Each of us took turns sitting in the Iron Throne and getting our photos taken by a professional photographer who'd been standing in the shadow cast by one of the columns.

As Annie descended the stairs, David stepped up to me and whispered, "Is it time?"

I nodded, and a wave of nerves battered my senses.

David gently rubbed Joe's arm as he passed, then vanished through a side door. I stepped around the group so they were facing me, away from where David had gone.

"Everyone," I called. "Can I have your attention?"

I waited as the group gathered around, and silence blanketed the hall.

"We have some special guests I'm sure you'll all recognize." I paused to let the tension build. "And they're not just making an appearance today. They'll be joining us for the rest of the cruise.

"Sam's face was a comedy of emotions: first elation, then confusion, then consternation, then ... I wasn't sure what that last one was. The door creaking open behind them saved him from further facial contortion.

"A couple of old friends would like to make an introduction." I motioned toward the door.

Everyone turned, and Sam practically fell over.

"Ty?" Sam stepped forward. "What are you—"

"Gabe?" Miguel echoed.

Sam's eyes fell to Gabe. "Is that—"

"A baby—" Miguel continued.

Ty beamed, his gaze traveling from Sam to Miguel, then to the infant wrapped in a lavender blanket in Gabe's arms.

"Hi, guys ... and Annie." He looked behind Sam to smile at Annie. "We'd like you to meet the newest addition to our family. This is Mila."

Chapter Twenty-Seven

Tyler (and Gabe)

I'd known Sam for nearly a decade, and I'd never seen anything throw him off balance like he was when he stared down at Mila, then reached out and palmed her fuzzy little head. The smile that curled his lips was one I scarcely recognized. It was as if Miguel had inhabited his body and was smiling through his face, nearly connecting his ears with his lips.

And the only time I'd ever seen him shed a tear was when Coop had told us about his grandmother's passing and given Sam her note. That tore us all up.

As the gruff man stared down at the fragile babe, and she wrapped her tiny hand around his rugged finger, tears escaped and rolled freely down his cheeks.

"She's so beautiful," he breathed.

Gabe held her toward him. "Would you like to hold her?"

Sam would've stumbled back if Miguel hadn't been there to brace him. It looked more like Superman being offered a basket of kryptonite than my best friend getting to hold our daughter for the first time.

Tentatively, Sam stretched his arms and pulled her into him. She reached toward his face and cooed, her bright eyes sparkling in the chamber's torchlight. The others gathered around, forming a circle with Gabe, Sam, Miguel, and Mila at its center.

"When? How?" Miguel stammered.

I reached up and pulled Miguel into an embrace.

"We've been working through the process for nearly a year," I said.

"A year?" Sam looked up, eyes wide.

I nodded. "We didn't want to say anything in case it didn't work out. We tried one other time and things fell apart right before we met that baby. David really came through for us this time though."

"I'm just happy things worked out. You two are going to make great parents," David said.

"I'm lost," Nate said, stepping up to get a better view of Mila. "Why are you here in Croatia? I mean, it's great to see you and all, but—"

I chuckled. "We adopted her from a place here in Dubrovnik. That's why we needed David's help. He smoothed the way with the Croatian government. We only found out we'd been approved three days ago, so we needed help getting into the country."

"Why'd you name her Mila?" Ethan asked, squeezing his way between the legs of all the adults blocking his view.

I bent down to eye level with him. "That was what her mother named her. We thought it was pretty, so we kept it."

The boy screwed up his face, then asked, "What's her last name going to be?"

I smiled. "Rossi-Hyatt. She gets a hyphen. Isn't that fancy?"

He giggled and reached up to touch his forefinger to hers. "That's cool."

Each of the others took turns greeting Mila, rubbing her head or playing with her fingers or toes. She grinned and gurgled merrily, never crying or showing irritation at all the attention.

"Honey, I'm so sorry about Domino," Annie said, wrapping her arms around me so tightly I thought my lungs might burst. "I know how hard that can be."

When she pulled back, I gave her a tight-lipped smile and nodded. "I miss him so much, and I hate that she'll never meet him, but ..."I couldn't finish before tears streaked my face.

"I'm so happy for you guys. This is amazing." Miguel pulled me against his chest. "When do you have to go back to the States? Can we at least all have lunch together?"

One of Coop's hands landed on my shoulder, while the other patted Miguel's. "They're joining the cruise for the rest of the trip," he said. "I never gave up their cabin, remember? Dario should have it stocked with formula, a crib, and everything else they might need. In fact, Joe and David are joining us too. The good congressman promised to shed his dress shirt if I got him a cabin, and Joe says that's well worth the price of admission. You can thank me later."

David's face filled with color as Joe clutched his arm and wiggled his brows.

Miguel shook his head. "You really did think of everything, didn't you?"

Sam handed Mila to an insistent Annie, then turned toward our huddle. "Not everything. I don't see Jon Snow or Ghost anywhere. I'm pissed."

I cocked a brow at Cooper.

He leaned in and whispered, "He thought he was meeting the real Jon Snow, then it was just you and a baby."

I grinned toward Sam. "Sorry to disappoint, Dad."

"You and your little adoption stole a precious moment from me. It may take a long time for me to get over this," Sam growled, then grabbed me roughly, pulling me away from Coop and Miguel, and making Annie's hug from before look like a gentle caress.

"Gabe, help!" I gasped, pawing at my husband, who was completely ignoring me. "Sam ... breathing ... would be ... helpful ... here."

He squeezed harder.

"You little asshole, keeping this from me for an entire year," he said, humor filling his tone. "I'm so fucking proud and happy for you, Ty."

Proud. Sam was proud of me.

I don't know why that word struck such a cord, but it felt like someone had whacked my chest with a baseball bat. Breathing was already a struggle in his embrace, but that word stole the last of the air I'd managed to suck into my lungs.

Sam gripped my face with both hands and pressed our foreheads together, his gaze more intense than I remembered seeing in a long time. "I always knew that party boy shit wasn't really you. That right there is the luckiest little girl in the world. You're gonna be such a great dad, you hear me. A great one."

That's when I lost it. Right there in the Throne Room, before the Iron Throne itself, two strides from a US congressman and surrounded by the people I loved more than anyone in the world, I crumpled into Sam's arms and bawled like a baby—well, not *my* baby, she never uttered a peep, clearly determined to show up her new old man.

Chapter Twenty-Eight

Sam (and Miguel)

Ty, Gabe, and Mila settled into their suite a few doors down from ours. True to form, Cooper had everything already set up, including multiple sets of bottles for feeding, a fully stocked pantry with formula, a crib neatly made with ridiculously soft sheets and a plush blanket, and a plethora of stuffed sea-themed creatures to keep the little lady company.

Annie fawned over the baby nearly as much as Gabe did, insisting her motherly touch would make her feel more comfortable. Ty stepped on a landmine by referring to her as "Grandma," earning a stiff slap and stern glare from our resident Broadway star. Her actual age was irrelevant; she stated she self-identified in her forties, and any member of the Alphabet Community should respect her decision.

I kept as far from that conversation as possible.

David and Joe also settled into their suite, the last of the open berths in our section. David made a real effort to endear himself to the others, telling tales of being in Congress and joking like the rest of our misfits. Joe tended to fade into the background. Our eyes met a few times, but neither of us had the stomach to maintain a gaze longer than a heartbeat. Miguel was everything to me, and I had no desire to rekindle whatever Joe and I had before he dumped me for his boss, but it still felt weird seeing him again after all these years.

Cooper had arranged for dinner to be served in the Aviary, anticipating most of us might want a low-key meal together after such an eventful day. In classic, ironic Cooper fashion, he shoved me into the chair beside Joe, with Miguel and David seated across from us.

As one of the servers refilled my wine, Joe leaned over and broke our silence. "Feels kind of weird, doesn't it?" he whispered.

"The baby, the ship, or seeing you again?"

He grinned, and the stupid dimples that used to make me melt punctured his cheeks. "How about all of the above?"

I took a sip—well, more of a gulp. "Yeah, all of it."

"Miguel seems like a really great guy."

I glanced up to catch Miguel and David chatting like old chums.

"He's the best man I've ever known," I said. It wasn't simply the truth, it was exactly what I thought every time I saw him. We'd been together for six years, married for five, and I still couldn't understand how I'd gotten so lucky to snag him. He was the textbook definition of punching above my weight class—far above it.

"Is he always smiling?"

I choked on my wine and had to cough a few times to draw air. "Yeah, pretty much. It's fucking annoying. Nobody should be that happy," I groused through rebellious lips that twisted upward at the thought of how much shit Miguel took for being so damn happy.

Joe chuckled. "David's almost always on, if you know what I mean."

I cocked my head like a retriever, having no clue what he meant.

"He's a politician. He wears this mask in public. I guess it's hard to take it off sometimes." Joe's voice trailed off.

I turned and looked at him. It was the first time since we'd been reunited that I really examined my old lover. He was still the same handsome, youthful man, but there were lines where everything used to be smooth, and his eyes held something ... a depth I didn't remember from before. He was always smarter and more mature than guys his age, but this was different. It wasn't exactly a darkness; rather, it was a more serious cast to the bright hues I was used to.

"You guys okay?" I asked without thinking.

He started, as if I'd woken him from a memory. "Oh, yeah, we're great." He took a quick sip of wine, something he did the first time we'd had dinner together when he was nervous about something I'd just asked. "David's winning reelection pretty easily now that the state Republican Party redistricted, packing all the Dems into his district."

I waited, but he stared at some indistinct point in the middle of the table.

"But?" I asked.

His eyes slowly rose to meet mine. He started to say something, then his lips clamped shut and his eyes fell.

"It's okay. You don't have to tell me anything. I mean, it's not like—"

"It's not David or me … or us. We're great, I promise. It's just … I want us to be friends."

Now it was my turn to stare blankly. "Oh."

"I always wanted that, even after things didn't work out between us." He took a far longer sip of wine this time and lowered his voice. "When we went to dinner that one time, I guess you, I don't know … you surprised me."

I looked up to find the deep sincerity I always saw in his gaze. "You were a lot more, I don't know, more—"

"More than a dumb mechanic?" I laughed as much as spoke.

Something akin to horror crossed his face. "I didn't mean—"

I laughed, this time more full-throated. "Yeah, you did, and it's okay. I get that a lot. People assume if I have grease under my nails, there's not much between my ears. No reason you wouldn't, especially since the bulk of our conversations consisted of grunts and groans."

"There might've been a few 'oh shits' thrown in there too," he said, grinning broadly.

I laughed again. "That was all you, fragile boy."

"Fragile?" He scoffed. "As I recall, I took everything you had, and you nearly threw out your back, old man."

"Hey!" I protested. "That was an old sports injury."

He rolled his eyes. "Miguel played sports, not you. You're just old."

"Maybe. I'm definitely getting there," I said, shaking my head. "It feels good to laugh with you again."

He nodded. "We always did laugh a lot."

We sat in silence a moment. I couldn't stop listening to the chatter around us, pulling tight about me like a favorite blanket. These were my people, my family. Coop had been right about bringing us together.

"You and David should come over to the house. We can grill out. Looks like Miguel and David have already hit it off."

Joe eyed me without turning his head, then slowly turned my way. "I'd like that."

"Me too."

"You guys look like you're plotting over there. Should we be worried?" David pointed between Joe and me with his wine glass, then nudged Miguel. "Can't leave them alone for a minute, can we?"

"I'm a cop. You don't have to tell me to keep my eyes peeled with this one—" Miguel gestured toward me, his grin wide as ever.

"Hey, I don't know what you're talking about. I'm pure and innocent."

From down the table's length, Annie's cackle pierced the clamor. "Sam Prescott, you may be a lot of things, but you have never been pure nor innocent," her slightly slurred voice sang.

I wanted to play it straight, to act offended or defensive, but she was already tipsy and we hadn't even started the main course. "I'll have you know—"

"Oh, Sam, quit while you're behind. Speaking of which, why don't ya stand up and give us a twirl so I can see that precious booty."

The blaze that traveled from my chest up my neck and into my cheeks was apparently visible, because the entire table erupted, and any semblance of order fell to the mighty sword of chaos.

And so it remained until the last of us stumbled to our cabins for the night.

Chapter Twenty-Nine

Miguel (and Sam)

THE COASTAL CITY OF Messina sat only a few miles across the water from the pinky toe of Italy, on the Sicilian island whose shape reminded me of a paper football we used to flick across tables just to annoy our parents. I'd never heard of the place, but Cooper swore we'd love it, claiming he'd done all the research, then verified his findings with Dario once we boarded the ship.

Of course he had.

At this point in our trip, I was less worried about one of the ports being a flop than I was worried what Cooper might pull while our feet were on land. He'd proven himself to be a true master of surprises.

Sam and I were both beginning to feel cooped up. We weren't trapped. Every day we stepped onto dry land to explore another new city, and even when we were aboard the ship, there were more shops, shows, restaurants, swimming pools, casinos, games, and parties than we could ever experience. Still, neither of us had worked out since starting the trip. My muscles were tight and beginning to ache, and Sam ... Sam was getting downright grumpy.

So, rather than join Steph, André, Nick, and Ethan on the Godfather vs. Mafia Tour, which sounded cool as hell, we found an excursion more fitted to our particular need.

We went kayaking around the island.

The sea was calm and crystalline blue, the wind was crisp and cool, and the views of the ancient Sicilian coast were breathtaking.

The only other couple, a pair of rowers on the Spanish national team, dared us to beat them. We weren't on a course. There were no finish lines. We were simply racing around a massive origami pigskin with no end in sight.

For four hours. Four hours of paddling. Four hours of paddling against Olympic rowers.

By the time we wobbled back aboard, I could barely push our cabin door open.

"I can't feel my arms," Sam said, flopping face-first onto the bed.

I wanted to laugh, but my body wouldn't allow the effort. I simply fell onto the bed perpendicular to his prone form and rested my head on his back, like some human pillow.

Neither of us moved—hell, we didn't even speak—for several long moments.

"Whose idea was that?" I asked.

The rumble in Sam's chest vibrated through the back of my head. "Yours, I believe."

"Fuck me. Why did you listen to me?"

Sam laughed again. "I ask myself that so many times."

"Ha ha. Very funny. You needed exercise, remember? You were getting pissy and snapping at the children, remember? Coop was about to sick Dario on us, remember?"

He rolled over, tossing my head off him to thunk on the bed.

"Yeah, I remember. I really did need it, even if I may never move again."

A knock sounded at the door.

"Fuck. Why does that knock sound happy, like the person smiled through their knuckles just to taunt us?" I asked, not moving.

Sam remained still too. "I hate happy people."

I grunted.

"I heard that smile."

"I was not—"

He sat up and leaned over so our heads were upside down looking at each other, like we were the dogs eating spaghetti in *Lady and the Tramp*, except on a bed … upside down. Okay, not like the movie at all, but still.

"I'll get the door. You lay there and recover," he said, planting a kiss on my lips, almost making the pain worth it.

The knocks sounded again, this time more insistent, less happy.

"Coming," Sam yelled as he pushed himself off the bed.

He opened the door to find Steph, knuckles poised to rap again.

"Oh, hey, Sam."

"Steph!" I called from the bed without daring to move.

"Did I interrupt—"

"Nope," Sam said. "We're far too sore for you to interrupt anything."

"Oh, okay," he said, drawing out the last word like he didn't understand why we were in pain. "So, um, a few of us are taking Ethan down to the kids' area. He wants to play ping-pong, and we thought you guys might want to join."

I kept quiet and waited to follow Sam's lead. He was actually great with kids and would love nothing more than to play games with Ethan, but the thought of doing anything more than crashing in front of the TV sounded like a herculean task.

"I think we're toast. Tomorrow's New Year's Eve, and we want to be well rested for whatever insanity Coop has planned," Sam said, following exactly the script I'd been writing in my head. Good job, Sam.

"You think Coop has something planned for tomorrow night?"

Sam laughed. "New Year's Eve in Mallorca? You think Coop would miss that chance to spring something on us?"

"Fair point," Steph conceded. "Alright, I'll let them know Mom and Dad are too old to play."

"There was a time when we liked you," Sam said, not missing a beat.

"You love me and you know it." Steph laughed. "Catch you guys later. Enjoy *Walker, Texas Ranger* ... or are you two more the *Murder, She Wrote* kind of couple?"

"Okay, I'm shutting the door on your nose now," Sam huffed.

Steph laughed as the door closed, then called out, "See you guys. Love ya lots."

Sam hobbled his old, sore ass back to the bed and resumed his role as my man-pillow.

"He really fits in, doesn't he?" I said.

Sam chuckled. "Yeah, he's just enough of a smart ass to fit right in."

THE NEXT MORNING, AS we prepared to disembark on the island of Mallorca, our little cadre divided into three distinct units.

Joe, David, Ty, and Gabe, along with Mila, chose a relaxed day, which included a bus tour, lunch at a winery, and an early return to the ship. Nick and André promised Ethan a tour of the caves of Drach, which claimed to be one of the island's great natural wonders—as if the island itself wasn't stunning enough. Apparently, there were canoe rides through the caves that ended at the Majorica pearl factory, where participants could enjoy a classical music concert in an amphitheater within the caves. While the adventure within the caves and the acoustics of the concert were appealing, the idea of paddling anything, even a canoe on a lazy river, made my biceps throb, so Sam, Steph, Nate, Coop, Annie, and I chose the more daring, less physically demanding path. We signed up for a hot air balloon tour of the island.

We'd made it down the gangplank and were about to hunt for taxis to our respective activities when Coop shouted for everyone to wait a moment.

"I have a quick announcement," he began.

"Oh shit. Here it comes," Sam said. "He's flying us to Paris for a party at the top of the Eiffel Tower."

I snorted and elbowed my hubby. "Shh. Let the boy have his moment."

"Yes, dear," he teased.

Coop cleared his throat. "We need everyone back and ready to ... ready for our next part of the trip at six o'clock. I mean, we leave at six, which means we all need to be back aboard by five so we have time to get cleaned up, dressed, and ready to go. You will want to wear your best party outfits for what we have planned. It's going to be a great New Year's Eve."

Without any further explanation, Coop grabbed Annie's arm with one hand and Nate's with the other, and hauled them toward a waiting car, forcing Sam and me to jog to catch up. The others, shaking off their confused expressions, finally broke to begin their day's quest.

"MY HEART IS STILL racing," Annie said as we stepped up the gangplank.

I glanced back to find Cooper grinning like an idiot, wedged in between Annie and Nate, just like he'd been when we'd left for the balloon ride. Arm in arm, I half expected them to break out into a chorus of—

"Weeeeee're off to see the wizard ..." Annie's voice dispelled any notion of escaping the obvious cliché. Coop joined in, harmonizing fairly well. When Nate tried to add his bass to the tune, the wheels came completely off the bus.

"Dear God," Annie exclaimed. "Are you truly tone deaf, Nate?"

"Annie!" Nate clutched his pearls in mock offense.

Coop nearly fell overboard laughing. "He absolutely is. Worse, even," he sputtered as we reached the top of the walkway and stepped aboard.

"Coop? You too?" Nate protested. "Guys, Miguel, help a brother out here."

I shook my head. "You sounded like someone was beating a baby seal to death. You're on your own, brother."

Coop roared as Annie threatened to hyperventilate. "A baby seal," she rasped. "I think I might've just peed myself."

The crew welcoming us aboard stared with mouths agape as we laughed our way down the hall toward our cabins. By the time Sam and I reached the safety of our stateroom, my sides hurt from all the hilarity.

"I can't remember laughing so much. This trip's been ... a trip," I said, stripping off the boots I'd worn in anticipation of a hike that never materialized.

"You're so good with your words, babe. Such a smart copper."

I huffed. He was gonna pay for that. "Fuck off. Get over here and show me how much you love me."

Sam cocked a brow as I grabbed his arm and yanked him across the room. I threw him onto the bed on his stomach, one arm behind his back like a suspect I was about to cuff.

"Help! Police! I'm being—"

"I am the police. Now shut up and take it like a man." I fell on top of him with my full weight and knocked the air from his lungs.

I teased his ear with my lips. "You're so fucking hot in those jeans," I muttered. "I wanted to rip them open and fuck you senseless in that damn balloon."

My cock throbbed against his ass, even through both our jeans.

"Fuck," he muttered into the comforter, wiggling his butt so my dick pressed between his cheeks. I groaned at the motion and clamped my teeth on his lobe.

"I want you so bad, Sam," I breathed.

He was still for a second. "We don't have time," he said, prying his face free of the bedcovers. "We have to be off the boat in thirty minutes, remember?"

"Thirty? I only need five." I ground against him, prompting a groan to escape his lips.

"Crap, babe. You'd better stop, or—"

"Or what?" I bit his lobe again, this time harder.

"Ah! Fuck—"Whatever he was going to say was cut off by three sharp knocks on our cabin door. Both our heads whipped up.

"Sam, Miguel, hurry up. Coop's about to wet himself over us being on time," Steph's stupid, disrespectful, ill-timed voice shouted. Something beeped, and our door opened. "Hey, my card works for your—"

We stared up at him. He gaped at us.

"Uh, dudes, sorry. I, uh, didn't know, um, shit ..."

That's when Sam lost it, and the mood shattered.

"All good," I said, pushing up off Sam, which shoved him further into the mattress. "I was just helping stretch Sam's back. He gets tight. Old age, you know."

"Looked like you were about to stretch something else," Steph quipped.

"Damn right he was. Want to watch?" Sam asked, propping up on an elbow.

"I, uh—" Steph's eyes flew wide as his hand raked through his hair. "Maybe I should, you know, go, Coop might need something—"

I stepped toward him and grabbed his shoulder. "He's kidding, Steph. Just breathe."

Steph sucked in a deep breath. "I mean, it's not like I haven't dreamed about …"

His words froze as Sam and I gawked at the dream he was about to unfurl. We really liked Steph. He was a good guy and had proven himself a great addition to our little family, but we didn't want anyone coming between us, especially our most intimate moments, and I doubted Steph truly wanted that either. But I would've been lying if I said his naked body hadn't entered my dreams. I was a guy, after all, and he was freakin' hot.

"Okay, I'll, um, let you get changed. Coop says … never mind. See you downstairs."

He vanished as quickly as he'd arrived.

"You really love teasing the boy, don't you?" Sam grinned up at me. "If we were a different couple, we would've already made him our boy. He's delicious."

I stared down at my husband, considering. "Would you want to—"

He shot to his feet and wrapped his arms around me. "Absolutely not. Not even for a moment. No. Period. End of statement."

"Sheesh. So forceful," I teased.

He kissed me deeply, and I thought we might end up back on the bed. "I love only you, Miguel Nuñez. In another lifetime, maybe in this one a few years ago, I would've jumped all over that. Other couples can do that, and I'm happy for them. I'm no prude, you know that, but I don't want that, not with you." He pulled back and held my head with both hands, as he'd done so many times before. "You changed my life, Miguel. You changed *me*. You make me want to be a better man every day, and just when I think I can't love you any more, the sun rises again, and I see you sleeping beside me, and my heart swells."

"Sam ..." I choked out.

He kissed me again. "If I die having never been with another man, I will be the happiest guy on the planet. Unless—" He froze, his eyes fixed on mine. "Unless you want—"

"God no," I said quickly. "Never. Sam, *never*."

Our lips met again, this time hunger was replaced by the warmth of the sun on a wintry morning, all comfort and brilliance and the promise of a beautiful day.

Chapter Thirty

Cooper (and Nate)

Annie was the last to arrive. Her maroon dress sparkled in the waning sunlight, and her hair, held up by a thousand pins, somehow looked like a Hollywood artist had designed it.

"Sweet Jesus, you look amazing," Nate said, taking her hand as she stepped onto the planks of the dock.

"Aw, sweet boy, keep talking. Tell me more," she said, pretending to blush when I knew she was loving every minute of it.

While she had chosen formalwear for her "going out on the town" outfit, the rest of us were dressed in tight jeans and even tighter T-shirts. We looked like a gay boy band about to tear up a stage in front of a gazillion screaming girls who thought they had a shot but were sorely missing the whole point of the phrase "boy band."

I scanned our group, enjoying the sight of all my friends in one place again. Ty and Gabe were the only ones who knew my plan for the evening. Mila's presence was a blessing beyond measure, but having a baby along complicated everything. After a brief conversation, they agreed it would be better for them to enjoy a quiet evening aboard the ship with their daughter. They would receive a few surprises, delivered by Dario, so I didn't feel too bad for them missing the evening with the gang.

"Alright, everyone," I shouted above the tooting horn of the ship that was slowly pulling away from us. Worried glances stole nearly everyone's gazes from me as they watched the massive boat drift away. "Our helicopter is waiting on the other side of that parking lot."

Ten pairs of eyes slammed into me.

"Helicopter?" Nick said, voicing the word I knew was hammering each of their minds.

I grinned and nodded. "Come on, we've got to stay on schedule."

We strode across one parking lot, past the port's main building and into an overflow lot that had been closed for the day. A slow, rhythmic thumping echoed off the building's walls, as a sleek helicopter, painted royal blue with gold trim, came into view.

"Holy shit," Sam said behind me.

By the time we reached the pilot, who stood beside the boarding door, the others had expressed similar surprise, some in far more colorful language. Ethan yanked free of André's hand and bolted past me, skidding to a stop just before slamming into the startled pilot.

"This is so cool, Uncle Cooper!" he shouted over the helicopter's heartbeat. His eyes darted from the blades to the nose, then to the tail, then back to me. Smiles on the faces of my friends was one thing, but the abject joy and excitement bursting from this child ... it made my heart soar in ways few things ever had. "Are we really getting in this thing?" I laughed and nodded. "You're going first, little man. We'll all follow your lead."

"PAPA!" he shouted and waved at André, who was still at the back of the pack some distance from the chopper. "Hurry! You and Dad have to follow me. Uncle Cooper's rules!"

I'd never really wanted to be a father, but in that moment, watching wonder bloom in Ethan's eyes, I felt a small fraction of the delight parents must feel each time their child experiences something new.

A moment later, the last of our clan climbed aboard, and we settled into the plush leather seats of the Eurocopter EC155, one of Europe's most luxurious passenger helicopters. Nate squeezed in beside me, his head on the same swivel as everyone else's.

"I always pictured the inside of a helicopter like on *M*A*S*H*: pretty much bare walls and a few uncomfortable fold-out seats." He rubbed his fingers across the smooth leather armrest. "This is fancy."

"Reminds me of Marine One," David said absently.

Ethan's face remained plastered to the window, but everyone else's head turned.

"You've been on the President's helicopter?" Miguel asked, his eyes wide.

David nodded. "A few times. It's pretty impressive. Same leather as this bird, but the presidential seal is embroidered in each headrest, and there's a lot more comms equipment on board. The President has to be able to work wherever he is."

Heads bobbed as if we all understood. I was fairly certain none of us could relate.

Joe reached over and grabbed David's hand, then raised it to his lips. Their eyes remained fixed on each other. It was a simple gesture, but in that one kiss, they shared their bond with our family.

"You two kids," Annie said, waving a hand. "It's just beautiful to see."

I snuck a peek at Sam. He was smiling in Joe's direction, while Miguel's meaty hand squeezed his leg.

The pilot's voice sang through speakers mounted to the ceiling. "Okay, folks, we have a short one-hour flight. The skies are clear and there's no wind. Should be a smooth ride. If you'd like to begin your New Year's celebrations, there's champagne in the cooler. Enjoy the flight."

Whomp ... whomp ... whomp, whomp ... whomp, whomp, whomp ...

Annie squealed and threw her hands in the air as the chopper lifted off.

Between takeoff and landing, I lost track of the number of times I was asked about our destination. For once in my life, I managed to keep my lips sealed.

Precisely one hour after we left the lot on the southwestern tip of Mallorca, the pilot's voice broke through the chatter: "Ladies and gentlemen, welcome to Ibiza."

The chatter that persisted throughout our flight was nothing compared to the pandemonium that broke out after that announcement.

"Coop! Ibiza? For New Year's?" Annie's scream threatened to crack the poor chopper's windows. She unbuckled her seatbelt, threw herself across the laps of men seated between us to wrap her arms around my neck, and planted the most awkward, slobbery kiss my lips had ever endured.

"You're such a good boy," she said, stroking my hair like I was her pet beagle, then allowed herself to be lifted and returned to her seat by those wanting their laps back.

"Dude," Steph said, going full surfer in his excitement. "This is going to be radical. Like, I don't even know what to say, dude."

As the chopper touched down on top of a building that housed our dinner destination, Sam leaned over to Miguel. "We're headed to one of the wildest party places in the world, and Ty's in a cabin with a baby. How ironic is that?"

Miguel's head fell back against the rest as he laughed. "You need to text him pics all night."

"We all do," Sam agreed.

The door slid open, and our pilot extended a hand to Annie.

"Thank you, young man," she said, taking his hand, then pretending to slip so he had to catch her.

"Oh my," she said, slowly pulling back from where her lipstick left its mark on the upper chest of his uniform. "I'm afraid I've marked you, dear. I think that means you belong to me now."

The pilot, a late-twenties, clearly ex-military man, flushed crimson and stumbled harder over his words than she had out of the helicopter. "Uh, m'am, I, uh—"

"She's kidding, airman. Relax," David said in his best command voice.

The pilot's eyes snapped up, and he nodded once toward David.

Annie, not one to follow orders, stretched up on her toes and gave the man a peck on his cheek. "That's for later."

David lost his stern composure as the flush returned tenfold to the poor man's cheeks.

Once everyone had deplaned—de-choppered? Gotten off? Ew, no. Once we were all out of the helicopter ... yes, that will do—we marched across the rooftop toward a door where a man in a charcoal suit and crimson tie waited.

"Mr. Hawk?" he asked.

"That's me," I said from behind David, who'd beaten me to our mark.

"I am Saviero. I will be your host for this evening's meal." The man inclined his head. "Welcome to the Ibiza Terrace."

"Thank you, Saviero," I said, turning to watch the others catch up.

"If you would follow me, please," he said, turning to open the door. "Watch your step. We must only go down two flights, but the stairs are very short."

Moments later, we were seated around a circular table large enough to comfortably seat fifteen. The restaurant proper sat one floor below and held enough tables to seat more than one hundred guests. The space in which our table was set, however, was only large enough for our party, giving us a breathtaking view of the sunset, the sprawling city of Ibiza, and the privacy of our own open-air terrace.

The moment our butts hit cushions, servers appeared from behind curtains with bottles of champagne and appetizers, which consisted of small plates of paper-thin tartar, oysters, and deep-fried ham-filled fingers the server called *croquetas de jamón*.

Food flew out of the kitchen so quickly it was hard to keep up, but the courses were light, so there was never a moment where the meal felt heavy. A round of sautéed cauliflower with a white sauce, and ravioli filled with langoustine came next, followed by the main course: a choice of sea bass, lamb, or steak, which they called *entrecot.*

"I'm surprised everyone isn't drinking as quickly as they're eating," David said, waving a fork around the table at the wine in half-filled glasses. The breeze blowing in off the sea made the sheer curtains flutter and flames atop the candles across the table dance.

"I think they got the memo that we have a long night ahead. Look"—I pointed toward the opposite side of the table—"even Sam's pacing himself."

David grunted through a mouthful of fish. "What do you have planned tonight? Anything my press secretary will need to clean up later?"

I hadn't thought of that, but the idea of putting David in a compromising position was at once terrifying and utterly hilarious. I nearly spat my steak into the center of the circle.

"Sorry," I said to David, avoiding the curious gazes of those around. "You made me think of something funny. I mean, I was thinking about what you asked, you know, of your press secretary having to clean up a mess, which almost made me wish I'd thought of that sooner because it could've made for a really fun prank—not that pulling pranks on members of Congress is something I do all the time; I mean, it's not like you guys need help stepping in shit. Oh shit. I didn't mean you ... you know what I mean. Congress isn't exactly squeaky clean, and besides, we're half a world away on New Year's Eve, so you really shouldn't worry about the press over here, though I'm sure there will be lots of cameras and you know how much people like to post on social media and you are kind of famous and sort of hot and all, not that I want to do anything with your hotness or your congressional-ness, if that's a word, which it isn't, but I just made it up, so there."

David blinked, then reached for his glass without taking his eyes off me and sipped. And blinked again.

I smiled and stuffed more steak into my mouth so I couldn't say any more.

"Do you have a wedding planned?" he asked.

This time I did spit the steak across the table, clearing the center and nearly reaching Sam on the far side. Everyone stopped talking and turned toward me.

"Uh, sorry, guys. I kind of"—I pretended to cough and grabbed my chest dramatically—"got something caught. I'm alright. No need to panic. It's out now."

Nine pairs of eyes blinked. And blinked again.

"So, wedding?" David whispered.

I took a long gulp of wine.

"You did the whole proposal thing, and I heard it was beautiful. This would be a magical place to get married," he said, raising his glass.

I smiled weakly, then leaned toward him and whispered. "I thought about it, but Nate's mom would kill me. Like, literally kill me. Cooper guts everywhere. Kind of like my steak tonight."

David choked on his wine and had to dab his shirt with his cloth napkin while laughing.

"Besides, I thought Nate would want to be part of the planning. Proposing is one thing, but the actual knot tying is something else. If we're going to be partners forever, we should start by planning together, don't you think?"

David set his soiled napkin on the table and eyed me a moment, then his lips curled upward. "Cooper, I think that's one of the wisest things I've heard in a long time."

I tried to process why including my future husband in planning our wedding was wise, but came up empty.

"Do you have any ideas? Have you two talked about it yet?" he asked.

I nodded. "We've tossed around a few ideas. Neither of us really wants to wait a long time, but we need to coordinate with his family. Lord knows his mom will want to play a big part."

"She sounds like something else."

"You have no idea," I said, then quickly added, "She's wonderful, don't get me wrong. She's just ... a force of nature. Think Annie, but Latina."

David's brows raised and his mouth formed an O.

Dessert arrived, a strawberry sorbet with shavings of dark chocolate and a salty crunch I couldn't identify. It might've been the best thing I ate that night.

"Mr. Hawk."

I turned to find Saviero standing behind me.

"Your cars are waiting. I know it is only nine o'clock, but the streets will become impossible soon. I fear if you do not leave now, you will have to walk most of the way."

"Thank you, Saviero. You have my card?" I asked.

"Yes, sir. You were kind enough to note the gratuity as well. Your party is ready to go."

"That's great. Thank you, again. The meal was amazing."

Saviero beamed and inclined his head. "It was our pleasure, Mr. Hawk. I hope you have a wonderful evening."

Chapter Thirty-One

Nate (and Cooper)

Our cars inched forward, stalled by the throng of festively clad partygoers milling about.

"This is nuts," Coop said, pressing his nose against the window of the car in the same way Ethan did against the opposite window.

"You knew it would be," I said. "This is Ibiza, one of the party capitals of the world."

Our driver, Paulo, whose broken English held an accent that didn't match any of the Spanish residents we'd met, spoke without turning his eyes from the crowded road ahead. "This is nothing, Mr. Cooper. The streets, soon they will be unmoving."

Coop and I shared a confused glance.

"Is that not right? Unmoving? The people will be ... how you say ... on top of each other."

Nick snorted.

"Oh," Coop said, throwing poor Paulo a lifeline. "You mean it will be so crowded we won't be able to move?"

"Yes, yes. *Sí*," Paulo said, a wide smile splitting a face that would've been handsome if not for the childhood acne that clearly played havoc with his complexion. "It is good thing you have special pass."

"Coop, what have you done now?" I asked.

He grinned and motioned zipping his lips and tossing away the key.

I let my head fall back on the seat and groaned.

We rode another fifteen minutes, listening to the music of open-air cafés and restaurants, and the cheers and shouts of those who had begun their celebration hours before the appointed hour. Ethan was a sun, bulging at the seams, ready to burst in every direction and sear anyone nearby. We were nearing the heart of the island's official New Year's celebration, where many of the women wore costumes and the men were mostly shirtless and wore feathered headdresses or eye masks.

"Bird theme?" I asked.

Coop shrugged.

Paulo spoke. "We are island. Birds are always ... in season? Is that right words?"

"Yes, perfect," Coop said, patting Paulo on the shoulder.

André leaned across the seat and whispered to Coop, "We will stay until a little after midnight, but will need to get our little monster to bed soon after."

Coop nodded and fished a key card out of his pocket. "We have rooms at a hotel just up the street. I think it's a two-block walk. I've already checked us in, so you won't need to do anything special, just go up to your room. They should already have a rollout bed set up for Ethan."

André shook his head as he took the card. "You really do think of everything."

I knew Coop hadn't always carried himself with confidence, growing up with parents who basically abandoned him to sports, and the loss of his grandmother had left scars that might never fully fade. And yet, over the course of this trip, I'd seen the light that was Cooper Hawk shine more brilliantly than at any time since we'd met.

Sure, he'd inherited more money than we could ever spend, but it wasn't about the money. He might've gone overboard with this vacation, but he was generally a frugal guy. We lived in a comfortable, modest house, and his ten-year-old truck was the same one he was driving when we'd first met.

No, this was deeper. It was how he carried himself, how he thought and made decisions, how he didn't question his own instincts at every turn like he used to often. The Cooper I met a few years ago would have second-guessed his choice of dessert, even if there was only one option on the menu. But now, he was fully in command of his decisions and unafraid to take risks, especially when the payoff for those chances benefited his closest friends.

I rested my head on his shoulder and squeezed his arm tight.

"Hey, you," he said, his hand running through my unruly hair. "Everything okay?"

I looked up, stared into his eyes, and knew the words I uttered to be the greatest truth I'd ever spoken. "Everything's perfect."

His kiss nearly turned me into a puddle of mush right there in the car.

"Eww," Ethan said, failing to shatter my bliss. "They're kissing, Papa." I peeked around in time to catch André's smile. "Yes, they are, son."

"We are here," Paulo said, bringing the car to a stop, then pointing across the passenger's seat. "There is the entrance to the VIP area."

"Thanks, Paulo," Coop said. "Happy new year. Stay safe tonight."

"You too, Mr. Cooper. You boys have fun."

We stepped onto the sidewalk and waited for the others to gather, then headed to the entrance marked "VIP" in elegant golden script. Coop whipped out a stack of laminated passes, and the bouncer waved us through with barely a glance.

I'd been so lost in thought that I hadn't realized the celebration was being held on a long stretch of beach. Three massive stages were set up with the sea as their backdrop, and endless wooden planking created dance floors above the sandy shores.

"This is so beautiful," Annie said. Her arm was entwined with Steph's, and her off-hand patted his forearm as she spoke.

The VIP section consisted of several roped-off areas: one nearest the stage, one off to the side where several bars were surrounded by high-top tables and a smattering of couches and lounge chairs. This area was also portioned by sheer billowing curtains that offered a sense of exclusivity and privacy. Finally, a small stretch of beach was roped off for the exclusive use of premier pass holders.

The general area was already shoulder-to-shoulder, but the VIP section remained relatively empty. A muscular shirtless man with stunning gray eyes and jet-black hair strode up with a silver tray.

"Would you like a bite?" he asked, his soap-opera voice sending a tingle up my arms.

"Of the food or—"

"Sam!" Miguel scolded, then turned to the hottie server. "Ignore him. He's a barbarian."

The server's eyes roamed Sam like a copier scanning a page, then he grinned up at Miguel. "You two could bite whatever you wanted."

"What is it with you two?" Steph asked from behind.

The server craned his neck, then cocked a brow. "Bring him too. Lots of biting."

A second server, a woman in a one-piece swimsuit styled like a tuxedo, strode up with a tray of champagne flutes. "Champagne?"

"Yes, please," Sam said, snatching a glass from the tray and stepping to the side. "And thank you for saving us."

She inclined her head and grinned.

The male server stepped back. "It is a long night. You are not safe yet." He clamped his teeth so they clicked loudly, then spun and returned to the kitchen area to refill his tray.

Annie cackled. "Sam, you are in way over your head."

"That makes it so much hotter," Miguel growled in her ear, earning a startled squeal.

I'm not sure what I expected from the music, but classical notes drifting across the water was not it. Clearly, the Spanish had a different vibe for their celebrations than any I'd attended back home.

I was about to say something when the orchestra on stage played a final note, rose, and bowed, then began packing up their instruments.

Thump-thump ... thump-thump ... thump-thump ...

A low, pulsing heartbeat began playing over speakers pointed in every direction. A wave of excitement raced through the crowd, and cheers began to rise in time with the heartbeats.

Thump-thump ... thump-thump ...

Faster ... and louder ... and faster ... and louder ...A lone electric guitar began playing a heavily accented Spanish melody clearly known by every native in the crowd. Their claps and screams grew as the music swelled.

A second guitar added a swift countermelody to the first. Then a third seasoned the pot with harmonies. Throughout, the heartbeat pounded, sending vibrations through my chest like I was standing on stage.

By the time the singer began her first words, new arrivals had streamed into the VIP area, filling the area to capacity in mere seconds. The instruments wove a complex, fast-paced song that had everyone's hands in the air, bouncing and screaming, all while swaying in time with the heartbeat. Nick had Ethan on his shoulders, his tiny arms stretched toward the sky as he giggled freely.

Men and women danced in each other's arms. Women swayed with women, and men writhed with men. Some were drunk—or on their way there—others were high, while more were simply riding high. A few wore formal attire, while most danced in little more than a few threads knotted together.

No one cared or even noticed.

The party was all that mattered. The celebration. The feeling of absolute liberation.

The Spanish song ended and another played. On and on, until a DJ appeared in a booth perched high above the beach. He was hot and sweaty as he spun the first record, his beefy arm raised above his head where one finger tapped out the beat.

And Deborah Cox sauntered onto the stage.

"Oh. My. God. That's Deborah *fucking* Cox!" Joe yelled, his voice jumping two octaves higher than normal.

"Hey, Ibiza," Deborah yelled through her microphone, earning a wild round of screams from the crowd. "Are you ready for the new year?"

The screams grew louder.

"I can't hear you!" Deborah taunted.

The crowd roared.

"Then let's do this!" she called. "You better get those lips ready. You've got twenty minutes to find Mr. or Miss Right Now, so get moving!"

Another roar mixed with raucous laughter.

Then the beat jumped, the familiar intro of "Nobody's Supposed to Be Here" cut through, and the crowd shifted into another gear.

Cooper ripped off his shirt and tucked it into his belt, then grabbed the bottom of mine and forced me to do the same. Midway through Deborah's first song, he grabbed my hand and pulled, leading me to a set of stairs that led to a small circular dance floor surrounded by a metal railing. The moment we stepped onto the platform, I felt movement I hadn't noticed before. The stage was rotating. Coop had brought me up onto a spinning dance floor.

From there, we could see the whole beach, all three dance floors and stages, and even most of the city. I looked down to find Sam and Miguel pointing up at us and waving. The others caught on, and in an instant, hundreds around them joined in.

"You'd better wave back," Coop said, his goofy grin a heady contrast with his sexy, sweaty, shirtless chest.

I raised a palm toward our friends, and a cheer rose from the VIPs. "They have no idea who we are, do they?"

"Nope," Coop shouted over the music. "It's just an excuse to scream."

I rolled my eyes and let my husband-to-be pull me toward the center of the tiny stage. There was only room for three or four couples, so we pressed together, our slick skin sliding each time we bumped.

Deborah's next song began, and a massive digital timer appeared above the stage. It read, "10:00," then began ticking down like some giant sports clock above an arena.

Thousands of fingers pointed toward the clock, and another ripple of excitement shot across the beach.

Coop's hands gripped me as we danced, pulling me toward him. Our eyes locked. I couldn't help myself. I pressed my hands to the sides of his head and pulled his lips into mine. The beach exploded in color and light, and cheers bellowed around us.

5:49 ... 5:48 ... 5:47 ...

My eyes closed again and there was only Cooper, only us. His arms wrapped around me, and his tongue teased my own. His kiss was passion and fire, longing and love and lust. His touch was everything I'd ever wanted or dreamed of. And it was all mine. It would be mine that night, and for every night, for the rest of our lives.

I could barely believe it.

My hand brushed back his hair, more to feel him, to press against him, to let him feel how badly I wanted him every moment. His hands roamed my back, his fingers teasing and probing and digging. The friction from his chest rubbing against mine made my cock pulse, and I felt his own erection throbbing beneath his jeans.

The music grew faster. Our kisses deepened.

The crowd began chanting something, but we didn't care. The world was a blur, a background, of no consequence.

Cinco ... cuatro ... tres ... dos ... uno ...

Our stage spun faster. My heart pounded.

Coop's teeth sank into my bottom lip.

"I love you so damn much, Cooper," I managed through gasps.

Coop couldn't be close enough. His lips couldn't press hard enough.

I needed him with everything inside me.

¡Feliz Año Nuevo!

The beach erupted. Flashes of color and brilliance exploded as fireworks lit the cloudless sky. Partygoers cheered and kissed.

We turned in time to see Deborah surprise a stagehand, grabbing him roughly and bending him back for a sloppy kiss. Cheers and laughter swelled as she let him go and he staggered off stage.

Coop pointed, and I followed his gaze to find Sam and Miguel locked in an embrace, and Nick and André kissing while Ethan, still perched on Nick's shoulders, chanted "Happy new year!" to anyone nearby. Joe and David were nowhere to be found, but Annie had trapped poor Steph and was getting a celebratory kiss of her own, much to the excitement of those gathered around.

"You did this, Coop," I said, my eyes brimming. "You brought us all together, gave us this ... all this." I waved my arm around. "I'm so damn proud of you, so proud to be your fiancé."

He kissed me again, then muttered, "I can't wait to call you 'husband.'"

"It can't happen soon enough."

Chapter Thirty-Two

SAM (AND MIGUEL)

THE SHIP ARRIVED IN Ibiza the next day as scheduled, and the few passengers who weren't utterly spent from a night partying and ringing in the new year stepped off to enjoy a final shore leave.

André, Nick, and Ethan had returned to their hotel around one o'clock, while David and Joe slipped out just after midnight so they could christen 2024 with a roll in the proverbial hay back at our hotel. The rest of us, including Annie, danced on the beach until the sun rose.

Around noon, Miguel and I dragged our hungry, exhausted, and very hungover asses downstairs to forage for food. Coop, Nate, Nick, André, Ethan, and Annie were already seated at a series of tables that had been mashed together to form one long surface at which our group could eat.

"I don't know what meal this should be, but it better include coffee," I growled as I flopped into the chair beside Annie. "Why are you smiling and happy and shit?"

She giggled. "I'm always smiling and happy. I don't recall shitting anywhere near this table though. Is that a Spanish thing?"

"It's a Sam thing. He's just a lousy morning-after date," Miguel said, sitting next to me.

"I hate you both. Officially. Now, where's the coffee?" The curl at my lips belied my gruff words.

As if on cue, a silver pot appeared over my shoulder. "Café Americano?" the server asked.

"Uh, if that's coffee, yes," I said.

"Sure you don't want a shot of espresso?" Miguel asked.

I shook my head. "I want the pounding in my head to stop, not to never sleep again."

"He's such a gentle flower," Annie teased. Miguel had the nerve to chuckle and nod his head.

"Now I hate you both."

Miguel and Annie somehow connected telepathically, leaned in and kissed my cheeks at precisely the same time.

"Is that a Sam sandwich?"

I glanced up to find Steph grinning as he took his seat across from us.

"Yeah, this is what you could've had, if only—"

"Sam Prescott!" Annie said, pulling back from her kiss and slapping my shoulder. "Your husband is sitting right beside you."

"Whose idea do you think it was?" I winked as she gasped in mock alarm.

A second later, she leaned across me to whisper to Miguel, "Now that's a move I'd like to see."

And the pair of them laughed together again.

"They ganging up today?" Steph asked, his eyes flitting between Annie and Miguel.

I nodded. "I might need a save before this is over. Speaking of saves, I don't remember seeing much of you on the dance floor last night. Did you find someone to, um, celebrate with?"

Steph colored. "No, none of that. I've never been a big partyer. Besides, I was flying solo, and that's never as much fun."

Annie snickered.

"Annie?" I said.

She shook her head.

"I know waterboarding techniques. You will break," Miguel said through a grin.

Annie glanced to a perplexed Steph, then up to me. "I may have seen Steph texting a certain flight attendant just before midnight."

I hadn't realized the others were listening, but in that moment, all heads snapped toward Steph.

"Dude," Coop called from the other end of the table. "You holding out on us? How much have you and Mr. Floppy Hair been talking behind our backs?"Steph flicked his own floppy hair back. Crimson was creeping up his neck.

"We might have talked once or twice," he said.

A chorus of "oohs" and "aahs" rose across the table.

"Come on, Steph. How bad is it? Have you done the nasty on FaceTime yet?" Nate waved his phone in the air.

Steph's color deepened. "No, of course not. I mean, not that I wouldn't, if, you know ... shit. Why am I talking to any of you?"

"Once a Mango ... " Nate joked.

Steph laughed at that. "I'm screwed when we get home, aren't I?"

Nate nodded. "Screwed like an Ikea lightbulb in a lamp."

Groans greeted that one.

"What?" Nate held up his palms. "That was a good one."

"No, Nate, my brother, it wasn't," Steph said.

"So? Are you going to see him again? What was his name?" Annie asked.

"Jack. His name is Jack. And yeah, I think we're going to try to meet up when we get home. I'm not sure how or when, but ... I think I like him."

Another round of "oohs" rippled.

We'd nearly made it through lunch without Steph serving as the brunt of anyone else's jokes when Annie set her fork down and held her hand across the table at him.

"What?" Steph asked, glancing toward the salt and pepper shakers that were well within her reach.

She cocked a brow. "I know he sent you pictures. I saw you looking last night. There was a lot of skin on your screen. Hand 'em over."

I thought Steph might crawl under the table right then.

"Don't make me come around this table, young man. You know I'll do it," Annie said in her best annoyed mother's tone.

Reluctantly, Steph unlocked his phone and flipped to a particular image then handed it to her.

"Oh my!" she exclaimed, holding one hand to her chest. "He's stunning ... and those tits—"

"Annie!" Miguel said, sounding like he was about to come to Steph's defense.

I reached over and grabbed the phone from her hands and angled it so the rest of the table could see. A shirtless pic of Jack standing in front of his bathroom mirror stared back.

"Whoa, those are nice tits. And look at those tiny little nipples—" I pointed at the screen.

Steph was quick, I had to give it to him. His hand was across the table and snatching his phone before I'd even seen him coming.

"I'm glad you approve," he said to everyone and no one in particular.

"Have you seen the goods?" Annie asked.

"Annie!" Miguel protested again.

She shushed him with a wave. "Well? Have you?"

Steph held the phone below the table so no one could grab it. "No, thank you very much. I happen to be a gentleman."

Annie cackled. "You haven't asked. Chicken. Give me your phone. I'll get you a dick pic in seconds."

"Annie Lynn Marie!" Miguel snapped.

"That's not her name," I said.

Miguel shrugged. "I know, but I don't know it and she needed to be scolded properly, using a full name, so I made it up."

Annie stared at Miguel for a heartbeat before doubling over.

"Annie Lynn Marie, I love it," she said through tears. "Is that my drag name now?"

"Oh, Annie," Steph said. "Don't ever ask a group of gay men for your drag name. It won't end well for you."

Joe and David went into town after lunch, determined to make the most of the few remaining days of vacation. The rest of us dragged our tired butts back aboard the ship and prepared for our final night at sea. By prepared, I mean we went back to our respective cabins and passed out. Nothing says "nap day"

like New Year's Day for couples who aren't used to staying out late anymore.

Miguel traced circles on my back as I tried, unsuccessfully, to drift off.

"This really has been an amazing vacation," he said.

"Mm-hmm," I mumbled into the pillow.

"How much do you think Coop dropped over these two weeks?" His fingers stilled. "I mean, think about it. The flights alone had to be ten grand each, and there's what, ten or eleven of us? He probably got a group deal on the cruise, but still, that had to be another ten thousand or more. Then that helicopter. I don't even want to know what that one-hour flight cost."

"Don't forget the two hotel stays, all the meals, and little things in between," I added.

"Shit, you're right." Miguel whistled. "I bet he's spent a couple hundred grand, maybe more."

His fingers began circling again as he processed the numbers. I'd almost lost consciousness when he said, "How much do you think Marjorie really left him?"

I grunted, more interested in dreams than Coop's inheritance.

"Yeah, you're right," he said, assuming what my grunt meant. "It's none of our business, but still ..."

I didn't hear whatever he said next because sleep wrapped a blanket around and pulled me close. When I woke, the sun was setting across the other side of the island and the ship was getting ready to depart on our final leg. I stretched and wiped the sleep from my eyes, then glanced over to find Miguel fully dressed and primping in the tiny bathroom.

"Hey there, handsome," I said.

His head turned, comb stilled in his hair, and he smiled. "Good morning, sleepy head."

I propped up on an elbow, unwilling to leave the warmth of the covers.

"What's got you up and dressed? I don't remember Coop announcing any plans for the evening."

Miguel pulled the comb through his hair, then pointed with it toward the built-in shelf near the door. "A note came. We have a dinner reservation in thirty minutes. Rise and shine."

"Ugh." I flopped back on the pillow. "I was hoping we could do room service and be lazy."

He chuckled. "It's our last night together. You think Mr. Hawk would allow such a travesty of justice?"

"Look at you, using fancy words when I'm just trying to keep my eyes open." My heart warmed at his grin. I threw back the covers and slowly levered myself off the bed. "Where's dinner tonight?"

"The Aviary. Coop's having it catered in. His note said he wanted to have one last family dinner together without all the other passengers around."

"Oh boy. That sounds like more surprises."

Miguel grunted as he struggled with a particularly stubborn lick of hair. "Who knows? I say we just roll with whatever he does and enjoy it. It's not like we can stop the Coop train anyway."

I laughed. "That's for sure. He's as much a force of nature as his grandmother was."

Miguel froze.

"What?"

He turned toward me. "I hadn't thought of that before, but you're right. Coop is so much like Marjorie. She would've done all this and more. I mean, she kept her wealth fairly low key, but she'd do anything for those she cared about."

"Yeah, that's true," I agreed.

"You should tell him. It would mean a lot, especially coming from you.""Why coming from me?" I asked.

"Because you were the first of us to meet Marjorie. She fell in love with you before she knew us."

"I wouldn't say—"

He pursed his lips. "You know what I mean. She loved you, and you know it. It would mean the world to Coop for you to tell him how much he reminds you of her, how much her spirit moves in him."

I sat on the edge of the bed, staring out the window at the gentle sea, unable to think of a reply. We'd talked of Marjorie many times, of her kindness, of the day she'd brought her late husband's car into my shop, and how she changed so many lives through her passing. We'd never really talked about how she'd shaped Cooper though.

That was hard to swallow, because there could be no more important fact in her life than how she raised and guided her grandson. He'd been so lost until she'd taken him in. It was her hand on his shoulder that urged him forward, her words he sought when the nights grew dark. It was her strength he borrowed when his own ebbed. Even to this day, with her gone, I knew her presence comforted him.

"I don't know about saying something tonight," I said moments later. "Maybe we should do something for him when we get home. It just ... I don't know. It feels like Marjorie deserves more than just a few words, you know?"

Miguel set his comb down and came to sit beside me, draping his arm around my shoulder. "I know exactly what you mean, babe. Let's think about it, come up with something perfect for Coop ... and for her."

THERE WERE NO SURPRISES that night, beyond the endless stream of food that Dario and his team laid before us. It seemed every buffet aboard the ship had found wheels and rolled into the Aviary.

Joe and I sat next to each other and chatted throughout most of the meal. Whatever ice that had formed when he'd ended our ... whatever we were ... years ago had melted and dried. We were simply two friends who genuinely enjoyed each other's company now, and I knew in those moments we would be in each other's life for many more to come.

Ethan spent most of the evening avoiding his meal, preferring to fawn over twelve-week-old baby Mila. She glowed at the child's attention, smiling with nearly every word he spoke and gripping his finger with her chubby digits like a champ. I can't remember a single moment in all the years Ty had been my best friend that I'd seen him so enraptured as when he watched the pair of children together. I never would've imagined my party boy pinup would contort his whole body around a baby's little finger like some Cirque du Soleil artist around a rope. Gabe was even worse. The adorable, dimpled, floppy-haired deaf guy who'd stolen Ty's heart was a veritable puddle of mush watching their new daughter smile.

André's hand was rarely far from Ethan's back, though his protectiveness was unwarranted. Annie sat on the other side of Mila and cooed at the baby almost as much as Ethan did.

André and Nick watched their son with the same awe and adoration as Ty and Gabe with Mila.

What was it about children and parents? Was there some special magic the universe imbued when a little entered a family? Was there a Mushy-Gushy Fairy who sprinkled love dust all over the place to turn rough-and-tumble men into hopeless—no, hopeful—piles of man-goo?

Eww. That sounded gross.

Miguel and I had no desire for kids, but seeing the others with their children gave me a moment's pause. It was impossible to ignore the joy in their eyes and the pure innocence in the faces of their children. It was beautiful.

Miguel held my hand through much of the meal, our fingers interlaced and dancing as music drifted through the lush foliage of the Aviary. He and Steph, who was seated on his other side, joked and laughed like old brothers who'd lost each other and were now reunited.

At one point, when the servers' diligence had outmatched my stomach, I sat back and soaked in the scene. Coop and Nate whispered at the far end of the table, making me wonder if, indeed, there was another surprise in the works. The hum of chatter was broken only by the ring of laughter.

Everything felt good. It felt right. This truly was my family.

As Dario and the servers set the last dessert on the table and retreated, Coop clinked his glass and stood.

"Everybody, can I have your attention?"

"Oh boy. Here we go," Miguel whispered in my ear, his fingers tightening against mine.

Coop continued, "So, a few announcements. First, the ship arrives back in Barcelona around ten a.m. Our flight is at five twenty p.m. Even with our priority status, it will take some time to retrieve our luggage, so we should probably go straight to the airport from the dock. The Delta lounge has a full menu for Delta One passengers, so we won't need to scramble to find lunch. Any questions?"

When no one asked anything, Coop sat and dug into his chocolate lava cake.

"Huh, no surprise," Miguel said.

I chuckled. "You sound disappointed. Has my baby gotten spoiled on this trip?"

He poked my ribs. "Like he said in *Pretty Woman*, 'We need a little spoiling over here.'"

I shook my head. "I'm not sure that's how the quote goes."

Coop's voice cut off whatever Miguel was about to say.

"Oh, sorry, I almost forgot." Coop waved his fork. "The Mangoes season opener is in March. Since Nate, Steph, and I will already be there, it seemed like a great excuse for another little get-together. Under your seats are vouchers for a plane ticket to Memphis. You'll need to make your own reservations, but the tickets are paid for. Between our house and, um, our other house we rent on Airbnb, we have room for everyone. Just let me know who's in so we can plan for tickets to the game."

"Surprise," Miguel said, reaching up and pinching my cheek.

I slapped his hand away, but grinned through the gesture.

"Getting us back together is the best possible surprise. I love it," Miguel said.

"Yeah, it really is," I agreed, as my eyes drifted around the table.

Chapter Thirty-Three

STEPH

I DON'T KNOW WHAT Coop did for us to get hand-and-foot service, but Dario had our luggage loaded into the black cars before we'd even set foot on dry land. We literally strode past the hoard of passengers gathering to wait for their luggage and climbed into our cars with barely a glance back. We reached the airport with hours to spare.

Lunch in the Delta lounge was another surprise. Coop had mentioned they served a full menu for Delta One passengers, but I figured that meant we'd get the same food as everyone else, just served on nice plates.

Oh no. That was definitely *not* the case.

Uniformed attendants walked us to a private section of the lounge, handed us menus, and explained we could also ask for off-menu items and they would do their best to procure them at restaurants throughout the airport. Being a Mango, I made a decent-enough living, but this entire trip had given me a peek into a world I'd never experienced. From the way many of the others reacted, they shared my wonder at the overwhelming service we received everywhere we went.

My phone buzzed as I raised a wine glass to my lips.

DeltaOne: Hey, mister.

"Who's that?" Sam, who never missed a thing, leaned over to sneak a peek at my phone.

I clutched it to my chest. "Nunya!"

"So mature," he chuckled. "Tell Sky Mattress we said hi."

Heat flared in my eyes. "He's not—""Hey, Miguel," Sam said, ignoring me. "Sky Mattress is texting Surfer Boy. Come watch."

Every head turned toward me. Great.

"Leave the boy alone," Nate said. "Mangoes need love too, you know."

That earned a round of jeers and laughs. I used the distraction to punch a quick reply.

Me: Hey, you. What's hangin'?

DeltaOne: About nine inches.

I nearly dropped my phone. Sam eyed me, a shit-eating grin spreading across his face.

My phone buzzed again.

DeltaOne: Gotta jet. Literally. See you soon.

Well, shit. That was fast.

"Why do you suddenly look so disappointed? No dick pic still?" Sam teased.

I took the mature route and stuck out my tongue. "No, no dick pic, Mom. I'm a gentleman, remember?"

"More like a lady, from what I've seen," he quipped, earning more laughter from the peanut gallery.

"Thanks a lot," I huffed. "He had to go. Guess he was boarding or something. He likes to text before he gets on a flight."

A chorus of "oohs" swelled around the room.

"You two text enough to have a routine? Wow," Sam said.

Miguel chimed in, "You like this one, don't you?"

I tried looking away, but Miguel's gaze was like some damn parental magnet forcing my eyes toward his, so I nodded, keeping my lips from betraying me and saying something I knew would be used against me.

"Just remember," Sam said, wagging a finger toward me. "We have to approve before you get serious. House rules."

I opened my mouth to argue, but nothing came out.

"Don't argue with your mother," Miguel said, a grin playing at his lips.

I hung my head. "Yes, Dad."

Others chuckled, and I heard the phrase "Steph's been adopted" come from someone across the room, followed by more laughter.

Sam reached over and patted my leg in a most maternal gesture. "Don't worry, dear, your family loves you."

I grinned back. "That's what worries me."

A COUPLE HOURS LATER, our group stood alone in the Delta One boarding line, waiting to be allowed onto our plane. The pre-boards and uniformed military were called, then the desk attendant welcomed us aboard. We made our way down the narrow sky bridge and were greeted by a perky brunette in a white shirt and purple vest.

"Welcome aboard, Mr. Hawk," the brunette said, glancing at Cooper's ticket to ensure he was entitled to the sacred Delta One section. "Good afternoon, Mr. Stringer. Welcome, Mr. Prescott, Mr. Nuez, Mr. ..."

When I stepped up to have my ticket checked, the young woman's brows rose. "Oh, Mr. Breeden. It's *so* nice to see you aboard." Her eyes licked me up and down like I was a frozen treat on a hot summer's day.

"Your seat is 1A," she said without checking. "Right up front, where I can watch you ... I mean, take care of you."

"Uh, okay, great. Thanks," I sputtered, scrambling past as quickly as I could. I could feel her eyes on me as I wobbled down the narrow aisle toward my front-row seat.

I stowed my carry-on, sat, and began perusing the Delta One goodie bag, when a familiar voice nearly startled me out of my seat.

"Hey, handsome. Champagne?"

I looked up to find wild black hair flowing in every direction. Swirls of rich, creamy cocoa stared down at me, and I suddenly forgot every word of my mother tongue.

"Jack?"

A tray of champagne flutes hovered just above my lap as he leaned down and whispered, "Told you I'd see you soon. When you told me you'd be flying home today, I arranged to take this leg. Happy new year."

He winked, reached across my body to set a flute on my side table, then stepped past my seat to offer drinks to the others, leaving me speechless and staring at the Delta logo painted on the wall ahead of me.

Annie, seated in the pod beside me, reached across and patted my arm. "Someone's going to have a great flight. Let's hope he gives full service."

Behind us, Sam and Miguel burst out laughing.

"Thanks a lot, Annie."

She grinned and winked. "Anything for my surfer poodle."

"Aww, Surfer Poo. I love it," Jack said as he passed by with an empty tray, mischief screaming through his features. "I think we just found your first nickname. How special."

I groaned and slapped my palm over my face, desperate to avoid the eyes I knew were boring into me from every direction.

Thankfully, the successive waves of menu items kept Jack and his cabin mate scurrying to keep up. As much as our boys teased, they ate even more. It wasn't until the second dessert was served that Jack had a moment to breathe. He motioned with a finger from the attendants' galley, so I unbuckled and hobbled three strides to face him.

"Have a seat," he said, lowering an attendant's chair and patting the cushion, before lowering one across the galley and sitting to face me.

"It really is good to see you." A smile crept into his eyes, and all snarky banter fell away, leaving a genuinely nice guy blinking at me.

"You too," I said. "I was pretty surprised when you texted me on the cruise."

"Why's that?"

I shrugged. "I don't know. We'd just met. I mean, you were working. You must get hit on all the time up here."

He grinned. "I feel like a bartender in a gay club some days, but the Delta One section tends to weed out the really creepy ones. It's mostly couples spending the coin to fly with me."

I blew out a breath, realizing I'd been hanging on his answer, hoping he wasn't some ... sky mattress, as Sam so eloquently put it. Thank you, baby Jesus.

We chatted for hours, only stopping a few times when he needed to make rounds to collect dishes or serve yet another round of something delicious. By the time the pilot announced our final approach, I'd completely lost track of time. We'd talked through the night and into the morning.

I reached up and helped Annie retrieve her carry-on bag as we prepared to deplane.

"He sounds wonderful, Steph."

"Yeah, he does, doesn't he?" I tried not to grin like a goofball.

"When are you going to see him again?" she asked.

"I'm not sure. He gets free flights, so I hope we'll be able to plan a visit soon." I grabbed my own bag and dropped it to the floor. "It's not as easy as just making dinner plans though. Once the season starts, I'll be all over the place, and he'll still be flying—"

She gripped my forearm and made me meet her gaze. "You listen to me, Steph. If you like him, and he's good to you, you find a way. You hear me? Don't you end up my age and ..." Her eyes fell. "You don't give up until you've really tried, alright?"

I swallowed a lump and nodded, as Annie fell into my arms and held me tight. "I promise."

As if on cue, Jack appeared behind me. "Hey. Guess this is where you get off."

"Not like he'd like to," Sam shouted, loud enough for the Delta Comfort section to hear. Our whole gang laughed as I blushed.

Jack glanced around. The brunette attendant, now waiting for the plane's door to be opened, nodded his way, a toothy grin parting her lips. His hand shot forward, cupped my cheek, as his lips pressed into mine for the briefest, sweetest kiss ever to break the flight attendant code on a plane. I nearly fell over from his touch.

"I will see you soon, Surfer Poo," he whispered.

Annie snickered behind me. Thankfully, the rest of my sodden lot didn't hear him.

"I ... I can't wait," I said.

And then the cabin door opened, we filed out of Delta's most coveted section, and our normal lives resumed.

EPILOGUE

Cooper (and Nate)

Annie sang the National Anthem, Miguel tossed out the first pitch, and Congressman Reese, our David, graced the jumbotron with a smooch when the massive screen flashed his and Joe's faces to the world, surrounded by a cartoon heart and comedic smacking sounds.

Ethan's cheers were loud enough to be heard over the twelve thousand assembled fans.

That night, the Mangoes beat the Sarasota Starfruit 7–2. Nate hit two singles and a homer. Steph drove in four of the team's RBIs.

The back of his jersey read, "Surfer Poo," a one-night-only tip of the hat to Annie who'd insisted the gesture would be good for his future love life.

He and Jack had only seen each other twice over the past three months, but Annie was convinced there was magic in the works, and she was determined to help it along. Before the night ended, she'd texted Jack four different images of Steph's back to ensure he saw the nickname sewn onto his jersey.

As the teams fled the field, Sam, Miguel, and I made our way down to the tunnel and into an office the team had designated for our use. I stripped out of my jeans and Mangoes jersey, donning dark pants and a T-shirt, then a crisp white dress shirt. Whoever invented the little button replacements for shirts was a sadist, because my fingers refused to get them through the little holes.

"Here," Sam said, grabbing the shiny button thing out of my hand. "Let me help you."

"Thanks." I smiled up weakly. "Guess I'm a little nervous."

"It's okay," he said, his voice oddly soothing, unlike his usually gruff growl. "You're going to do great, Coop. This is your night."

I nodded again, unsure how to respond.

Miguel handed Sam my bow tie, and, to my utter amazement, Sam began tying it around my neck.

"What?" His brows rose with the corners of his mouth. "Can't a mechanic know how to tie a bowtie?"

"Uh, okay, sure. I mean, wow."

Miguel chuckled. "Articulate as ever. That's our boy."

I glanced to him. His eyes were so ... full, his smile so soft. I'd grown so used to a broad grin on Miguel's face that the gentle, almost wistful twist to his lips caught me unaware.

Sam straightened the knot and stepped back, eyeing me up and down. He blinked a few times, then nodded. "You look amazing," he breathed, and I swear his voice broke.

"Sam?"

Miguel put his arm around Sam. "Coop, there's one more thing we need to do before you go out there."

"Can we sit down for this?" Sam said, his voice shaking.

"Guys, you're scaring me. What's wrong?"

Miguel smiled as he wheeled a couple of office chairs next to one near me. "Nothing's wrong at all. In fact, everything is almost perfect."

"Almost?" I asked.

Sam removed a small box from his jacket and set it on the desk.

"Coop," Sam said. "There's something we never told you … after your grandmother died."

I sat forward, my every sense on alert.

"When her will was finally read, there was one last instruction she left her attorney. Mr. Whisker visited our house in the days after her funeral and delivered a note, along with this box. She wanted you to have these, to have part of her … " Sam's voice finally failed.

Miguel didn't dare attempt to speak. He just motioned to the box.

My hand shook as I slowly reached up and took it, then opened the lid. A folded note nearly fell out before I grabbed it. I unfolded the paper and immediately recognized Grammy's script.

My Dear Boy,

Today is such a special day. You are starting a new life, writing a new chapter, and joining with one who will love you like no other. On this beautiful day, allow an old woman to offer a few words of advice:

First, laugh every day. You'll live longer, and your days will be filled with joy.

Second, don't forget to love yourself, as you love another.

Finally, love with your whole heart. Hold nothing back. I know it's scary, but if you truly love with everything you have, you will never know regret.

This is how I loved your grandfather. It's how I loved you.

But enough of that. Inside this box are the wedding rings we exchanged when we were first married. That gaudy thing you saw me wear came many years after. These were the bands that bound us together.

I want you to have them. Use them however you choose, as your bands, or in some other way that reminds you of us. Hopefully, in this small way, we will be with you every day and bring you comfort.

My sweet Cooper, I love you more than life itself, and I am so, so proud of you. Enjoy this day, soak it in. It's your day. It's your beginning.

I love you.

Grammy

It took a good ten minutes to dry our tears.

I pulled out the ring Nate and I had chosen and held it beside the box with Grammy's rings. Nate hadn't wanted anything fancy or unique. We'd settled on simple platinum bands. Still …"What do I do, guys?"

Sam reached over and pressed his palm into my shoulder. "You do what your heart tells you. This is your day, Coop. I know she'll understand, whatever you choose."

WHEN THE ORGAN BEGAN playing the wedding march, the ten thousand fans who remained for the post-game ceremony stood, and a hush fell over the stadium. I looked from the dugout toward the pitcher's mound where Nate stood, his uniform replaced with a sharp black tux. To his right, Steph and two other Mangoes stood, still in uniform, per his choice. To his left, Annie glittered in one of her finest red-carpet gowns. The rest of our friends formed a semicircle behind them, just in front of second base.

My foot crunched grass as I stepped from the dugout, and the crowd began to clap. By the time I stepped onto the infield, the applause was thunderous.

I could barely breathe. I couldn't take my eyes off Nate.

For the first time since we'd met, he looked paler than me, which almost made me laugh.

"Hey, you," I said as I stepped onto the mound.

He smiled back. "Hey."

The crowd quieted as the music stilled, and the officiant, who happened to also be the Mangoes' in-game announcer, clicked his mic.

"Ladies and gentlemen," the announcer's voice boomed. "Tonight, a Mango takes the final turn, on Mango field, for the first time."

The crowd roared.

He continued, "Nate and Cooper asked that we be brief, so let's play ball!"

Another wild cheer.

Nate took my hands in his, our eyes never wavering.

"Nate Stringer, do you take Cooper Hawk to be your lawfully wedded husband, to have and to hold, in sickness and in health, through wins and losses"—a chuckle rippled through the crowd—"until death do you part?"

Nate swallowed hard. "I do."

"And Cooper Hawk, do you take Nate Stringer, a reasonably good fielder but outstanding batter, to be your lawfully wedded husband, to have and to hold, in sickness and in health, through one championship after another, until death do you part?"

I squeezed Nate's hands. "I do."

"Do you have rings?" the announcer asked.

I froze.

Nate's brow scrunched. "Babe?" he whispered.

I reached into my pocket. The ring Nate and I had bought floated loose. I pulled it out and held it between us, staring at it like some foreign object.

The announcer made to speak.

"Wait, please," I said, my hand trembling.

I glanced back to where Sam stood with Miguel's arm wrapped tightly around his shoulder. He nodded once.

Without thinking, I shoved the ring back in my pocket and reached into my coat, retrieving the box.

Nate and the announcer's heads cocked at the same time. I let out a nervous laugh.

"Sorry, that was … you two were like … never mind."

I opened the box, and Nate's eyes widened. Still, confusion remained in his eyes.

"These were Grammy and Grandpa's," I whispered.

Nate's hand rose to support mine, and the smile I loved more than sunlight brightened the night. "They're perfect, Coop."

I turned to the officiant and nodded. "We have our rings."

He gathered himself and motioned. "Do you have vows?"

"We do," I said.

I pointed to the ring I thought was closest to my size, and Nate took it and placed it on my finger.

"Cooper, from the first day we met, you've baffled me. I never know what's coming out of your mouth or how long it will take. You make me laugh more than anyone I've ever known and have the biggest heart of any person alive. I love and respect you so much. One day, I hope to be more like you."A rumble of sniffles made its way through the crowd.

"Cooper, I promise to love you with everything I have and everything I am every day I draw breath. I will hold you, cherish you, protect and guard you—even though, as you said on our first date, you could kick my butt in ten directions without breaking a sweat."

Now laughter rang from the stands.

"Coop, I promise to be yours forever, if you will have me."

And my heart leapt into my throat. The fucker hadn't told me about that line.

I took the remaining ring and slipped it onto his finger. Sam had worked his magic and both bands fit perfectly.

"Nate Stringer, I could indeed kick your butt in ten directions without breaking a sweat. Never forget that."

The crowd's laughter grew.

"Nate, I fell in love with you that first night in the Bluebird. The way you supported your friend, the way you treated the server, the way you looked at me, not even knowing me, how could I not? You stole my breath, even while you dropped your dumplings."

Nate fought back a laugh at that.

I smiled and steadied myself for what I'd memorized next.

"Nate Stringer, when you cry, I promise to wipe your tears. When you're scared, I promise to hold your hand. When you laugh, I will laugh with you. When you're hurt, I will take that pain and make it mine. When I say I love you, I mean that I will love you forever. You are my soul mate, my best friend, and I want to spend forever with you. This ring—Grammy's ring—means eternity, and whatever the future holds, I promise that we will face it, no matter what, because we can do anything as long as we have each other."

Nate stared, tears welling in his eyes, as his fingers gripped my trembling hands.

Annie sobbed behind me, and even Steph, standing behind Nate, had to wipe a tear.

"I love you so damn much," Nate said, his lips quivering.

"Well, then," the announcer cleared his throat. "By the power vested in me, as a legally ordained minister in the state of Tennessee, I pronounce you married. Let's see that first pitch!"

Nate didn't wait for the crowd's cheers. He grabbed my head in his hands and kissed me with everything he had. My legs nearly buckled, but Ethan was there in a flash, wrapping his arms around one leg, hugging me with every ounce of strength in his tiny body.

The organ began a raucous round of "Take Me Out to the Ballgame," and thousands began to sing, none louder than our own Annie, and fireworks lit up the Memphis sky.

DID YOU KNOW? YOUR reviews are more than simple words of encouragement, they help me rank on Amazon and reach more readers.

If you loved *A Nashville Spicy Christmas*, please leave a review filled with stars.

Don't forget your free gift . . . click here to tell me where to send your free copy of My Accidental First Date.

Books by Casey

About the Author

Casey Morales is an LGBT storyteller and the author of multiple bestselling MM romance novels. Born in the Southern United States, Casey is an avid tennis player, aspiring chef, dog lover, and ravenous consumer of gummy bears. Learn more at AuthorCaseyMorales.com.